Feeling defiant, Erwyn kicked a rock. The fist-sized stone flew into the air and landed against a tree with a loud "*Yeowtch!*"

Did he just hear what he thought he'd heard?

With Chesric looking on, he rushed to pick up the rock. Rolling it over in his hand, he examined it. It seemed ordinary enough. Solid, like a rock. He dropped it back on the ground.

"Did you *have* to do that?" the rock moaned. "As if I'm not sore enough already."

"You . . . you can talk!"

"Of quartz I can talk. I'm a roc."

"Now, hold on just a second. You're a rock, but you can talk?"

"I thought we'd established that already. You're a little slow today, aren't you, kid?"

Erwyn glared at the creature. "So how come none of the rest of these rocks talk?" He picked up a gray-brown pebble and threw it against a tree. Not even a whimper. "See?"

"Geez, of all the sorcerers in the world, I've gotta run into a *genius*. I'm a roc, kid. *R-o-c*. Roc. A big bird . . ."

Other TSR® Books

Go Quest, Young Man

K.B. Bogen

GO QUEST, YOUNG MAN

Random House and its affiliate companies have worldwide distribution rights in the book trade for English language products of TSR, Inc.

Distributed to the book and hobby trade in the United Kingdom by TSR Ltd.

Distributed to the toy and hobby trade by regional distributors.

Cover art by Walter Velez. ©1994 TSR, Inc. All Rights Reserved.

TSR is a registered trademark owned by TSR, Inc. The TSR logo is a trademark owned by TSR, Inc.

First Printing: September 1994
Printed in the United States of America.
Library of Congress Catalog Card Number: 94-60103
ISBN: 1-56076-898-3

9 8 7 6 5 4 3 2 1

TSR, Inc.
P. O. Box 756
Lake Geneva, WI 53147
U. S. A.

TSR Ltd.
120 Church End, Cherry Hinton
Cambridge CB1 3LB
United Kingdom

Since this is my first book, there are a lot of people to thank. So here they are, listed in alphabetical order by last name. Okay, everybody, take a deep breath.

Thanks for everything to:
Robert A., Leo B., MaryAnn B., Buddy B., Lynn B., Shelly B., Darlene B., Art B., Michael C., Jack C., Duane E., Tom F., Mike H., Bev H., Dixie H., Royce H., Criss H., Joy L., Katherine K., Scott M., Kim M., Warren N., Sharon P., Teresa P., James P., Richard P., Robert R., Nancy S., Robert S., Darla T., Larry T., Leigh T., Mark T.,

and especially to:
Cal B., Flip B., David B., Keith C., Jody H., Sean H., and Brian T.

You all know who you are. And if you don't, see me at the intermission.

Prologue

Here begin the adventures of Erwyn, Journeyman Sorceror Extraordinaire. At least, I hope to be someday, for my sake.

Are you ready for this, you stupid journal? I absolutely hate writing in you. I hated writing in you through six years of Sorceror's Apprentice School, and I'm not too thrilled about it now. How do you feel about that, huh? Personally, I think this journal stuff is responsible for me talking to myself all through school.

At least that's over with! I've survived the best rudimentary education the school has to offer. Now I'm supposed to go forth and learn about the world in general and magic in specific, and get back. Without getting killed.

That's it. Just spend four years, alone, wandering around a world peopled with dragons, evil magicians, giants, and all sorts of other nasties, and return unscathed. Easy, right?

You know, it's probably going to be a very long four years.

He paused to shove his straight brown hair out of his eyes. This would never do. Too wishy-washy. Too sarcastic. Too . . . truthful. He ripped the page out of his book and tried again.

Today is the first day of my journey, he wrote with a flourish. *Nothing happened. Absolutely nothing. That's right, nothing. I am filling this page with nothing but the word nothing. I hope it continues.*

1

Decisions, Decisions

(Or, How to Choose a Direction When All Are Equally Bad)

Orcs never sleep and are impervious to swords. However, they cannot swim and are particularly susceptible to lightning.

Sorcerers Almanac
Section Five: On Things to Watch Out For

Erwyn stuck his book in his pack. He needed a place to hide for the next few years. But where? Looking around, he made a mental note of directions to avoid.

That sinister-looking forest to the north, for example. A likely hiding place for bears, or tigers, or some other perfectly nasty creature. Like the seven-foot-tall orc running out from under the trees, for example. Better to skip that direction.

Wait a minute! Erwyn stared at the dark figure racing toward him. It was an orc, all right. Big and ugly and mean. And running at full speed—straight toward him!

What kind of spell would protect him against one of those monsters? Fire wouldn't work; orcs weren't very flammable. Wind, rain, foxfire? No good. Metal detection or scry spell? Very funny.

He wondered briefly what his *Sorcerers Almanac* would have had to say about the situation. He vaguely remembered it containing an entry about this sort of thing, but he couldn't remember the details.

With the orc running toward him, there wasn't time to dig the book out of his pack, even if he had brought it with him, which he hadn't. It was too late to worry about it now, in any case.

Maybe he could levitate himself out of the way. But levitation would take time, lots of it. So would protective wards. But then, standing there trying to decide what to do didn't help much, either. He needed something quick. Summoning all the energy he could, he cast a sleep spell.

The orc kept coming toward him.

What now? Hastily, he called up the levitation spell, trying to build it in his mind.

The creature was close. Close enough for him to see the wild light in its red eyes. Close enough for him to see its rippling muscles and long, sharp claws.

Erwyn finished the spell just in time and started to lift himself off the ground. He got about two feet up when . . .

Zzzzap! A burst of crimson flame surrounded the beast. It froze, a mere yard away from the startled sorcerer.

Erwyn lowered himself back to the earth. What kind of magic could immobilize an orc? And more important, who controlled it?

Suddenly, the monster teetered, rocking on frozen feet, then crashed into the dirt. Behind it stood a short, thin man with a few ragged wisps of gray hair fluttering across his bald pate. Several black smudges marred the starched white robe that hung from his sloped shoulders, its sleeves stiff around bony wrists.

The man stepped forward, kicking the monster with one steel-shod toe. The monster clanged.

"Yep, the bigger they are, the harder they are."

"Who are you?"

The man looked up at Erwyn as though he'd just noticed

his audience. "My name's Robert. Orc-Out Exterminations. We specialize in pest control. *Big* pests." He kicked the orc again, then pulled a book from a pocket of his robe and walked around the creature, making notes.

"You kill orcs for a living?"

"Sure do. Pay's great, hours are okay, and I get lots of fresh air and exercise."

He returned the book to his pocket before taking out a silver pendant with a large purple stone.

"So, uh, is exterminating orcs hard work?" Erwyn watched him, fascinated.

"Harder than some, easier than others."

"What can be harder than exterminating a seven-foot monster with metal scales, long sharp claws, and a bad temper?"

The exterminator thought for a while. "Elves."

"Elves?"

The man nodded. "Elves. Nasty, insidious little critters. They get into your castle, it's almost impossible to get rid of 'em."

He pointed the pendant at the orc. A beam of purple light shot from the stone. It enveloped the body, then got smaller and smaller and smaller. So did the orc. When the light cleared, the huge creature had been reduced to the size of a small doll. The exterminator wiped his forehead on his sleeve and took a deep breath. With a trembling hand, he put the pendant away.

Erwyn had a good idea of how much energy the man had used to shrink the orc that small. "So elves are really hard to get rid of?" he asked.

"Sure are. Compared to them, an orc is just a troll in the park." He pocketed the orc and headed back the way he'd come.

Erwyn watched him leave. He'd never seen an elf, didn't know anyone who had. And after his conversation with the Orc-Out man, he didn't think he wanted to.

What had he been trying to . . . oh, yeah: which way to

go?

North? The forest. Uh-uh.

He turned to the northeast, where the Impassable Mountains loomed against the pale blue sky. Impassable! Somebody's idea of a joke, no doubt. They were nothing of the kind, having numerous perfectly good trails all through them. But mountain climbing tended to be both cold and wet. No thanks.

He turned even farther, to the east, where the small town of Burgdell lay. Gentle puffs of smoke curled up from rooftops peeking through the trees. The scene reminded him of the hearthfires back home, so . . .

> *Petty squabbles are bound to arise between people in close proximity to each other. Watch for the telltale signs of smoke and refugees.*
>
> Sorcerers Almanac
> Section Three: On People and Their Influence

It looked peaceful enough in the afternoon sun. A promising beginning. Erwyn hoisted his pack onto his shoulders and headed toward the small cluster of buildings. As he trudged through the knee-high grass, he breathed a sigh of relief.

Free at last! he thought. No more spending ten wonderful hours a day sitting on a hard stone bench listening to old Picklepuss Potterby drone on about bats' wings and newts' eyes and the dried blood of witches (which, he'd discovered, didn't come from the real thing).

No more enchanting evenings in Nasty Nazurski's caldron room trying to learn spells that frequently did not want to be learned. At least not by him.

Nope. Here he was, setting out on a four-year jaunt to seek out useless knowledge, destroy perfectly harmless dragons, and rescue stickily sweet damsels from their homespun distresses.

What had he gotten himself into? As he understood it,

the idea of the journey was to survive, using wits and magic. Not a pleasant prospect. He only knew a few basic spells, and as for using his wits . . . well, maybe he shouldn't dwell on that.

Of course, he could have married Heatherlyn instead of going to the school. At least, that's what his father had threatened him with.

* * * * *

"That will be quite enough, Erwyn." King Alizar'n had plainly been in a bad mood that morning. "Either you take that entrance exam, or I announce your betrothal—tonight."

"But, Dad," Erwyn whined, "have you ever *seen* Princess Heatherlyn? Everything she owns is pink!"

"That's a most becoming color for a young lady."

"Even her dog?"

"Well, I'll admit that may be going a bit far. But she's young. She'll grow out of it."

"Fat chance," Erwyn muttered.

"What did you say?" His Daddyship, the king, didn't seem too pleased with his heir.

"Nothing. Sir."

King Alizar'n had the upper hand, and they both knew it. "Well, what's it going to be?"

"What if I don't pass the exam? Do I still have to marry ol' Princess Dither-lyn?"

The king stared over his bushy crimson beard at his son. His equally bushy eyebrows drew together, forming one long, red, fuzzy line on Alizar'n's forehead. A sure sign he was miffed.

"What, exactly, do you have against Heatherlyn? Besides her pink poodle, that is?"

"Well . . ." Erwyn paused for a moment to take a deep breath. "She's skinny, she's always got huge black circles under her eyes, her nose is too long, her voice squeaks, and she kisses me all the time."

"Someday you might not mind the kissing part."

"During sword practice?"

"According to the reports I've gotten from your instructors, being kissed by girls during practice is the least of your worries."

Lords, is he going to bring *that* up again? Erwyn groaned softly.

"Look, Son. I've taken about all I can stand of this nonsense. Make your decision now, or I'll make it for you."

"But what if I don't pass? Heatherlyn's likely to paint *me* pink next!"

"Oh, all right." Alizar'n rolled his eyes toward the ceiling. "If you take the test and don't pass it, you don't have to marry the princess. But if I think you failed on purpose . . ." He left the last part hanging, but Erwyn got the message.

"How in the world could I do that?" he asked innocently. He had hopes, though.

So the matter was decided, and Erwyn took the Sorcerous Evaluation Test.

Unfortunately, he passed.

* * * * *

Erwyn hauled his mind back to the present. The faint trail he'd been following took an unexpected turn—downward. He suddenly found himself sliding down the path, trying to stay on his feet, gravel and loose dirt slipping out from under him.

Somehow he made it to the bottom intact, leaving behind only a few strips of skin and the pocket of his best breeches. He didn't feel like going back for them.

He'd found the way into Burgdell, though. He stared longingly down the narrow dirt road. Not too far ahead, a nice warm bed with his name on it waited. . . .

Erwyn paused, one foot hanging in the air. Somewhere in front of him, he heard the rumbling of what could only be horses' hooves. They were headed his way. Fast.

"Oh, no. Not now!" Erwyn moaned. Everything had been so peaceful.

Frantically, he looked around for cover. As it happened, the only thing available was a small bush at the side of the road. It would have to do.

He dove behind the bush as the first of the horsemen rode into sight around a bend in the road.

Seconds later, they drew abreast of him, their mounts' hooves throwing clouds of dust into Erwyn's eyes. There were about a dozen riders, and they stank of dirt, and sweat, and fear. Fortunately for Erwyn, not one of them noticed him crouched behind the shrubbery. They were too busy.

As soon as the last of the horses passed, Erwyn coughed, clearing his throat of dust. When he could breathe again, he got up, dusted off his clothing, and checked his pack.

"I wonder what they're running to. Or from," he said to himself. He turned toward the town.

Then he heard the sound again. Horses. Coming his way.

"I wasn't really expecting an answer!" he screamed to whatever deity was causing the trouble.

He dove back behind the bush. Somehow, the small sprig of vegetation didn't seem adequate protection against whatever could frighten a dozen grown men. Erwyn might be a little on the thin side, but he was pretty tall, and it was a short bush.

He tried vainly to scrunch down lower. The thundering of hooves from the second party of horses told even his inexperienced ears that the second group was *big*.

"What I wouldn't give for an invisibility spell!" he muttered.

Actually, he *did* have an invisibility spell. Sort of. But it never seemed to work right. Every time he used it, instead of becoming invisible, he turned into a copy of whatever he happened to be near at the time.

And after the experience with Master Hexis's dog . . .

2

BENCHED

(Or, Do You Mind? You're Sitting on My Head!)

Into each life a little rain must fall. For some people,
however, it's a thundershower.

Sorcerers Almanac
Section Two: On Weather and Its Effects

Erwyn sighed, remembering what a perfectly awful day it
had been.

It had started out as a fairly typical day at school. It
rained. It poured. Rivers ran through the courtyard, and
waterfalls fell from the roof. As usual, the current crop of
Third Level Apprentices hadn't learned to turn off their rain
spells when they got done.

Due to the weather, Master Gordrun, the Applications
teacher, moved his class into Nasty Nazurski's caldron room.
So, of course, Master Nazurski just had to have brewed a
particularly vile-smelling concoction the night before. The
room reeked.

"Okay, class, everyone find a seat, and we'll begin. Today
we will demonstrate our Fifth Level Invisibility Spell."

Erwyn shifted uncomfortably on his seat, trying hard not
to breathe, hoping the stench wouldn't interfere with his

control. He knew the spell well enough, but the students were supposed to practice, and he'd been too busy. Now he wished he'd found the time. He really hated trying a high-level spell without having a chance to test it first. One never knew when something might go wrong.

"Axelrod, if you will please demonstrate first." Gordrun nodded to the skinny blond at the end of Erwyn's bench.

Axelrod, the third son of Bentstaff, a blacksmith some-where in Balgris, jumped up and began singing the spell.

Erwyn winced. Everyone had his own method of imple-menting spells. Some recited incantations. Some used potions or incense. Some sang. Some sang off-key.

Axelrod finished his aria and disappeared from view. Gor-drun made a note in his lesson book. Then he picked up a spray bottle and squirted its contents in the general direc-tion of Axelrod's last location. The boy reappeared, grinning broadly.

"Very good, Apprentice Axelrod. You may return to your seat."

The Applications teacher worked his way down the row. Each student sang, squeaked, recited, or whatever, his way into invisibility. Gordrun squirted each in turn. Finally, he reached Erwyn.

Erwyn stood, carefully recalling the spell. He didn't sing or recite or boil potions. He just *felt* it build inside him. When he completed the spell, he released it. But instead of disappearing, he felt himself sink toward the floor, almost like melting.

When he tried to look around, he couldn't. He couldn't find his eyes. He felt funny, too. Long and narrow and hard, with four feet on the ground. Sort of like—like one of Nasty Nazurski's stone benches!

Oh, no! He couldn't have, could he? Of course he could.

Master Gordrun tried the spritzer. It didn't work. It was meant as an antidote to the invisibility spell, not whatever Erwyn had conjured.

"Erwyn." Gordrun sounded worried. "If you can hear me,

try doing the spell again. You know, like when you repeat a foxfire spell to stop it."

Erwyn tried, but nothing happened.

Dis-spell wouldn't work, either. It only worked for the person who'd cast the spell. And Erwyn couldn't cast it because the dis-spell was Sixth Level and he was only a Fifth. He didn't know how yet. Most of the low-level spells didn't require it, anyway. And Gordrun's spritzer took care of the rest.

Well . . . most of the rest.

In the end, it took three days for the Masters to unravel his mistake. They might have managed it faster, but old Falwrickel, the librarian, had gone home to visit his family. No one else was quite sure what to do.

In the meantime, Master Nazurski wasn't about to waste an opportunity. Since he had an extra bench, he crammed more students into the room.

For three days, Erwyn was sat on, kicked, and generally mistreated. He had an itch where someone had spilled something sticky on his pants. He had blisters on his hands and feet, and a bruise in a very tender spot where a crucible had hit him. He might have looked like a stone bench, but he was still a sixteen-year-old boy, and when they finally restored him, he had to stay in bed for the rest of the week.

When he recovered, he returned to his classes. For once, the weather was sunny, and Master Gordrun held the Applications class in the courtyard.

"Now that we're outside, where very little damage can be done, would you care to attempt the invisibility spell again, Apprentice Erwyn?"

The entire class backed away, leaving Erwyn in the middle of an empty circle about twenty feet in diameter.

He gulped and nodded. He'd never figured out what he'd done wrong earlier. Neither had the Masters. So he had no choice but to try it the same way as before.

Nothing happened.

"Apprentice Erwyn, we're waiting."

He tried again, with the same result—none at all.

"I–I don't know what's wrong, Master Gordrun. I'm trying, but it doesn't seem to work!"

Gordrun sighed. "Never mind. Why don't you go stand by that tree and think about it for a while? Maybe you're just nervous."

"Yes, sir."

Leaning against the old oak, Erwyn went over the spell in his mind. He even dug out his spellbook and reviewed the procedure. But he couldn't figure out what was wrong. After a few minutes, Gordrun came over.

"Think you can handle it now, son?"

"I guess so, sir."

Erwyn tried again, building the spell slowly, carefully. At last he felt he was ready and released the spell.

For a moment, he thought it hadn't worked. Then he felt himself stretching and growing, sprouting leaves and roots, until a second tree, exactly like the first, stood in the courtyard. Erwyn would have screamed his frustration, if only trees had vocal chords.

At least this time they knew how to undo the damage. Master Gordrun ran to get the supplies to reverse Erwyn's mistake. He returned quickly, but not quickly enough.

Master Hexis, the cook, had decided to take an afternoon stroll—with his dog. The tiny brown-and-black-spotted mutt decided the new tree was the perfect place to relieve his bladder.

It took Erwyn nearly a month to get the smell out of his leather boots.

* * * * *

Erwyn shook his head to shake the memory. No, he wasn't going to attempt *that* again. He knew the dis-spell now. They taught it to him as soon as he recovered from being a tree for an hour. But he didn't want to spend even a tiny slice of his life looking like that stupid bush.

The first of the second group of horses finally galloped into sight, the noise almost deafening him. Erwyn gasped and stared. There were hundreds, maybe thousands of them. Well, at least a hundred.

They rode five abreast, armor and weapons glinting wickedly in the sunlight. And here he sat, with nothing but one small, stupid bush to keep him from being trampled. While he racked his brains for a way to save himself, the first of the horses reached him.

Without breaking stride, the horses split around Erwyn and his bush. He covered his head with his arms, waiting for one of the horsemen to finish him with a well-placed stroke of the sword. But it never happened. They streamed past without even seeing him, intent only on the larger prey.

"Whew!" Erwyn wiped his forehead with his sleeve. "This place is awful busy for a little bitty town in the middle of nowhere."

He picked up the pack, dusted himself off again, and thought about the situation. Perhaps he should go somewhere else instead.

Then again . . . Erwyn considered his other choices. Might as well go ahead and check out Burgdell anyway, he decided. Maybe those horsemen were just passing through. After all, they were headed *away* from the town.

He reached the next rise and stopped. Before him lay Burgdell in all its glory. The remnants of it, anyway.

Smoke rose in lazy curls from the charred remains of the buildings below, and he knew he wouldn't be staying in Burgdell, after all. Ashes make lousy protection from the weather.

Now what should he do? If he stood there too long, he'd probably sprout roots. Again.

Travel southward was completely out. That way lay the Sorcerer's Apprentice School, and he couldn't go back there. Not yet.

South of the school lay Irvingdell, which was, Erwyn recalled, currently in the midst of a little spat with its neighbors, Martindell and Arbordell, over some property owned by the now-defunct hamlet of Curtisdell.

Sheesh! Couldn't the people around here come up with some more original names for their towns? Immortality through town-naming. Humph! There wasn't a single real dell within miles of this area.

So he turned west. Virtually unknown territory.

Erwyn himself had never traveled farther west than the school. Neither had anyone else he knew. Why should they? They had everything they needed; there was no need to go anywhere else. Now he needed to.

He looked toward the setting sun, shading his eyes against the glare. All he could see were vast grasslands rippling in the cool autumn breeze.

"Looks good to me," Erwyn said to no one in particular. At least there were no smoke signals, escaping armies, or raging monsters to be seen.

Besides, there ought to be something of interest in a land no one ever explored, at least no one he knew personally. He might even be able to have some fun while he tried to stay out of trouble.

Having made his decision, Erwyn shouldered his pack, shoved his hair back into place again, straightened his cloak, and set out to find his calling. He didn't expect to find it on the first day.

He was right.

3

Westward Ho!

(Or, It's Barbaric but, Hey, It's Barbaric)

Selecting the least threatening of all available options does not necessarily mean you won't get hurt.

Sorcerers Almanac
Section One: On Getting the Lay of the Land

Only two hours of full daylight remained as the young would-be sorcerer headed in his chosen direction. And it was a good thing, too. After two hours' walk, he was completely exhausted. No wonder magic-users tended to be pale, emaciated wisps of humanity. Too much time sitting on hard stone benches.

He scanned the grassland for a suitable campsite. And there it lay, the perfect location, right in front of him. Complete with a tree and a bare spot in the grass, just right for building a fire.

Erwyn stood there a moment, staring.

"A tree. Sure. Right in the middle of nowhere. How convenient."

It also seemed a little weird, since Erwyn didn't remember it being there a few minutes ago.

However, since it was available, and he couldn't think of

an alternate plan of action, he figured it would do. Shrugging, he sat down with his back to the tree and began rummaging in his pack.

"I wonder why there's just this one tree right here in the middle of . . . shit!"

They didn't give him a tinderbox! He searched through his pack again. Nothing. It never occurred to him that they wouldn't even give him a tinderbox.

"Of all the stupid, inconsiderate . . ." He went through the contents of his pack once more. "That's the last time I let someone else do my packing!" One spellbook, a journal, two clean tunics, a pair of pants, a dull knife, and dinner for one. What was this, the super economy model? There wasn't even an instruction book on how to live life to the fullest on zero gold pieces a day. Of course, that might be what the *Almanac* was for.

In the end, lack of proper equipment forced him to use his flame spell to start a fire in the pile of branches he'd gathered. He glared at the twigs angrily and built the spell in his mind.

> *Never build a fire directly beneath a low-hanging branch.*
>
> *Sorcerers Almanac*
> *Section Four: On How to Have a Safe Trip*

"Yikes!" He scrambled back from the small firepit. Flames shot up from the branches, licking hungrily at the tree limbs above.

He damped down the flow of power, embarrassed that he'd let his emotions interfere with, or add to, the spell.

"As soon as I find some sign of civilization," he groused, "I'm going to get myself some proper equipment and a real bed and some warmer clothes and . . ." He paused, sighing. "And a way to pay for them." Maybe he could get a job selling used carriages.

Griping to himself about primitive living conditions,

Erwyn set about making camp. Dull routine stuff, making camp. Especially since all he really had to do was build a fire, fix dinner, and lay out his bedroll. And he already had the fire.

He shot another nervous glance skyward at the branches overhead.

Dinner was simple, but tasty. His refrigeration spell had kept the ham and potatoes fresh until time to cook them. Unfortunately, he had no cooking utensils, unless he counted his knife.

Cursing once more, Erwyn tucked the potatoes among the hot coals, then levitated the ham to hover just above the flames. While dinner cooked, he pulled his journal from his pack.

> *A journal of your adventures can be a valuable asset. If you can't remember what you did wrong, you can't avoid doing it again.*
>
> *Sorcerers Almanac*
> *Section Four: On How to Have a Safe Trip*

He paused a moment trying to decide. Should he write about what actually happened on his trip, or spice things up a bit? He finally settled on a blatant lie ("creating fiction for fun and self-gratification") and began writing.

> *I walked for hours and hours before finding a suitable place to make camp. Choosing a huge, gnarled old oak for my campsite, I ripped from it branches as thick as my arms with which to build a fire.*
>
> *As I sat eating my supper, which I caught and killed myself, several large, unidentifiable hairy beasts came to glower at me over the flames. Undaunted, I repelled them with a few of the multitude of powerful spells at my disposal.*

Erwyn sat back to reread his latest passage. It needed something more. . . .

One of the beasts dared to approach me, snarling and growling as he advanced. I think I shall have his carcass for breakfast, as I have already roasted it. I hope he's tender.

That should keep them entertained, should anyone ever actually read the thing.

Smiling to himself, Erwyn closed his book and turned his attention to supper. His knife served as spoon, fork, and, of course, knife. A bit awkward, perhaps, but he managed rather well.

The air made a perfect plate, though. He levitated the food to a comfortable height and dug in. Toward the end of supper, he started playing with levitating his food right up to his mouth.

Children, even eighteen-year-old children, he decided, are easily amused. What the hell, it was fun.

After he ate, Erwyn slid gratefully between his blankets, glad for a chance to rest. He did remember to set his wards before he went to sleep, though.

It took him a few minutes to relax, slipping into the proper meditative state.

In his mind's eye, he saw the blue network of energy woven (theoretically) around him each time he set the wards. But was it his imagination, or were they really there? Who knew? Moreover, who cared?

Erwyn thought of it as just a mental exercise, anyway. He didn't think it really worked.

Whether the wards worked or not, he was so tired that even the ground felt comfortable. He fell asleep almost immediately.

The next day, however, was different. The ground might have felt comfortable the night before, but it certainly didn't this morning.

Erwyn tried some exercises to help relieve the ache in his muscles. Once he'd worked out the majority of the kinks, he stood next to the firepit, rubbing his hands together in anticipation. Spell practice was his favorite part of the day.

He actually liked using magic when no one—such as a teacher—was watching.

"Let's see, how did that wind spell go again?"

Concentrating, he recalled the form of the spell and gave it a trickle of energy. One had to be very careful about these things. . . .

Lightning zapped the ground by his feet as a small thunderstorm appeared over his head. "Whoops! I hate it when spells feel so much alike!" Oh, well, if he were perfect, he wouldn't need to practice, and the storm did make a nice portable shower.

He tried the wind spell again. This time he got it right.

While the warm air dried his clothes, he rushed through as many of his spells as he felt there was time for. Safely, anyway.

At last, he felt ready to resume his travels. But which way to go? Should he keep going the same direction as yesterday, or not? He needed a goal—a landmark or some sort of guide.

The wind spell blew itself out, leaving only the gentle breeze blowing across the knee-high greenery. It produced a series of waves in the grass, like the ripples on a pond. Very pleasant. Very boring. And not very helpful.

Farther to the west, Erwyn spotted a thin, dark line at the horizon. Perhaps a forest. Perhaps an illusion caused by the distance. He couldn't be certain.

Oh, well. It was as good a choice as any. At least if he continued in the same direction as he'd started, he would know more or less which way to return, just in case.

Something about the mysterious line of black seemed to pull at him, sort of a *yearning* to explore that mysterious darkness.

"You're getting weird, Erwyn," he said to himself.

It felt right, though, and his feelings were about all he had to go on. Of course, instinct wasn't really his best resource. . . .

The air around Erwyn suddenly resounded with a loud,

harsh screech. Looking skyward, he was amazed to see a very large, very angry-looking bird plummeting toward him.

"Indecision can be *such* a problem!" Erwyn had just enough time to snatch up his book and pack, and race headlong toward the line of darkness he had just been thinking about.

The actual details of the terrain blurred around him. Long tufts of grass grabbed at his ankles, slowing him down when he needed speed.

Erwyn risked a glance backward. The bird was less than twenty feet behind him. No way could he ever outrun such a creature.

So this is the end of my glorious career, he thought ruefully. He began to think that perhaps Heatherlyn wasn't so bad after all.

The grass finally got him. He tripped, sprawling headfirst onto the ground.

He lay still, eyes closed, heart pounding.

Stupid! I really ought to watch where I'm going when I race through tall grass while being chased by an outraged giant bird, he thought. I'll have to remember that, if it ever happens again.

The bird skimmed past, its long brown tailfeathers brushing the back of Erwyn's head. He tensed, ready to feel the sharp bite of talons in his unprotected back.

He smelled the warm, grassy scent of the animal. Its wings swished as it passed over him. But it didn't hurt him. Scared the hell out of him, but didn't hurt him.

Astonished, Erwyn opened his eyes, looked up, and saw the bird soar higher. Probably preparing for another attack, he decided. He sucked in some air, almost wishing he could just lie there, waiting for the end.

Quit, however, was a four-letter word. One of the worst, in Erwyn's opinion. So, instead of waiting for the bird to finish him off, he staggered to his feet and resumed his mad dash across the grassland.

The edge of the grassy area must have been closer than

he first thought. What had earlier seemed a dark line on the horizon rapidly resolved itself into the mottled green of forest.

The blurred brown line of trunks beneath a crown of leaves promised safety. If he could reach it.

The grass thinned, allowing Erwyn to speed up. He raced as fast as he could across the last few yards.

Behind him, the bird shrieked a challenge.

This is it, Erwyn thought.

He dove beneath the trees. His legs screamed in protest, cramping painfully. His chest heaved.

The bird shrieked again, no closer than before. Rolling onto his back, Erwyn looked across the field.

The huge, feathered creature settled into the grass near the tree where Erwyn had been writing in his journal. And, incidentally, right next to his erstwhile campsite.

"Wait a minute!" Erwyn sat up suddenly. His head reeled, both from his exertions and from the questions racing around in his mind.

What the hell was going on? Why did that stupid bird chase him, anyway? Why did it stop? And why could he still see the tree after running away from it for a small slice of forever?

Did the forest get closer to the tree, or did the tree get closer to the forest? Either way, it simply didn't make any sense.

Erwyn leaned against the nearest tree to watch the bird. From this distance, the creature was huge, nearly as tall as the tree.

He shuddered, thinking how close to death he'd probably come.

The bird was quiet now, just resting (or was it roosting?) in the grass. It didn't even seem to notice him watching it from the edge of the forest.

His heart finally slowed its wild beating, and his legs seemed usable, if a little wobbly. Slowly raising his pack once more, Erwyn turned toward the shadowy trees.

The pull he felt before was stronger here. The green-tinted darkness seemed to beckon, drawing him into the forest.

For a moment, he felt a twinge of anxiety. Then the moment passed, and he found himself eagerly giving in to the summons.

4

A Walk in the Wood

(Or, Pardon Me, I've Just Stepped on My Tongue)

The Western Wood provides an interesting assortment of engagements for the seasoned adventurer.

Sorcerers Almanac
Section One: On Getting the Lay of the Land

Little sunlight penetrated the trees overhead, and the air became chill. Erwyn shivered and pulled his cloak tighter about him.

His feet made no noise in the layer of decaying leaves on the faint trail. The world through which he passed was green, dark, and quiet.

Too quiet, he thought. Everything seemed fuzzy. Unreal. He frowned, trying to concentrate. There was something he needed to do, someplace he had to go. It was so hard to think. . . .

His head jerked up as he came to his senses.

"Must have been walking in my sleep," he muttered, looking around.

He realized suddenly that he was headed toward a definite goal. Only he had no idea what that goal was. His feet did, though, and they were carrying him there without consulting his brain first.

"This is not a good idea, Erwyn. You're going to get yourself into trouble." Somehow, the comment didn't cheer him as much as it used to.

He tried to break stride, force his feet out of rhythm. When that didn't work, he tried to trip himself on a convenient root. No luck. His feet stepped over it without a hitch. It was the first time he'd ever had any difficulty tripping over anything.

He was a prisoner in his own body, and it seemed to work better without him.

I certainly hope this isn't a permanent condition, he thought. A tight knot of fear began forming in the pit of his stomach.

He looked at the trees. There wasn't even anything he could use for a landmark when he got out of this mess. *If* he got out of this mess. Every tree looked the same: long, straight trunks and silver-green leaves. Identical.

A feeling of panic began at the base of his neck. He could tell it started there because the hairs were standing on end.

What if there is no way out? he thought. What if the forest is enchanted and . . .

Enchantments. Sorcery. He'd spent six years training to work magic. There had to be some way to break the forest's spell. But he just couldn't think.

Then again, not being able to think had never stopped him before.

"Calm down," he told himself. "You're supposed to know how to handle these things. Think of something!"

"Right. Think of something when I can't even think. Neat trick."

He'd heard somewhere that the first sign you're going crazy is when you start talking to yourself. The second sign is when you start answering back. . . .

Okay, so he was crazy. No one ever accused him of being normal.

Erwyn laughed at his private joke. The laughter helped. His fear evaporated, along with the spell that held him.

Most of it, anyway.

He still felt a slight pull onward, though not as strong as before. He could resist it. But should he?

Not knowing what else to do, he continued deeper into the forest. He didn't want to admit, even to himself, that he was kind of curious about the whole situation.

"Hello, Erwyn."

The force that had drawn him into the forest stopped.

So did Erwyn.

He looked around, trying to see who spoke.

"Uh, hello," he finally said to the air.

The owner of the voice didn't seem inclined to show up in person. The only thing Erwyn knew for certain was that it was definitely female. And very seductive. In fact, he felt chills when he heard it. He wondered briefly if the disembodied voice had a body to match.

He waited a few minutes, but nothing else happened. The voice was silent. Since there wasn't much else he could do, he decided to check out his surroundings.

He stood in a small open space in the trees. The ground was smooth and cleared of leaves. At the center of the clearing sat a large stone.

The stone was almost perfectly round and very flat on top. The sun found its way through the trees, and shafts of light illuminated the rock. Tiny motes of dust danced in the beams.

"I've been waiting for you," the voice finally spoke again.

The glowing particles gathered together, getting brighter.

"Sure. Whatever you say," Erwyn replied, shading his eyes against the glare. Maybe he should just find the nearest exit now and save himself trouble in the future. Except for one problem: Forests don't have exits. The path out seemed to have disappeared, too.

The voice had come from the light, and it was a good bet it belonged to whoever, or whatever, had been jerking him around like a puppet. A way out would have been really handy.

At last the light dimmed, and Erwyn lowered his hand, but neglected to shut his mouth.

Beside the stone stood a lady like no other Erwyn had ever seen. Of course, he hadn't seen too many ladies recently. Only sorcerer's apprentices, and they all tended to look alike after a while. Even the girls.

The lady had long golden hair, an oval face, emerald green eyes, and a tall slim figure. She wore a close-fitting blue dress girded with a chain of flowers.

All right, so she was beautiful. Erwyn still didn't like being dragged around like a life-size doll, and he suspected her of being the culprit. He shut his mouth.

The lady gestured, and he felt a sudden urge to sink to one knee in front of her. He took a couple of jerky steps toward the stone. Then his brain took over.

Why should he kneel to this woman? Good manners didn't need to be forced. Besides, he'd already sworn allegiance to his father. King Alizar'n would be royally frosted if Erwyn changed sides all of a sudden, enchantment notwithstanding.

With all the willpower he could muster, Erwyn remained standing a few feet in front of the woman. He faced her, waiting. For what, he had no idea.

Finally she spoke, her voice sending shivers up his spine. "You have come, then, my champion." She smiled as though nothing unusual had happened.

It was pretty unusual to Erwyn, though. He stared at her, raising his eyebrows for emphasis. "Champion? What *are* you talking about?"

Something snapped like an invisible string, making him take an involuntary step backward. The path seemed to have reappeared, too. Her hold on him had finally been completely broken. For the moment.

"I have waited for you, knowing you would come." She smiled again and tossed her hair over her shoulder.

Erwyn thought he heard the muted sound of tiny bells when she moved.

"Though, perhaps the word 'champion' is a bit melodramatic."

"Try 'a bit premature.'"

Laughing, she beckoned to him. "Come, sit here with me."

She gestured to the flat stone, then seated herself. The bells jingled again.

He watched her for a moment, acutely aware of a growing uneasiness within him. That tickly feeling started at the base of his neck again.

He wasn't particularly fond of nasty surprises. This woman, while admittedly very beautiful, was an unknown quantity, and a magic-user to boot. Magical nasty surprises were the worst kind.

The lady clasped her hands and looked up at him expectantly.

Erwyn hesitated another second. Maybe he was just being paranoid. Who could be sure? With a shrug, he walked over and plopped down beside her.

"So what's going on?" he asked, rubbing his left leg, which had developed a sudden cramp. He was more tense than he realized. Or maybe it was a leftover from his morning run.

"I need someone to perform a task for me, and I believe you are the man for the job."

"I'd really rather not, if you don't mind. You see, I'm in the midst of a—"

"Journey. Yes, I know. I can see by your patch that you are a journeyman." She lightly touched the puce and yellow guild patch on his chest, then smoothed his cloak over it. "Still, I am in need of help, particularly the magical kind."

"With an entrance like that, you need magical help from me?" Erwyn was incredulous, to say the least.

"It *was* pretty spectacular, but I needed to get your attention. You have to admit it worked."

"Yeah, it worked all right. You got my attention, but I doubt if I'm your 'champion.' As magic-users go, I'm pretty limited. I barely made it into Apprentice School."

"Trust me, you'll be perfect."

"I can't agree with you there." Erwyn sighed. "I know my basic spells pretty well. Setting protective wards, lighting fires, that sort of thing. But not much more. I'm afraid I wouldn't make a very good champion." Why was he telling *her* this stuff?

"Believe me, you are much more than you seem. And you *are* the right champion. I know, and I am always right about these things."

"Assuming, just for the moment, that you are correct," he sighed, martyrlike, "just what is it you want me to do?"

"Rescue a damsel in distress."

"Ye gods, not that!" Erwyn jumped off the stone and away from the lady, stumbling as his leg cramped again. "I promised myself four uneventful years of traipsing around the world without actually doing anything. And I never go back on my word," he said, then added to himself, "not if I can help it."

"Oh, but you must! For my sake, if for no other reason." Tears glistened in her eyes as she turned a stricken face toward him.

"Don't you go trying your feminine wiles on me," he exclaimed. "I'm immune, at least mostly. I am *not* going to rescue your damsel. No way. I hate damsels!"

"You're not . . ." She arched an eyebrow at him.

"No, of course I'm not. I mean, I like girls in general. It's just that I can't stand damsels. Especially the kind who are in distress. Too gushy, too sweet. Yuck!" He shuddered.

"I'll make it worth your while." The tears stopped suddenly, and a slow, sultry smile replaced them. She gazed at him through tear-dampened lashes.

"That won't work, either." Blushing, Erwyn backed a little farther from the lady and closer to the edge of the clearing.

"How about money? I have gold. . . ."

"Well . . . I could use some money about now," Erwyn

said, pausing to think.

He tapped his chin thoughtfully. Something wasn't quite right. She was trying too hard.

Finally, he shook his head. "Nope, I don't think so. It's just not worth it."

The lady sat back from the edge of the stone, shoulders slumping slightly. "What could I offer you to get you to do this little thing for me? What payment would you require? How can I persuade you to help me?"

"Offhand, I can't think of a thing."

Erwyn gazed at the lady for a while. What, exactly, *would* make damsel-rescuing worthwhile? Not much. Except, perhaps, information.

"Okay. For starters, you can tell me your name."

She hesitated a few moments. Then, sighing heavily, she answered, "My name is . . . Sharilan." She watched him closely, as though looking for a reaction.

"Sharilan. That's very pretty. I don't see why you wouldn't want to tell me."

She smiled, relaxing visibly. "Is there anything else?"

"Yes, as a matter of fact." Erwyn looked at her with what he hoped was a compelling stare. "I would like to know *why* you want this particular damsel rescued. If you can give me a really good reason, maybe you can convince me to change my mind. But it had better be good!"

Sharilan sighed again. "I was afraid you would ask me that." She rose and paced gracefully around the stone. "I guess if you've got to know, you've got to know."

5

Sharilan's Story
(Or, Rats! I Forgot the Popcorn!)

Evil comes in many guises, some quite pleasant to the eye.
When in doubt, just say "no."

Sorcerers Almanac
Section Five: On Things to Watch Out For

Sharilan proceeded to tell Erwyn a long story, the substance of which follows.

Years ago there were born to a poor woodcutter two daughters. One, named Sharilan, was as bright and sunny as a spring day. Her hair was as golden as sunlight, her eyes green as grass. She would sing and dance the day away, always with a smile on her face.

The other, Fenoria, was as unpredictable as a thunderstorm. One minute wild and excited was she, the next minute angry and threatening. Hair as black as a raven's wing hung to her shoulders, and her eyes were dark as jet.

Both girls were beautiful, talented, and intelligent. And they loved their father and mother very dearly.

As different as the two girls were in looks and temperament, so they were different in desire. Sharilan wished nothing so much as to spend her life in the study of magic and science and art. Fenoria, however, wanted to find the right man, settle down, and start having the woodcutter's grandchildren.

This division of interests earned the approval of both the woodcutter and his wife. As long as one of their daughters remained to give them the grandchildren they desired, and to take care of the two of them when they grew old, the other could do as she wished.

Time passed, as it always does, and the girls grew into very beautiful young women. Their plans had remained consistent, and now those plans were about to come to fruition.

Sharilan passed her childhood in diligent study of the arts and sciences, as well as those aspects of magic which were available to the people at large. When she entered her sixteenth year, she prepared to enter into an apprenticeship with a noted wise woman, who would lead her along the path she chose.

Fenoria learned to cook, clean, and sew, and to perform the myriad chores required of a good housewife. When she entered her sixteenth year, she prepared to marry the son of a prominent businessman, who would lead her down the aisle she chose.

Unfortunately for them both, someone else made other plans for the two of them. A powerful noble had fallen in love with Sharilan and plotted to make her his bride. Hubert, Baron of Gorlick, was a very wealthy man, with many prominent connections. When Sharilan, naturally, turned down his proposal, he purchased the aid of a notorious dark wizard.

With his purchased spells, the baron locked poor Fenoria in a huge, empty castle. He surrounded the castle with a high wall of rosebushes with giant thorns. An evil, firebreathing dragon stood guard over the castle, in case someone should manage to win through the thorny wall.

After imprisoning Fenoria, the baron told Sharilan that her sister would stay imprisoned forever, or until Sharilan consented to become Baroness of Gorlick, whichever came first.

Still Sharilan resisted. As long as Fenoria was unharmed, there was still hope. She would not give in to the baron's demands.

Outraged, Baron Hubert tried to hack his way into the castle to take his anger out on poor, innocent Fenoria. He failed.

No matter how hard he tried to cut through the bushes, he made no progress. The thorns and roses grew back as fast as he could cut them down.

Consulting once more with the wizard, Baron Hubert learned that nothing could harm Fenoria within her prison. He had, after all, only wanted some place to stash Fenoria until Sharilan relented. However hard he tried, the Baron would not be able to get through the wall of roses. So, after much screaming and hair-pulling, he purchased another set of spells from the wizard.

With the new spells, he imprisoned Sharilan within an enchanted rock in the middle of the Western Wood, where no human had ever before set foot. From time to time, the Baron would return to the stone to ask Sharilan to marry him. Always she said "no."

Unbeknownst to both the wizard and Baron Hubert, the woodcutter and his wife also consulted a wizard. The wizard they found was a kindly old man who had a fondness for cherry pie. So, in exchange for two cherry pies (and everything else the couple owned of any value), the old man managed to put a "rider" on the Baron's second spell.

When Baron Hubert used his purchased spell, the rider changed part of it. Sharilan would not be imprisoned in the rock permanently, unable to do anything on her own behalf.

Instead, once a year she would be able to leave the rock of her own volition, attract the attention of any passerby she could (by means of an enhancement of her own spells), and try to recruit a champion to free her.

Moreover, the champion need only free one sister, and both would be freed. Unfortunately, there seemed to be a shortage of passersby in the Western Wood.

"So you see," Sharilan continued, "since I know of no way

to defeat the spell which holds me, it seems simpler to send someone to free Fenoria, which in turn will free me. And you're the first person I've been able to find." She batted her eyelids.

Erwyn looked at Sharilan for a few minutes before speaking.

"What a load of horse do-do!"

"What do you mean by that? You—you don't believe me?" Sharilan looked shocked.

"Pardon my language, milady, but that has got to be the worst pile of crap anyone has made me listen to in years!" He rose indignantly, feeling his face flush.

"You've gone to all this trouble to lure me in here just to tell me that? It sounds like you've been reading too many fairy tales and have used pieces of the plots from all of them to make up a story. Forget it! I'm not your champion, I don't like damsels, and I'm not going. I've half a mind to pack up my things and leave. In fact, I think I will."

He paused, glaring at her, then picked up his pack. He turned to where the path continued through the woods, on the opposite side from where he had entered. He took two steps forward before Sharilan called out to him.

"Wait! All right, I'll tell you the truth."

Erwyn turned back toward her, allowing his pack to slide to the ground. Then he stood watching her, arms crossed over his chest.

"The truth is," Sharilan said, sighing, "Fenoria ticked off some old witch, and if I can't talk someone into freeing her, I'll have to go home, get married, and try to pretend to be domestic for the rest of forever."

For a moment, she looked thoroughly disgusted. Then she glanced up, pleading. "I can't think of anything more boring than having some schmuck's brats and taking care of my parents for the rest of my life. I love my parents but . . . *blech!*"

Erwyn stood there, laughing helplessly. Sharilan watched him, her eyes narrowing in anger.

"What do you mean by laughing at me like that?"

Someone had used a refrigeration spell on Sharilan's voice, and tiny blue sparks danced on the palms of her hands.

The significance of the sparks escaped him.

He tried to stifle a chuckle as he replied. "I'm not laughing at you, Sharilan. Not exactly." The chuckle finally erupted as a loud hiccup. "I guess I'm really laughing at myself. You see . . ." He hiccuped again. "That's the very same reason I went to Sorcerer's Apprentice School. My father gave me a choice between magic or marriage. And given *that* choice . . ."

Sharilan thawed. "I see." Hope shone in her eyes as she added, "Then you'll do it?"

"I don't know. I still hate rescues and can't stand damsels. But if there isn't too much resemblance between the *real* Fenoria and the one in your story, maybe she's not too sticky. Perhaps I can handle her. At least it might help pass the time."

He paused, uncertain whether he was doing the right thing. Then he took a deep breath and, looking straight into Sharilan's eyes, he gave her his answer. "Okay. I guess I'll give it a whack. I can't promise you I'll succeed. I wasn't kidding about not being very proficient at magic."

"That's all I could ask for," Sharilan almost purred. Then she added, "I can help you, a little."

She waved her hand, and on top of the stone a small tree branch appeared. At least it looked like a tree branch. Only when Erwyn picked it up, he was surprised to find that the branch seemed to be made of some kind of stone.

The detail was exquisite. As he studied it, he could see knots and grain as though it were real wood, stripped of its bark and turned to stone.

"This wand may help you, if you can learn its secret," Sharilan told him. "Unfortunately, that is all the help I can give. It supposedly belonged to the witch who has my sister, but I don't know what it does. Maybe it will help, maybe it won't."

Erwyn slid the branch into a pocket in his tunic. The school's tailors designed the pocket to hold such a wand, but he wouldn't be given one of his own until he became a Master in his Art. The wand itself was worth a little damsel-rescuing. It might even count as credit toward his Masters. *If* he could figure out how it worked.

The branch settled comfortably into the pocket. Its weight felt reassuring somehow, as if it belonged there.

Once more, he shouldered his pack, preparing to leave. "I don't know how much good I'll be to you or your sister," he said, smiling hesitantly, "but I'll give it a try."

Feeling gallant, he took her hand and kissed it. Then he turned and walked into the trees.

He had only walked for a few minutes before a disturbing thought occurred to him: If Sharilan was only just learning magic, how could she have made an entrance the way she did?

And how did she acquire a wand that belonged to the witch who imprisoned her sister? And why did she need *him* to rescue said sister? And how could he be sure Fenoria was Sharilan's sister, anyway?

Erwyn did not believe in coincidence. And, as far as he knew, witches who could imprison damsels in guarded castles did not make mistakes like leaving wands lying about unguarded. Moreover, now that he thought about it, he realized that Sharilan never actually told him where to find this guarded castle with its distressed damsel. And, in the second version of the story, she hadn't mentioned being spell-stuck to that rock.

Ergo, Sharilan had lied to him. Again. She might not have fooled him with her first story, but she certainly suckered him with the second.

Of course, there might have been more to the story than the words. He thought about the spell that had brought him to her and wondered how many more spells she knew. Unfortunately, the only way he could learn exactly what was going on, without having to confront Sharilan again, was to find this Fenoria person.

Then again, he *could* just skip the whole thing and get on with his life.

Unfortunately, the whole business smacked of mystery. Erwyn hated unsolved mysteries almost as much as he hated damsels.

6

A Bump in the Knight

(Or, One More for the Road)

Night falls quickly beneath the shelter of a forest.
                                    Sorcerers Almanac
                    Section One: On Getting the Lay of the Land

Well, mystery or no mystery, the time had come to continue his wanderings. Or more precisely, his escape. While he still could.

That proved to be more difficult than it sounded. Sometime during his interview with Sharilan, the sun had set.

"Crap! I can't see a damn thing."

Erwyn paused, balancing on one foot while he rubbed the big toe on the other.

"Damn tree roots!"

His leg cramped again, and he crashed helplessly into a pile of damp, musty leaves.

"This will never do," he proclaimed loudly to anyone—or anything—who might be listening.

He stretched his hand out before him, palm up. How did that spell go again?

He started to look through his pack for his spellbook. But it was so dark that he wouldn't be able to read the book without the very spell he sought. He couldn't even see well enough to find the book.

"Well, here goes nothing!"

Carefully, he built the foxfire spell, centering the spell on his palm. A tiny ball of light appeared over his hand.

As he slowly added power to the spell, the foxfire glow increased until it gave off as much light as a small torch. He lowered his hand. The sphere wobbled a little, then steadied itself at chest height.

He dropped his hand to his knee and the tension left his shoulders. He was glad he got the spell right. No telling what might happen if he got foxfire mixed up with something else. He grimaced at the thought. With his kind of luck, it would be something worse than a small thunderstorm. Possibly even lethal.

While he finished rubbing the knots out of his leg muscles, he stared at the trail, or at least what he could see of it in the small ball of light. Whether or not Sharilan was on his tail, he hadn't the energy to do anything about it. He was just too tired to go anywhere.

This seemed like as good a place as any, so Erwyn decided to camp right where he was. The path continued in two directions beyond his small circle of light, the way he'd come from, and the way he was going. At least he couldn't get lost. Theoretically.

The trees grew far enough apart along the path to allow room for a fire, and the lowest branches hung well above his head. It seemed safe.

Besides, he had a sneaking suspicion it wouldn't be a good idea to leave the trail. He probably wouldn't find a better place anywhere away from it, but he might find something else. And the something else might be hungry.

Speaking of which . . .

He set about gathering dry branches to make a fire and clearing away the dead leaves around his chosen spot. The foxfire ball followed him. That was good.

He smiled to himself. It gave him a warm feeling to do

something well.

Returning to the center of the path, he prepared to lay his fire. He felt like being artistic and decided to try something new. After a few minutes of futzing around, he had a passable cone made of twigs, like a small tent. Then he began his spell to light the wood.

A loud crash in the underbrush broke his concentration. Fortunately, he hadn't gotten far enough into the spell for it to be dangerous. Whatever made the racket was either very clumsy or very strong. Maybe both.

Assuming the latter, Erwyn tensed. He should be prepared for flight. Or something.

Once again, he ran through his small collection of spells. What would work against whatever beasts prowled these woods? Wind? Nope. Refrigeration? Uh-uh. Fire? Maybe. Levitation? Not with all those trees.

He heard another loud crash, closer this time.

"Oh, the hell with it!" He grabbed his pack and started to run. The fireball followed him.

"Oh, great!"

The foxfire ball made him a perfect target. Whatever was out there couldn't help but see him. He could either face the beast, or extinguish the ball and kill himself stumbling around in the dark. Not a pretty thought.

Besides, the creature could probably see in the dark.

Another crash.

Then again, maybe it couldn't.

Suddenly the creature burst into his haven of light, and he didn't have to worry about it anymore. Erwyn stared, mouth open.

It was an old man, in full antique armor, complete with broadsword and lance, minus horse. His helm sat askew on stringy gray hair, while a huge, bushy gray mustache hid most of his face. He was dirty and rusty and—Erwyn sniffed —smelly.

"Aroint thee, varlet! I'll hack off thy tail and hale out thine innards!" The man swung his sword in Erwyn's direction.

The old boy's completely nuts, Erwyn thought, leaning away from the blow. The guy sounded as if he'd come straight out of Sharilan's fairy tale.

Erwyn watched, incredulous, as the knight swung his sword again, close enough to make the young sorcerer a little nervous.

"Excuse me," Erwyn began, clearing his throat. "Would you mind terribly not waving that sword quite so close? You might hurt someone. Possibly me." Erwyn ducked and the sword whistled past his ear.

"Stand still, thou mangy lizard, while I lop off thine head." The knight swung again, this time missing his mark completely. He spun around in a complete circle, barely managing to keep to his feet.

"I will *not* stand still, and I am *not* a lizard, mangy or otherwise!" Irritated, Erwyn allowed his voice to rise. In fact, he practically screamed in the old man's face.

The old man stopped, blinking in Erwyn's direction. "Art thou not a foul, fire-breathing dragon, who sears maidens with his very breath?" he asked in a tremulous voice.

"Nope. I may be a little foul, but I don't breathe fire, and I don't care much for charbroiled maiden. I prefer a nice, juicy steak. Rare. With lots of catsup."

"I beg yer pardon." The old man squinted, rubbed a grimy, gauntleted hand across his eyes, and squinted again. "I thought ye were that pernicious dragon I've been chasing for the past twenty years."

"Sorry, not guilty. I'm still a couple years shy of being twenty. But I'm certain that if you keep crashing about in the underbrush awhile longer, something will turn up."

"Oh, that's all right. I think I'll just rest meself here by yer fire." The old man sat down in the middle of the path, rusty armor creaking as he lowered himself to the ground.

"But I don't have a fire yet!" Erwyn cried, exasperated.

"That, too."

The knight looked down at his knees while Erwyn stared in confusion. After a few moments, the old man started snoring. Loudly.

Cursing under his breath, Erwyn sat down beside the firepit. He'd knocked down his carefully built teepee of sticks, scattering the pieces everywhere.

Regathering the wood, Erwyn tried again, but his hands shook too much. Probably only frustration, but he just couldn't get the wood to cooperate. So much for being artistic.

Finally, Erwyn gave up on design and just piled the sticks into a heap and lit them. While he watched the flames lick hungrily at the wood, he thought about the missing tinderbox.

Now that he thought about it, the school hadn't given him much of anything, as far as tools for survival went. He carried the required equipment, plus a small amount of jerky he'd sneaked out of his room at the last minute. Not much. The *Almanac* had been optional, and he hadn't thought he'd need it. It wasn't much help in an emergency, unless you already knew what it said. And you couldn't eat it. Additional food supplies had been on the "officially forbidden" list.

Of course, it was possible the school sent journeymen out without any supplies to force them to rely on their magical abilities for survival, to stretch their powers. Or maybe the teachers at the school were a bunch of power-mad sadists who enjoyed putting people into difficult situations. Either way, it was a pain in the posterior.

Erwyn sighed and fed more wood to his fire. Once the fire burned briskly, he dismissed the foxfire ball with a wave of his hand. That done, he nibbled on a piece of jerky from his pack and contemplated his future. The next four years of it, anyway.

> *Worrying too much about everything is bad for the digestion. On the other hand, not worrying enough could be fatal.*
> > Sorcerers Almanac
> > Section Four: On How to Have a Safe Trip

The more he thought about it, the more certain he became that Sharilan was using him for something. Or planning to.

Okay. So maybe he simply stated the obvious. Question was, what did she plan for him? And, while he was on the subject, why *him*?

Erwyn started to go over in his mind everything he knew about the situation. After a few minutes of trying to think of something, he gave up. It was easier to list what he *didn't* know.

He didn't know where to find Fenoria, or even if she existed. He didn't know if Sharilan could be trusted, so anything she told him was therefore suspect. And he didn't know how he would survive if problems like this kept cropping up all the time.

Sharilan couldn't seriously expect him to find the castle without directions. Come on! Let's get real, here.

Erwyn once more considered removing his guild patch, getting a respectable job, and forgetting the whole thing. If no one knew what he was supposed to be, no one would ask him to do anything. Maybe.

Anyway, he had given his word to Sharilan, and until he had a good reason not to, he would have to continue with this quest of hers. His personal code of conduct would allow him no less.

Having come to this world-shaking conclusion, Erwyn turned to his studies. He read through part of his spellbook and worked on a few of the newer spells. Periodically, he looked up to see if the old man showed any signs of waking and (he hoped) leaving.

An hour and a half and six spells later, Erwyn decided that the old knight was simply not going to leave. He shook his head and shifted into a more comfortable position.

This was the part he liked best, even better than spell practice. He didn't really have a chance to enjoy it the last time.

Relaxing completely and closing his eyes, Erwyn allowed

himself to reach the meditative state required to set his wards. The familiar, welcome feeling of well-being washed over him.

He always felt so much more alive when he meditated. More confident. As if he could do anything he wished, just by thinking about it. It felt great. He could keep this up forever.

Only it wasn't a very good idea. Remaining in his trance-like state without a guard could be unhealthful, if not actually fatal.

Reluctantly, he turned his thoughts to the construction of the wards. He envisioned a hemisphere of blue lines, crossing to form a protective network. Then he expanded the vision to enclose himself, his fire, and, out of necessity, his companion.

Slowly Erwyn added to his mental image until the vision glowed brightly. His fingers tingled and the hairs on his arms stood on end.

Erwyn almost lost the spell then. He had never felt like that before. It was wonderful. Also scary.

He tried harder to concentrate, ignoring the sensation while he finished his spell. The dome covered a larger area than usual, so he took extra care to build it. The concentration it required helped him forget his troubles.

Maybe that was the difference. More to worry about, more concentration required, hence more noticeable effect. Then again, it probably wasn't.

Once finished, he opened his eyes. Across the fire, the old man still slept, his chin resting on his chest. There was nothing Erwyn could do about him until morning. He crawled between his blankets and pulled his pack toward him to use as a pillow.

The night was cool, holding a promise of winter to come. He spread his cloak atop his blankets for added warmth and snuggled deeper into his bedroll. His elbow brushed against the slender length of the wand in his tunic pocket.

There's something very odd about that wand, he thought.

I must remember to examine it. Soon.

But he just didn't have the energy. The wand would have to wait until some other time. He patted it a couple of times, then drifted off to sleep with his hand resting across the pocket.

He woke the next morning stiff and sore, as usual, from the trials of the previous day, but found no serious damage done. His cloak was damp from the morning dew, and not much sunlight had managed to penetrate beneath the trees for it to dry.

His unwelcome guest sprawled on the ground at the other side of the firepit, still snoring. Erwyn allowed himself a martyrlike sigh. He would get no help from that quarter this morning. Not that he expected any.

The fire had burned down to embers. After banishing the wards, he gathered some more firewood, and soon the flames blazed merrily.

While the heat penetrated his stiffened muscles, he opened his pack and got out his journal again. For a few moments he just sat rereading the previous paragraphs.

Then he pulled out his pen and began writing, filling in the details since his last entry. Perhaps he could keep his mind off his problems by ignoring them.

Though I had in no way threatened it, the huge bird attacked me viciously. I tried bravely to defend myself, but to no avail. The creature was too much for me. I snatched my pack and raced across the field of grass.

I ran for hours before I reached the forest. There was something strange about it, something hauntingly evil, hauntingly beautiful. Without a second thought, I entered the enchanted wood, determined to get to the root of the problem.

The sorceress within the wood tried to enslave me, but I fought valiantly to free myself. I would never give in to her demands, never, though my life should be forfeit. Finally, I fought my way clear of her spells and traps, and escaped.

Sharilan.

So much for the "ignore it and it will go away" approach. His mind kept returning to the woman in the wood.

He had a sneaky feeling it was important to find out what game she played, and what role she expected him to play in it. There was more to this business than simply freeing a girl from an enchanted castle.

He shook his head and continued his writing.

I was alive, but my tunic would never be the same. In her desperation, the sorceress had shredded my clothing. I was, however, determined to make use of the information she had let slip.

Somewhere, there is an unfortunate damsel in distress. It is my duty to save her, even if it kills me. I must press onward, into the jaws of death.

That might be closer to the truth than he wanted to believe. Lords! What kind of mess had he gotten into this time? So many questions and only one answer. And he was getting a little tired of "I don't know."

When in doubt, change subjects. Erwyn looked across the clearing.

"What do I do with you?" he murmured to his still-sleeping guest.

Erwyn thought for a moment and came up with an answer. He didn't know.

He couldn't leave him, alone and unprotected. Okay. So the old guy *did* have a sword and lance, not to mention plate armor. But other than that, he was defenseless.

On the other hand, Erwyn couldn't have him tagging along for the next four years.

On the third hand, if normal mortal folk never visited this wood, what in the name of the Four Hells was the old man doing here in the first place?

Here he was, barely into the first year of his travels and, rather than filling his days with the bliss of boredom, he'd had to deal with a quest, a mysterious mage, a damsel in distress, a mystery, a mysterious knight, and a bucket-load of unanswered questions. Erwyn never was very good at leaving unanswered questions unanswered.

Like the time he just *had* to find out how to work the Fourth Class levitation spell . . .

7

Up, Up, and Away

(Or, Dust the Rafters While You're Up There)

Curiosity and inventiveness can make the life of a sorcerer
both interesting and rewarding. A little caution is good, too.
                                        Sorcerers Almanac
                        Section Six: On the Successful Use of Magic

He couldn't wait a year to have it taught to him properly.
Nope. Not him. He went looking for enlightenment.

Late one evening, after classes were over and all good
little apprentices should have been meditating or practicing
their spells, Erwyn sneaked into the Applications Master's
library.

The Masters were in their private dining hall, laughing
over the "mistake of the day" and whoever made it.

The door had a simple iron lock. In no time, Erwyn
opened it, using his dagger and no feat of magic at all. He
didn't think that there would be any other sort of protection
set on that door. Okay, he didn't think.

He entered Master Gordrun's sanctum sanctorum quietly.
Before him stretched row upon row of leatherbound books.
Magic books, recipe books, and history books. Books with
ordinary letters stamped on their spines, books covered with

glowing runes, and books with no writing on them at all.

There was one book in particular that Erwyn sought: Gordrun's reference book. The instruction manual. The place where old Gordrun got the spells he used to torture his pupils. An ancient book, decrepit, and filled with all the spells a fledgling magic-user could possibly desire.

His heart beat loudly as he glanced furtively down the hall and carefully closed the door.

The book lay open on a high wooden pedestal on the other side of the room. A tall candle rested on a small shelf next to the book, illuminating the pages.

Erwyn started across the room. He was halfway across when . . .

Creak!

"Crap!" He froze, listening for any sound from the hall. It was probably the only loose board in the room, so of course he found it. Now the school would find him. He stood there for almost half an eternity, waiting, but no one came to investigate.

Sighing with relief, he managed to cross the rest of the room and reach the book without further mishap.

He stared at the pages of the book in front of him. "Wow!"

Before him were hundreds of incantations, gestures, potion recipes, and descriptions of magical devices. Each page was beautifully decorated with illustrations. Mythical beasts leaped though magical forests. Vines heavy with fruit twined about enchanted maidens. Small creatures peered out from beneath dew-laden leaves.

He felt a tightness in his chest and realized he'd been holding his breath. His fingers tingled as he turned the pages, savoring each of them in turn until he found the levitation spell he sought.

It was simple enough. He memorized the feel of it, the gestures involved. The spell seemed to sing in his brain. It was so easy!

He built the spell in his mind, giving it power from his

own store of energies. And pushed.

Then he realized he'd goofed. He was supposed to rise gently, like a feather. Instead, he shot upward like an arrow. It was wonderful.

Air rushed past him as he soared toward the vaulted ceiling. *Crack!* He floated near the rafters, rubbing his aching head.

"Oh, no!" He looked down toward the distant floor.

He'd forgotten one tiny detail. He knew how to go up, but he had no idea how to get back down!

He bobbed there, twelve feet above the book that could have been his salvation. Stranded as he was on the ceiling, he couldn't turn the pages to find the counterspell even if he *could* read it from there, which he couldn't.

"Erwyn, you've gotten yourself into a real mess, now." *That* was an understatement. "So what are you going to do about it?" Good question.

Being found floating against the ceiling would be extremely embarrassing and could conceivably get him suspended . . . er . . . kicked out of school. There had to be some way to get down.

While he hung there, wondering what to do, the door opened, and a black-clad figure shuffled into the room. Erwyn's heart stopped. At least, that's what it felt like.

It wasn't Master Gordrun, fortunately. Old Master Falwrickel stood just inside the door while the boy tried vainly to float out of sight.

Erwyn took a deep breath, preparing himself for a display of temper such as he had never seen. He was, however, disappointed.

The old man glanced once at the young apprentice dangling against the ceiling. Then he tucked his hands into the sleeves of his robe and bowed his head. But not before Erwyn caught the hint of a smile on the Master Sorcerer's face. The old man shuffled into the library, and the door swung gently shut behind him.

Master Falwrickel searched through the rows of books as

though Erwyn wasn't even there. Erwyn watched him, wondering.

With a cry of triumph, the old man pounced upon one small volume bound in red leather, then shuffled back toward the door. Just before he opened the door, he turned back to the boy, that smile still peeking out through his wrinkles.

"Apprentices get themselves into some of the most interesting predicaments, don't you think?" He paused, stuffing his book into a hidden pocket in his robe.

"You know," he added mischievously, "levitation spells work on other things besides people. Think about it." After which, he opened the door and left.

Erwyn thought he heard a soft chuckle as the latch clicked behind the old man. He considered the matter for a minute or two. "Other things besides people?"

He looked around. The room contained nothing except some musty old stuffed animals, a long wooden table, some writing materials, and lots of books.

Books? That was it!

Gathering his scattered wits, Erwyn recalled again the levitation spell. Carefully, he aimed the spell at the book below him, spreading it to include the candle as well. He frowned, concentrating a small portion of his energy on his goal.

Book and candle rose toward him slowly. It wouldn't do to crash them into the ceiling, too. But it certainly was hard work being careful.

Footsteps sounded in the corridor outside, and Erwyn's heart skipped a few beats. His concentration faltered. Book and candle fell toward the floor. Quickly, he "caught" them. The footsteps continued down the hall, leaving Erwyn weak-kneed (or a reasonable approximation, considering). Eventually, the book and candle reached him, and he leveled the spell off.

Erwyn hurriedly searched through the book for the correct counterspell. He found it with no trouble. The counterspell turned out to be only a little more complicated than the levitation spell, and he memorized it in minutes.

With all the control he could muster, he tried to lower himself, the book, and the candle gently to the ground.

Moments later, the book and candle landed on the table with a muffled thump, and he released the spell. Unfortunately, while the book and candle were safe, he wasn't. He fell the last couple of feet, his ankle twisting painfully beneath him as he landed heavily on the floor.

Erwyn returned the book to its stand and hurried to the exit as fast as he could. He locked the door on his way out, then limped toward his quarters and safety.

At least, he thought he was safe, assuming old Falwrickel didn't tell anyone. Boy, was he wrong!

The next morning at Applications practice, Master Gordrun had a surprise in store for his young pupil. "Today, students," he said, rubbing his hands together in anticipation, "we are going to make a slight departure from the norm.

"A few of you think you are ready to attempt some of the higher-level spells, so today we are going to let you try one or two. Apprentice Erwyn" —he looked directly at the boy with a predatory smile— "would you like to help me demonstrate the Fourth Level levitation spell?"

Erwyn never knew how he managed to keep from fainting.

At first, he thought Falwrickel had ratted on him. Not so, he learned later.

Each door had a simple iron lock, so simple absolutely *anyone* could open it. And each door had a warning spell on it, a magic burglar alarm. If the door was opened without negating the spell, the Masters would be alerted. After a reasonable time, someone went to check up on the intruder.

Apparently, the school not only tolerated such excursions, but actually encouraged them. Not openly, of course. But then, no one ever really tried to *prevent* an apprentice from sneaking into the libraries, by magical or any other means. After all, ingenuity and daring are desirable traits in a magic-user.

How long ago it all seemed. If anyone had told Erwyn a year ago that he would actually be thinking fond thoughts about Apprentice School, he would have used that levitation spell on the person just to see exactly how far is *up!* But now, he found himself honestly wishing for that quiet, peaceful time in his life.

Peace and quiet seemed to be in short supply these days.

8

Enlightenment

(Or, Where Magic Flows, Trouble Follows)

It is not natural for too many plants with magic properties to grow in the same area. If you find such a garden, find out who planted it and make sure both plants and people are friendly.

Sorcerers Almanac
Section One: On Getting the Lay of the Land

Erwyn closed his book and returned it to his pack. The fire had burned down again. Since he hadn't put much wood on it, he'd expected that. With his eyes on his still-sleeping guest, he rose and kicked the sticks apart, making a lot of noise in the process. No reaction.

He pushed a mound of dirt atop the embers, stirring the dirt and wood together, again loudly. The old man still lay snoring in his sleep.

Erwyn shook his head and refrained from laughing aloud. Not wishing to delay any longer, he hoisted his pack and got ready to leave. He walked about six feet before . . .

"Hold on there, young fella!" the old man's creaky voice sounded behind him. "I've a mind to tag along, if it's all right." He spoke like a commoner, with a thick accent. "I'll just get me things here." Bending slowly, he picked up the weapons he'd left in the now-damp grass. They weren't even wet.

"Actually . . ." Erwyn started to reply. He swallowed his answer before it escaped. Something more important had just occurred to him. "What happened to all that 'Aroint thee, varlet' stuff? You sure talked a lot differently last night."

The old man smiled nervously. "It was the first thing I thought of. I, uh . . ." He paused, fumbling for words. "I wanted some company."

"I think a simple 'Mind if I join you?' would have sufficed. Anyway, I'm probably not going the same direction you are." He smiled hopefully.

"Sure ye are, sure ye are." The old man laughed and stepped up to Erwyn's side.

"But which way are you going?"

"Old Chesric's goin' the same way you are."

"But . . ."

"Come on, young fella. Time's a-wastin'."

So Erwyn allowed himself to be towed along the path, muttering feeble protests all the way and cursing himself for being too spineless to stick up for himself.

While they walked, the old man kept up a running commentary on just about everything in their path.

"The Western Wood is a very special place," he was saying. "Take those trees over there." He gestured toward some trees to their left. "Do ye know what they are?"

Erwyn shook his head. "Nope," he replied without looking up, then added softly, "And only a short time ago, I actually *missed* being back in school!"

Fortunately the old man wasn't listening.

"Those're oak trees," Chesric continued. "Those're ash." He nodded in another direction. "And over there," he said, pointing somewhere to the right, "are some rowan trees. Hawthorn, cedar, aconite. So close together. Don't ye understand the significance of this?"

"No," Erwyn answered automatically.

Actually, he was looking down at his feet shuffling in the dirt and leaves. He didn't know what the old man was talking about. "What's so strange about it?"

"Well," the man said, fixing Erwyn with a hard stare, "it would be unlikely for 'em to just grow here by accident. Someone planted 'em here on purpose. Ye see, young fella, those plants have magical properties."

Erwyn stopped. "Huh? What did you say?"

The old man's voice changed as he reiterated, "I said, those plants have magical properties." For a moment, he didn't sound like a crotchety old peasant anymore. "Their wood is used in making wands and staffs. Mages use the leaves, nuts, and berries for potions and to ward off evil." He seemed to realize his mistake suddenly, and the peasant accent came back thicker than before. "Ye wear that on yer chest, and ye don't *know?*" He poked at Erwyn's guild patch.

"Well, uh . . ." He meant to say something about Chesric's accent, but instead retreated before the old man's verbal attack.

"Some magic-user ye'll be, assumin' ye survive at all. These here are the basics of magic. The tools of the trade." The man shook his head. "Ye should know 'em by heart."

Erwyn flushed guiltily for a moment, then made a half-hearted attempt at a defense. "There didn't seem to be much point. I'm not very good, anyway. I'll probably never need to know that much about the 'tools of the trade,' as you call them."

Wait a minute! What did he have to feel guilty for? He hadn't been *that* bad. He'd actually listened to most of the stuff his instructors tried to cram into his head, unlike some of his fellow students. When he bothered to show up for class, that is.

"Anyway," he continued aloud, "I don't think they ever told us *apprentices* anything about that stuff. It's probably the kind of thing we're supposed to learn while we're journeymen."

"Well, yer a journeyman, aren't ye?"

"Yeah, but . . ."

"So, now ye know." The old man turned back to the path. "Good thing I came along to help."

"Now, wait just a minute!"

Erwyn grabbed Chesric by the arm and hauled him back around to face him. Not an easy task, since the old guy still wore his armor.

"Who are you, really? And how come you know so much about an enchanted wood where supposedly no one ever comes?"

"I told you, my name is Chesric."

"And . . . ?"

"And what?"

"What are you? Who are you? What are you doing here? And how do you know so much about magic? Are you a spy from the school?"

"Bet ye didn't ask this many questions while ye were in that there school." The old man nudged Erwyn in the ribs. Then he became serious again. "I don't really know that much about magic, but I've got a lot of common sense. A staff made from ash works just as well to protect someone without the Gift as with it.

"Rowan berries, too. And hawthorn. And aconite. Don't need to be a mage to use them. As to *what* I am," Chesric said, shrugging, "I'm just an old knight on a quest—to nowhere."

"Nowhere?"

"And everywhere. I travel around the world, trying to find me a dragon. Occasionally, I hook up with some young fella who's still a bit wet behind the ears, and help him stay alive until they're dry."

"Now, wait a minute." Erwyn felt his face redden.

"Now, now. Don't go gettin' yer dander up. I didn't mean it as an insult. Ye've got to admit, yer a bit inexperienced." He smiled. Erwyn could tell because the edges of his mustache twitched upward.

The boy sputtered for a minute more, but the old man was right.

"Yes, I guess I am," Erwyn admitted. "I just wanted to make it through this by myself. Anyway, what business is it of yours?"

"And yer doin' a fine job, so far." The old man ignored the last question. "I just thought I'd tag along and see what kind of mischief I can get meself into. I figure a young journeyman sorcerer probably attracts all kinds of interesting people."

"What do you mean 'attracts all kinds of interesting people'?"

"You know. Magic attracts magic. And magic attracts adventure. Don't they teach you young folks *anything?*"

Erwyn stared at the old man for a moment. Magic attracts magic. Pieces of the puzzle began to fall into place. Since he'd left the school, he'd been beset by all sorts of unexplained and unexplainable events.

Like the army riding out of Burgdell just before he decided to go there. And the bird chasing him across the field when he couldn't make up his mind. Sharilan and the enchanted forest. Chesric finding him in that same enchanted forest. Everything.

Maybe that was it. "You mean I can't avoid trouble because, sooner or later, it will find me?"

"Somethin' like that."

"Sounds a lot like homework," Erwyn grumbled. "Cause and effect, huh? By using magic to survive, I get forced into a position where I have to use more magic to survive. Right?" This could be a problem. It could also be interesting. "So that business with Sharilan, and the bird and everything, was just the natural outcome of my using magic?"

Chesric had been smiling indulgently, but suddenly his expression grew serious. Some of the sparkle left his eyes. "Sharilan? What do you know of her?" His voice was stern, demanding an answer.

Noting the tone of voice, Erwyn looked toward the old

man. "I met her in this wood." He pointed the way they had come. "Back there. Why?"

"If she's mixed up in this, there must be more to you than meets the eye." Chesric looked at Erwyn critically, as though seeing him for the first time.

"I doubt that very much." The old man's scrutiny made Erwyn uncomfortable. "Who is she?"

"Sharilan is a most powerful sorceress—in the *old* meaning of the word." He raised one bushy eyebrow for emphasis. "She practices evil magic, human sacrifice, the lot. And she don't care one whit fer those she hurts in the process. If she sent ye on a quest, ye can bet her reasons weren't good fer anyone but her. Are ye sure that was the first time ye ever met her?"

"Yeah. I'd definitely remember her if I'd seen her before. You say she's an *evil* sorceress?"

"The worst."

Erwyn felt his knees begin to wobble, and there was a sinking feeling in his gut. He did remember the archaic method of practicing sorcery, and he didn't like it.

"Take it easy, boy." Chesric grabbed Erwyn's arm. "Here, have a sit. Ye look a mite green around the edges."

"Wouldn't you, if you just found out you'd had a close encounter with someone like that?"

"Ye've got a point."

"So why'd she pick on me?"

"I don't know fer sure. I *can* think of a few possibilities, though."

"Like?"

"Like maybe yer potentially very powerful and she's out to eliminate a future rival."

"Not likely. What are my other choices?"

"Yer either very unlucky, or so magic-poor that she figures she can use ye any way she likes."

"Could be either or both. But there's another possibility you've either overlooked, or deliberately omitted."

"Which is?"

"That I'm an agent of hers, sent on some sort of errand for her."

"I doubt that."

"Why?"

"Well, if ye were, ye wouldn't likely be standin' there tellin' me about it."

"Oh."

"Me, I favor option one."

"Whatever for?"

"Mostly because if it's true, then ye might be kinda fun to have around. Liven up an old man's final years."

"And if it isn't true?"

"Then yer goin' to have a mighty difficult time tryin' to stay alive. Sharilan don't hang on to a tool long once she's through with it."

"Great! So I've got to either learn a hell of a lot in a very short space of time, or I'm going to die. Is that it?"

"That about sums it up."

Erwyn felt one first-class depression building. "So I might as well just give up while I'm behind."

"I wouldn't recommend the givin' up part."

"What do you suggest? I'm not likely to become a super sorcerer overnight. I'm just not that good." He kicked at a pile of leaves in frustration. "Oh, I do pretty well at the basic charms and things, but you only need to have a positive score on the tests to be able to do that. But the advanced spells . . . I don't have much hope of mastering them. I barely got into the school. I didn't even score very high on the entrance exam."

Erwyn couldn't interpret the look Chesric gave him as the old man replied, "Boy, ye've got some strange ideas in yer head. Those tests don't tell ye how much magic yer capable of. They only tell ye how much magic yer capable of *at the time of the test!*"

"You mean, I *can* learn the higher-level spells?"

"Sure, if ye really want to. It's all up here." He tapped his temple. "Have ye been tested since ye went to that there school?"

"No. Maybe. I don't know. I suppose some of the tests they gave us might have been evaluation tests. It all runs together after a while." Erwyn sat down on the damp ground and put his arms around his knees. "Besides, they didn't give us the results of any of our tests, except for telling us whether we passed or failed."

"There, ye see? They've probably been testin' ye all along, and ye didn't even know it." Chesric clapped Erwyn on the back and reached down to help him stand. "By the way, I can't just go about callin' ye 'boy,' boy. How 'bout I just call ye Erwyn?"

He extended his arm, which Erwyn clasped firmly. It took him a few minutes to remember that he hadn't told the old knight his name. More important, Chesric had managed to talk at great length about a whole lot of things. Without really answering any of Erwyn's questions.

9

Brief Encounter

(Or, The Magic Gets in the Way)

Doing a good deed can often help cement relations between you and the natives. It may also lead to complications.

Sorcerers Almanac
Section Three: On People and Their Influence

"Doesn't this stupid forest ever end?" Erwyn shifted his pack and kicked angrily at a rock.

They'd walked forever, it seemed, and still hadn't seen daylight. Erwyn was tired and hungry. And to top it off, Chesric had kept up his running commentary on the unusual local flora.

At first, Erwyn tried to listen to what the old man had to say. It helped pass the time. Besides, if he kept his ears—and mind—open he might accidentally learn something important. But now his feet hurt. He wanted to see something other than trees and the back of Chesric's rusty armor.

He kicked another stone and watched it sail into a pile of decaying leaves. As he turned back to the path, he noticed Chesric watching him.

"Problem?" Erwyn planted his hands on his hips and stared back at the old man.

"Not yet."

"What's *that* supposed to mean?"

"Only that, considerin' where ye are, ye might want to stop abusin' the real estate. Before it starts abusin' you."

"Come on, Chesric. They're just rocks!" Feeling defiant, he kicked another. The fist-sized stone flew into the air and landed against a tree with a loud "*Yeowtch!*"

Did he just hear what he *thought* he'd heard?

With Chesric looking on, he rushed to pick up the rock. Rolling it over in his hand, he examined it. It seemed ordinary enough. Solid, like a rock. Feathery veins of blue-green shimmered across its shiny black surface. It didn't even rattle when he shook it.

"Well?" Chesric finally ran out of patience.

Erwyn shrugged. "It's just a rock. I think maybe we were hearing things." He dropped it back on the ground.

"Did you *have* to do that?" the rock moaned. "As if I'm not sore enough already."

"You . . . you can talk!"

"Of quartz I can talk. I'm a roc."

"But rocks aren't supposed to talk."

"Another expert. Listen, kid, I don't know where you get your information, but every roc in my band talks constantly. Imagine the noise! Sheesh!"

"Now, hold on just a second. You're a rock, but you can talk?"

"I thought we'd established that already. You're a little slow today, aren't you, kid."

Erwyn glared at the . . . creature. "So how come none of the rest of these rocks talk?" He picked up a gray-brown pebble and threw it against a tree. Not even a whimper. "See?"

"Geez, of all the sorcerers in the world, I've gotta run into a *genius*. I'm a roc, kid. *R-o-c.* Roc. A big bird. Understand? I'm under a curse."

"How'd you know I'm a sorcerer?"

"That puke and yellow badge on your chest. Don't you

look at your clothes when you put them on?"

"Hey, watch your mouth, if you've got one. I don't have to stand here and be insulted."

"Really? Where *do* you go to get insulted? Sorry, kid, reflex action. Let's face it, sittin' around on the ground for a few months ain't any way to learn good manners. I'm sorry. Really."

"Uh-huh. So, how'd you end up in this predicament, anyway?"

"Me and the little woman had a falling-out. She said I took her too much for granite. So, I went out with the boys to let off a little steam. I drank too much, and feeling a little boulder than usual, I picked up a pretty trinket to take home to Ruby. To make up to her." He sighed. "It was a real beauty, too. Simply marbleous."

"And?"

"And the trinket turned out to be some sort of magic power focus, and the old geezer who owned it was a wizard or something. He took it back, the old pyrite. Anyway, he started waving his hands and mumbling and pointing in my direction. Boy, was I petrified! And darned if the old boy didn't stone me. I've been sitting here ever since, waiting."

"Waiting for what?"

"For someone like you to do something about it."

"Me?" Why did *he* always have to do everything?

"Makes sense to me." Chesric finally stuck his nose into the discussion. "How 'bout usin' one o' them magic spells of yers?"

"Because none of my spells will work on this. There are some potions and ointments and stuff that might do the job, but I don't exactly have the equipment handy to make any. Standard spell-removal techniques won't work if a power focus was used." He paused, trying to remember. What had Chesric been droning on about? Oak, ash, thorn. Rowan, aconite, rosemary. He looked around. No thistle, no unicorn root, no . . .

"Aha!"

"What aha? What's that mean?" The stone rocked in impatience.

Erwyn grabbed the roc and knelt beside a large fern. He swept the fronds aside and dropped the roc into a patch of tiny white flowers.

The blue-green lines on the stone glittered among the dark green leaves. Suddenly, the stone exploded in a burst of violet light and pink mist. The blast knocked Erwyn and Chesric to the ground.

"Holy moly!" The roc towered over them, flapping its wings. "I'm free! How'd you manage it?"

"Holy moly. You're standing in a patch of it." Erwyn almost laughed at the bird's confusion. "As Chesric's been saying for hours, the Western Wood is a pretty strange place."

"And here I thought ye weren't even listenin'." Chesric beamed with—pride?

"Some things do sink in. Besides, I've had some prior experience with moly." An experience he'd never forget. If it weren't for the patch of moly Master Berdun had cultivated in the school garden, Erwyn might still be a bench in Nasty Nazurski's caldron room.

The roc flapped his wings, twisting and turning to be sure everything was all right. He bounded over to the young sorcerer.

"If there's anything I can do for you, anything, ever, you just let me know. Okay, kid? You can count on Rocky. Boy, oh, boy, I can't wait to see the guys. Thanks a million, kid. This is just terrific. Say, what's your name, so's I can tell everyone?"

"My name's Erwyn, and if you don't mind, I'd rather you didn't go telling everyone about me."

"Why not? You should be proud of yourself. You're the greatest."

"Because if you go telling everyone about me, it could be very inconvenient. Anyway, don't you think you ought to go see your mate first? After all, 'going out with the guys' got you into the trouble I just got you out of."

"Yeah, you're right. I guess I should. Thanks again, kid." He flapped his wings a few more times, causing the leaves to dance across the path. Then he launched himself into the branches overhead.

Erwyn watched, fascinated, as the trees parted to allow Rocky passage. He turned to smile at Chesric. The smile became a grin as he saw what lay behind the old man. Apparently, freeing the roc had freed them from the endless forest, as well. "You know, Chesric, sometimes you've got to abuse the real estate. If I hadn't kicked him, we would never have found Rocky. And if we hadn't found Rocky, we might never have found that." He nodded in the direction they'd been headed.

A few yards down the path, the trees opened up onto a valley bathed in the crimson and yellow rays of sunset.

"Great! Why don't we camp right here, under the trees?" Chesric said, laying down his weapons and a pack that Erwyn didn't remember seeing before. "That is, if it's all right with you. Yer the leader of this expedition, after all."

I seriously doubt that, Erwyn thought. Aloud, he replied, "Sure. That's just fine." He had the feeling the decision had been made without him, anyway, but couldn't think of a reason to argue.

Dropping his pack where he stood, he started clearing a space for the fire, like he always did. Chesric looked on for a few minutes, then left without a word. He returned with an armload of wood, but his armor was missing.

"What happened to your armor?" Erwyn asked, eyeing the rumpled, sweat-stained tunic and hose the man wore.

"Can't hardly move around comfortably in that getup," Chesric answered. "I took it off while ye was gettin' the ground ready." While he spoke, he stacked the wood and laid the fire.

Erwyn watched his companion. The old man built the fire with only three medium-sized branches and a few twigs, like a letter "A" with a beard.

It looked a lot faster and easier to build than Erwyn's version, but not as interesting. When Chesric finished, the boy composed himself, preparing to light the fire. He built the spell slowly this time. He didn't want a repeat of his earlier experience.

> *Never allow little distractions to interfere with the casting of a spell.*
>
> *Sorcerers Almanac*
> *Section Six: On the Successful Use of Magic*

Chesric watched the boy with interest.

Erwyn had just started to cast the spell when . . .

"Whatcha doin'?"

Erwyn lost it. Released prematurely, the spell zapped the first thing in its path. Which happened to be his sleeve.

"Shit!" He grabbed his cloak and wrapped his arm. Then he glared at the old man. "I *was* trying to get our fire lit. Now I'm trying to put my arm out. Why?"

"Wouldn't it be more appropriate," Chesric said carefully, "to use plain ol' flint an' steel, instead of wastin' yer energy on cookfires?"

Erwyn just stared at him. "Sure, no problem. I'll just pull one out of my pack here." He snatched at the bag. The flap flew open, scattering its contents across the dirt.

"One journal book." Erwyn held it up to make certain Chesric saw it. "One Beginning Spellbook containing thirteen, count them, *thirteen* meager little spells. No flint and steel there.

"One slightly dull knife, two relatively clean tunics, a pair of pants, and a packet of jerky I hid in my pocket before I left. No flint and steel there, either. Got any suggestion? Maybe I should just make up a spell to conjure them."

He tossed the pack on top of his belongings.

"That's all ye've got with ye? Don't they give ye some sort of travel guide or instruction manual?"

"As a matter of fact, we were told we could bring a copy

of the *Sorcerers Almanac*, but I decided not to."

"Would ye mind tellin' me why?"

"Mostly because I didn't think I'd need it. I mean, it's *huge*, about three inches thick. I didn't want to lug it around for four years when I wasn't planning on using it."

"That the only reason?"

"That's the big one. That and the fact that it's the most annoying and frustrating book I've ever read."

"Frustratin'?"

"Yeah. It's self-updating." That explained everything, as far as Erwyn was concerned, but Chesric seemed to need more. "How would you like to read something, then go back a little while later and find it's not the same? It changes to reflect whatever the current situation is. And the way some petty tyrants like to bicker . . ."

"I can see where that might be a problem. But aren't there likely to be times when it would be more of a help than a hindrance?"

The old man had hit on one of the things that had really been bothering Erwyn. Had he made a serious mistake in leaving the book behind? Even if he had, he didn't feel like admitting it to a virtual stranger.

"I like traveling on the surprise-a-minute plan. Bringing the *Almanac* would have taken all the fun out of the trip. Listen, I'm tired and sore and hungry. And the last decent meal I had was about two days ago."

"*About* two days?"

"Give or take a month, yes."

"Ye ain't sure?"

"Listen, Chesric. I was under some kind of spell when I entered the forest, and I have absolutely no way of knowing how long I was there before you found me. It must have been just a couple of days, but it seemed like a couple of years.

He gazed at the fire, then continued almost apologetically. "I haven't even found time to try hunting or anything. I've been pretty busy."

"No matter. Tonight we'll eat well. I'll be right back."
Chesric fumbled in his pack briefly, then disappeared among
the trees.

With the old man gone, Erwyn could finally enjoy some
time to himself. He rose and leaned against a tree at the
edge of the forest. The sun was setting in a glorious array of
oranges, reds, and yellows. Purple against the sunset, clouds
drifted lazily across the land below. In the waning light, he
studied the land.

Beyond the wood, the terrain became rolling hills, covered mostly in short grass. Here and there a darker spot
marked stands of trees, or maybe rocks.

Farther on, the hills rose higher, becoming mountainous.
Unlike the grasslands on the other side of the forest, this
land had character.

The sun finally sank between two peaks in the distant
mountains, cutting off most of the light and throwing the
hills into shadow.

In the semidark, Erwyn thought he saw something move.
And it was coming toward him. Fast.

"Chesric!" Erwyn called as loudly as he could, trying to
keep the hysteria out of his voice while he moved away from
the edge of the wood. "Chesric, where are you?"

Suddenly, being alone didn't seem like such a good idea.
Right now, he wanted nothing more than to see the rumpled old knight come stumbling through the trees.

10

All Fired Up

(Or, Strangers in the Night, Exchanging Lances)

Always know the terrain and be prepared to defend your-self against wild animals.

Sorcerers Almanac
Section Four: On How to Have a Safe Trip

The shadowy figure continued its advance toward the trees.

Erwyn backed into the circle of light made by the fire while chills raced up and down his spine. The fire's warmth helped, but his silhouette against the flames could probably be seen for miles. And Erwyn couldn't see beyond that light.

"Why me? Why always me?" he moaned.

He had already been through this once or twice before. And he had a feeling that this time he wouldn't face anything as harmless as a philanthropic old man.

Desperate, he thumbed through his mental spellbook. Lightning might work, if he could separate it from the rain. But could he direct it accurately?

The shadow pounded closer.

Maybe he could levitate into a tree.

But what about Chesric?

Sleep spell? Someone, or some*thing*, might get hurt if the creature fell asleep on top of it. Besides, it didn't work on the orc. How did he know it would work on this?

Closer.

Invisibility spell? Suppose he flubbed it again.

Closer.

Protective wards? Not enough time.

Closer.

Okay. He'd try the invisibility spell and hope the old man could take care of himself.

He stepped closer to the fire and concentrated, calling up the spell. With another glance at the approaching shadow, he carefully wrapped the spell around himself. And ended up lying on the ground, flames reaching toward the sky like hair standing on end.

A log shifted beneath him and he winced. His flames flickered in reaction. They tickled. And he'd thought being a fire would feel better than being a tree. Hah! He only hoped the flames were feeding on his energy instead of his clothes.

Quickly, he summoned the dis-spell and stood once more beside the real fire.

The shadow had almost reached the edge of the wood.

Erwyn looked around wildly. His eyes fell on Chesric's sword lying across the clearing. He dashed around the fire. Grabbing the weapon, he held it awkwardly by its hilt.

The sword seemed in better shape than its owner. The blade glittered in the firelight, its surface clean, its edge sharp.

The hilt felt uncomfortable in Erwyn's hands. Awkward. Clumsy.

Clenching his teeth, he grasped the weapon tighter.

"I sure hope I can use this thing." His voice came out barely above a whisper.

The sword slipped in his grip, slick with sweat. Before Erwyn was ready, the creature arrived.

Paws drumming on the ground, tongue hanging from its

mouth, a large black wolf thudded into the firelight. It skidded to a halt, staring at Erwyn across the flames.

The boy stood his ground, arms trembling from the weight of the sword (at least he told himself the shaking was just caused by the sword). He watched the beast warily. He could almost believe he saw intelligence in those eyes. An alien, animal intelligence. It wanted—it wanted him!

Slowly, the wolf took a few steps forward.

Erwyn held the blade between them. He tried to remember all the stuff his instructor had tried to drill into him when he was a child. But he couldn't. That was a long time ago. The only blade he'd used since then was his belt knife.

The wolf came closer.

Erwyn looked into the creature's eyes again. That intelligence he'd first seen . . . maybe it wasn't so alien after all. He lowered the sword slightly.

The wolf stood in front of him, its nose nearly touching his hand. It was just about to . . .

Chesric burst into the clearing, a pair of rabbits dangling from his belt. "Get outta here, ye mangy cur!" He threw a rock at the beast for emphasis. The wolf whimpered as the rock bounced off its back. Then it ran off into the night.

Erwyn dropped the point of the sword into the dirt. Sweat dripped in his eyes, and his hair was damp. He forced his fingers to release the sword so he could wipe his forehead with the hem of his cloak. His hands shook.

At the edge of the fire's glow, Chesric watched the wolf lope into the hills. Then he turned to Erwyn.

"Don't never treat a sword like that, boy!" He rushed forward, snatching his weapon from Erwyn's hands. Then he pulled a rag out of his pack and started wiping the blade. "Didn't anyone ever teach you proper care of weapons?"

"Yeah, about six years ago, before I got into that stupid school!" Erwyn retorted.

He was getting tired of being pushed and led around. First that bird, then Sharilan, now this.

"I was twelve years old! I've spent most of the last six

years sitting on a stone bench listening to old men talk about potions and spells and incantations and stuff. And, anyway, I've seen you drop that sword into the dirt at least twice since you decided to 'tag along' with me."

"That's different." Chesric shrugged off Erwyn's protests. He put his weapon away, then proceed to skin and spit the rabbits.

"Yeah, right."

The old man continued to prepare dinner, ignoring Erwyn's insolent reply. "Ye mean to tell me ye didn't want to go to that there school?"

He caught Erwyn off guard with that one.

"What difference does it make? I went."

Why did Chesric need to know whether or not Erwyn wanted to go to the school?

"Might be important later."

"Sure. Uh-huh."

"Would ye just stop selling yerself short and answer me question?"

"What was the question again?"

For a second, Erwyn thought Chesric would give up and strangle him. The old man exerted what appeared to be a massive amount of self-control, however, and restated his question.

"Did you or did you not want to go to the Sorcerer's Apprentice School?"

Shrugging, Erwyn replied, "Yes and no."

Chesric had picked up a stick to feed the fire and it broke with a loud crack.

Quickly, Erwyn added, "Mostly, I went to the school to avoid getting betrothed—to a girl."

"That's the best thing for a boy to be betrothed to," Chesric replied.

"You obviously don't know Heatherlyn. Besides, have you ever been to Caldoria?"

"Not that I recollect."

"I'll save you the trouble. Caldoria is a wretched little

kingdom, full of smelly sulphur pits and bubbling lava pools. Almost everything that moves is deadly, and some of the dead things still move."

Erwyn jabbed the end of a branch into the fire, twirling it around until sparks flew into the sky to mingle with the stars. A few sparks landed on the rabbits, to lie smoking on the golden brown skin.

He pulled the stick out and stared at the few straggly smoking leaves it still bore.

"You know, there's practically no plant life in Caldoria? What little there is falls into one of the previously mentioned categories." He looked up into Chesric's eyes. "The climate is hot, humid, and sticky, and so are the women. Dragons love the place."

"Still, the girl is more important than the place where she lives, isn't she?"

"Not this one. I think her personality was poured from a syrup bottle. I'm surprised she doesn't draw flies. Then again, her perfume would probably just drive them away." Erwyn stared into the fire, feeling chills race up his spine at the mere thought of getting close to the princess.

"I'd rather have had an intimate relationship with one of the sulphur pits than marry Heatherlyn." He grimaced. "At least they smell better."

"But what possessed ye to choose magic as the alternative?"

"Not what. Who."

"Huh?"

"My father. He always wanted to be a sorcerer, or a magician, or something, but his father wouldn't let him. So I got to be the lucky one. Magic or marriage. Some choice."

"What will ye do when ye finish yer studies?"

"*If* I finish," Erwyn reminded him. "I don't really know. I figured I had at least fourteen years to decide, assuming I made it through the Master levels."

"How do ye feel about being a sorcerer?" Chesric began pacing around the fire, tugging thoughtfully at his mustache.

What was this, a job interview? "I'm not sure. When I work a spell, it's like . . . well . . . like I'm one with the whole world. Like I can do anything. Even when I don't quite get it right, it feels . . ." Erwyn shrugged. "I don't know. I can't explain it."

"But ye don't know if ye want to dedicate yer life to it?"

"Not yet." How could one simple conversation make him so miserable?

Erwyn's shoulders slumped a little. He took another jab at the fire.

Chesric walked up beside Erwyn and put his hand on the boy's shoulder.

"Someday, yer going to have to make a decision, boy. But it don't have to be tonight. Decisions that affect yer whole life shouldn't be rushed, or they tend to make ye miserable. Let's eat supper and get some sleep."

The old man ate quickly, leaving Erwyn to himself. When he finished, he pulled out his bedroll and dropped onto the ground on the opposite side of the fire. Erwyn watched, amused, while Chesric snuggled between the blankets with a chorus of grunts and groans. Moments later, he was snoring.

The young sorcerer couldn't help laughing to himself as he finished his share of meat, then shifted into a more comfortable position. He ought to go to bed, too, but he knew he wouldn't sleep. Not any time soon.

He lay in his bedroll with his pack beneath his head and his cloak wrapped tight around him. The ground was hard under the thin layer of bedding. Or maybe it only seemed that way because his brain wouldn't shut off.

Becoming a sorcerer had originally been just a way to avoid getting married. The lesser of two evils.

He had been occasionally bored and frequently intrigued by his studies. Some things were interesting, others were not. Some were just plain fun.

But did he want to practice sorcery for the rest of his life?

Voluntarily? Good question. He drifted into a restless sleep with that question on his mind.

* * * * *

"Honey, don't you think it's about time you got up?"

Erwyn's eyes snapped open. He stared for a minute into the face of—Heatherlyn! Complete with library pallor, dark circles, and frilly pink nightgown.

"H-Honey?"

"Yes, dear?" She smiled, showing rows of sharp teeth.

He sat up, suddenly aware of his surroundings. Then he leaped from the bed as though it were full of hot coals. The covers slid to the floor.

Heatherlyn smiled again, like a cat, as she ran her eyes from his face to a point halfway to his toes.

Erwyn looked down and grabbed the coverlet, blushing.

"Don't play games, dear. Get dressed. Our guests will be here soon. And start the fire, will you?" Now she sounded like his mother.

Had he married Heatherlyn, after all, and just dreamed all the stuff about the school? But it all seemed so *real*.

"What are you waiting for? Light the fire." Heatherlyn frowned. That was worse than her smile.

Reluctantly, he searched the mantel for a tinderbox. There wasn't one.

Heatherlyn returned in a combination orange, off-black, and teal riding outfit. Well, at least the colors weren't the pastels she normally wore.

"What are you looking for, dear?"

Erwyn stared at his toes, trying not to look at her. He didn't want a case of the dry heaves so early in the morning.

"You told me to light the fire. I'm looking for something to light it with." Preferably a servant.

"Silly boy! Not that way. I want you to, you know . . ." She sidled up to him, putting her arm around his shoulder and winking dramatically. "Do the magic thing. Light it with your mind. I *love* it when you do that."

"Light it with my m-mind?" What happened? How could he be married to Heatherlyn *and* have gone to the Sorcerer's Apprentice School?

He knelt beside the hearth and tried to remember the right spell. It came easily to mind. Too easily. He started to direct it toward the logs on the grate.

"Could you please *hurry*, Erwyn dear? The combination of a cold room and the crackle of magic is so . . . stimulating." She ran a hand across the back of his pants. Pants he hadn't had on a moment ago.

The fire erupted with a boom, knocking Erwyn to the ground.

He sat up, checking his eyebrows for signs of damage. Nothing was singed but his sleeve from when Chesric. . . Chesric! Erwyn breathed a sigh of relief. Just a nightmare. He snuggled back into his covers and waited for his heart to stop pounding. With dreams like that, soul-searching at bedtime could be hazardous to his health.

11

Revelation

(Or, Castles in the Air Tend to Fall Down)

Rain is a common occurrence in both spring and fall.
Flooding is likely in low-lying areas.

Sorcerers Almanac
Section Two: On Weather and Its Effects

Erwyn sighed for the umpteen-millionth time. Lords, but this part of the country was boring! From a distance, it had looked wonderful, with lots of dips and curves. But traversing those dips and curves was just plain work. And to top it off, it had started to rain.

Chesric stopped long enough to glance unhappily at the cloud-covered sky. "You do this?"

"Certainly. I just love slogging around soaking wet and hip-deep in mud."

"No need to go gettin' sarcastic on me."

Erwyn shifted his pack and wiped the water out of his eyes. "Why are we taking this route, anyway?"

"Don't be askin' me, boy. *You* picked the direction."

"Not this time. I've been following you since we left the forest a small slice of eternity ago."

"Maybe, but yer the one who went into that forest in the

first place. From where we were, there was only two directions to go: into the mountains or back through the forest. We can wander all over these here valleys fer years, but one fact will never change. There's only one route through these mountains that's passable to an old man and an inexperienced boy. That's where we're headed.

"O' course, if ye've a mind to try something harder, like climbing a sheer cliff, or ye hanker to go visit Sharilan again, I'd be happy to change direction."

"That's okay," Erwyn said quickly. "The way we're going is just great."

He continued to follow Chesric's lead as they wound in and out of the hills for what seemed like months, even if it was only a few weeks.

The old man seemed to know something about the area. But to Erwyn, the journey was so dull he couldn't even make up something interesting to write in his journal. His brain was too numb—or maybe it was just waterlogged.

He found himself hoping for something interesting to happen. Something like an irate giant bird, or a curious wolf, or even an evil wizard. Nothing too dangerous or elaborate, just something to relieve the boredom.

He didn't have anything to do except walk, so he spent a lot of time thinking about his future. Five or ten minutes, at least. Something more than how to survive the next four years.

He realized he had come to an important crossroad in his life. He just didn't know what to do about it.

Chesric diplomatically left Erwyn to himself. He probably knew better than to interrupt someone working on a first-class depression. For that, Erwyn was grateful. He wanted to be alone. He wanted company. He wanted something to do. He wanted time.

Wait a minute! What did he have to be so morose about? He *had* time. Four years of it, anyway. Surely he ought to be able to figure things out by then. And if he couldn't . . . well, he'd just have to face that when the time came.

That evening they made camp in the shelter of some rocks. While Chesric hunted, Erwyn pulled out the wand Sharilan had given him. Rolling the length of stone between his hands, he examined every knot and curve. He had to figure the wand out. He just *had* to. Somehow, he felt it was connected to his future as a sorcerer.

Thoughtfully, he ran his fingers over the length of the wand, rubbing his thumb on each knot. He stopped, tracing one particularly unusual spiral carved into the surface.

As he studied the wand, wondering about its purpose and its origin, he finally learned the answer to one of his questions: the real reason he chose to learn about magic. Not just to get out of marrying Heatherlyn. If that were really the only reason, he'd have flunked out of the school a long time ago.

And not just because working magic made him feel more alive than anything else he'd ever tried. Sure, when he felt the buildup of energy as he worked a spell, he felt whole. But it was more than that.

The thrill of learning something new. That intrigued him. Learning spells from old books was fun, too. But the chance to create his own spells, the chance to explore the possibilities magic presented, that was why he stuck with it.

And why he tried to practice every spell carefully, memorize the feel of each when he cast it correctly. At least, the ones he thought were important.

And why he hadn't gone through with his plan to find a nice town and get a job. Never mind the fact that he hadn't found a town yet. Not intact, anyway.

He needed to know more about this wand and the woman who had given it to him. For good or ill, he would find out why Sharilan sent him on this quest. Although, without any solid information, he might have a bit of a problem.

He did have one lead, though. Fenoria. There couldn't be too many damsels locked up in storybook castles in the neighborhood.

Erwyn turned the wand around in his hands, wondering about the supposed castle prison with its wall of thorns and guardian dragon. He closed his eyes, imagining such a castle. He built a mental picture of it, from the foundation to the peaks of its towers. Could the wand, perhaps, lead him to it?

Nothing happened. Nothing tugged at him; no invisible string pulled him the way Sharilan had.

"What the hell?"

Erwyn looked up, wondering why Chesric's voice sounded funny.

The old man stood a few feet away, a pair of dead birds hanging from one fist. He stared at the ground between Erwyn and the fire. Erwyn followed his friend's gaze until . . .

He froze, his mouth hanging open in surprise. There before him sat a miniature castle, exquisitely detailed down to the turrets and arrow-slits. Just like he'd imagined it, but made entirely of sand!

Even as he sat gawking at the tiny structure, it crumbled onto the grass. Nothing remained but a small pile of damp sand, the sort Erwyn remembered from the beaches back home. He looked up at Chesric.

"Where'd it come from?" His voice squeaked. It always did when he was nervous.

"I thought you did it," Chesric replied in a hushed voice. "I've never seen anything like it. There ain't no sand fer miles around here. It'd take magic to make one o' those." He looked sideways at the boy. "You sure you didn't do it?"

"No, I'm not sure. But I don't think I'm up to finding out tonight." Erwyn rolled the wand in his hand once more before returning it to its pocket. He had a theory, but he wasn't prepared to test it. Yet.

Chesric wasn't about to let a little thing like a magical mystery get in the way of his dinner. "What d'ya say we get these birds cookin' and get down to some serious eatin'?"

Erwyn smiled. "Sounds fine to me."

In a few minutes, the grouse had been plucked, cleaned, and spitted, and were roasting over the fire. While dinner hissed and sputtered above the flames, Erwyn took his journal out of his pack and began a new entry, the first in over a week.

We've made incredible progress these past weeks, pushing ourselves to the limits of our endurance. A wolf attacked our camp a few nights ago. Chesric huddled against a tree while I vanquished the beast. This sort of thing has become so commonplace as to be boring.

While studying the wand Sharilan gave me, I learned to create huge, magical sand castles from thin air. I will give this new development a little thought. There must be some way I can devise to use sand castles as an offensive weapon. It could be a useful talent.

Erwyn returned his book to his pack. He wondered if, someday, he might not want a more accurate account of his journey. But he could worry about that later. The birds were done roasting, and his mouth had begun to water.

Halfway through his dinner, he realized he was eating as though he hadn't eaten in days. He slowed down to a more civilized pace and glanced up at Chesric, embarrassed.

"I was beginnin' to think ye were goin' to give yerself a stomachache, eatin' that fast." The edges of the old man's mustache twitched up. "After nearly a week of watchin' ye walkin' around like some sort of zombie, it's good to have ye back again."

"Was I that bad?" Erwyn had a mental picture of himself, stiff-legged, arms straight out, eyes glazed.

"Worse," Chesric replied, throwing the last of his grouse into the fire. The flames sputtered, licking greedily at the remaining bits of meat clinging to the bones. "I thought fer a while there I was goin' to have to put ye out of yer misery."

"I'm glad you didn't."

"Ye goin' to be all right, now?"

"Yes." Erwyn smiled, his voice warm. "I'm going to be

just fine." He pulled his pack into position and lay down. Before he went to sleep, he set his wards. No trance, no meditation. He just reached out with his mind and built the energy dome around the campsite. It was easy.

12

Foxfire and Ice

(Or, If at First You Don't Succeed, Try Something Else)

Travel in the mountains is not recommended during the winter months.

Sorcerers Almanac
Section One: On Getting the Lay of the Land

"I just don't understand it!" Erwyn punctuated the statement by jabbing his wand into the dirt. It hadn't taken him long to think of it as his own. "For days now, I've been trying to reproduce that stupid sand castle and—nothing!"

"Maybe yer just tryin' too hard."

There seemed to be no end to Chesric's patience. Just once, Erwyn thought, I'd like to see him lose his temper.

"Maybe, maybe not," Erwyn growled back, making another jab at the dirt.

They'd gone through this conversation at least once a day for the last week or so, every time Erwyn tried to duplicate his sand castle.

He'd tried it with and without the wand, lying down and sitting up, during meditation and at random times during the day. Nothing. He'd had no luck with the wand or himself.

Disgusted, he threw the wand to the ground and stood, jamming his hands into his pockets. It just didn't make sense.

Sure, he'd gotten more and more proficient at the spells he already knew. A little confidence worked wonders. Setting the wards had become downright easy. And now he even knew they worked.

A few days before, some wild animal had wandered into the network of energy, probably attracted by their provisions. When Erywn tried frantically to disentangle himself from his cloak to see what was disturbing the wards, his thrashing woke Chesric.

"Think I'll go find me a place where a body can get a little sleep," the old man grumbled before going out to hunt down the presumably dangerous beast that had awakened Erwyn.

He returned a few minutes later with the next morning's breakfast—a wild hen that had been out for a moonlight stroll. Embarrassed, Erwyn mumbled an apology, but as Chesric magnanimously pointed out, at least they had proof that the spell worked.

The trek through the rolling countryside was long and tiring, but not as tiring as it could have been.

Chesric favored crossing over the hills, but after climbing the first two, Erwyn began whining about the amount of effort involved.

"Can't we just go around?"

"I don't see why we should. It's shorter to go straight, and a little hike never killed nobody."

"It's only shorter if you fly. If you count the ups and downs, I'd bet the distance is the same. What good is it going to do us if we die from exhaustion before we've climbed them all?"

Chesric reluctantly agreed.

In spite of Erwyn's complaints, they finally reached the foothills of the mountain range called Snake Ridge, because, as Chesric said, "The mountains weave through the valleys like a snake through grass."

"The *mountains* weave? Haven't you got that backward?"

"Neither the mountains nor the valleys move, so what difference does it make, eh?" Chesric asked as they began to make camp.

When the evening's chores were finished, and Erwyn sat down, taking his journal from his pack, but he really wasn't in the mood to write.

He thought he'd found at least the beginning of some sort of talent. Surely the wand and the sand castle were the keys! If he could just find the right key.

Maybe he was wrong. Maybe the tiny castle was only a fluke or a manifestation of the wand.

It just wasn't fair! Every time he gained a little confidence, something happened to shake it.

Erwyn returned his book to its place without adding anything to his story. He didn't feel like writing fiction, and he wasn't up to talking to himself on paper . . . yet. He went to bed more than a little unhappy.

They found plenty of game in the foothills, and Chesric made use of their good fortune. The old warrior succeeded in bringing down a couple of the small mountain deer that inhabited the area. Then he constructed a tent from tree boughs, sort of a smokehouse to preserve a large portion of the meat.

"The trees are thinnin' out, and so will the game," he explained.

"If you say so," Erwyn replied. Having little experience in hunting, he was forced to take Chesric's word for it.

During the next few days, under Chesric's tutelage, Erwyn learned how to skin game. Or tried to.

"No, no, no!" That word was getting awfully familiar to Erwyn. "Ye don't hold the knife that way. Here, let me show ye again."

Chesric took the knife from the boy and, once more, attempted to show him the technique. After the fourth or fifth try, Erwyn began to get the hang of it. Sort of.

"Ouch!"

"Do ye think ye can skin that beast without bleedin' all over it?"

"Your concern for my welfare is touching."

"You'll heal, but human blood makes the meat taste *terrible*."

"When did you ever try human blood?"

"Never mind." Chesric shuddered. "I'll tell ye sometime when I don't have such a graphic picture in front of me. Now, bind up that nick in yer arm and finish skinnin' that critter. After we get the meat a-'smokin', we'll have a little instruction on how to use a sword."

"Great! Instead of a few small nicks, I can get some lovely gashes."

"Ye'll do fine, boy. Trust me."

Chesric was wrong.

"Yer supposed to stay on yer feet when ye lunge, ye know."

"Really? I'm so glad you told me before I bruised myself any more."

Erwyn hauled himself to his feet, brushing the dirt from his breeches. So far they'd determined that his elbow wobbled, his wrist was limp, and he couldn't lunge without losing his balance. It seemed he just wasn't cut out to be a man of arms, a fact that didn't bother him at all.

Chesric sighed, reminding Erwyn of his weapons instructor back home, the one who had to witness Heatherlyn's frequent displays of—affection.

"Maybe ye could learn to throw a knife?"

Erwyn eyed his belt knife. Its worn handle and ragged edge spoke of years of use and misuse. "This thing?"

"No" —Chesric produced a knife from his pack— "this one." He handed the weapon to Erwyn.

The design on the hilt depicted a hunting scene, the horses, riders, and quarry carved in perfect detail. The silvery double-edged blade glinted in the firelight.

"You want me to *throw* this? At what, a pillow?"

"How 'bout the knot on that tree over there?"

"But I might hurt it."

"Nah, ye can't hurt that old oak. It's tough."

"No, I mean the knife."

"Ye won't hurt that neither. Give it a try."

Erwyn held the knife's blade and started to throw.

"Not that way! Ye'll cut yerself again." Chesric gingerly removed the knife from the boy's grasp and replaced it, hilt first.

"But I thought you were supposed to hold the blade to throw a knife."

"Not this one. Ye could throw it that way a hundred times and never get it to stick. This way, ye don't have to take time to turn the knife. Ye just grab it by the hilt and throw."

He positioned the boy's fingers carefully before allowing him to try the skill.

The knife hit the tree sideways with a dull thud.

Chesric shook his head and patiently demonstrated a perfect throw. The knife landed, quivering, in the center of the knot.

"Would ye care to try again?"

Erwyn nodded, thinking fast. His second try worked. He buried the tip of the blade a good half inch into the wood, just above the knot.

"That's pretty good. Try it again."

The third throw landed in the same place Chesric's had.

"That's terrific, boy! I knew ye had it in ye. Since ye seem to do better with a shorter blade, maybe next time we'll try a little hand-to-hand fighting with it."

Chesric walked over to retrieve the knife.

Erwyn refrained from mentioning the levitation spell he'd used on the weapon. He didn't think Chesric would understand. He also didn't think it would help in hand-to-hand combat.

They remained at the same campsite until the meat finished drying. After that, their packs were heavier, but their hearts lighter. Food wouldn't be a problem, for a while at least.

When the two adventurers finally headed into the mountains proper, Erwyn began to worry about other aspects of survival. Like warm clothing.

Their trek across the valleys and into the foothills had taken them into the first weeks of winter. Here they were, about to fight their way through the mountains in the thick of the season, without anything in the way of proper cold-weather gear.

"Stupid, just plain stupid."

"Was that comment directed at me, young fella?"

"As a matter of fact, yes."

"So what's the problem?"

"The problem is, why are we going up into the mountains at all? It's the beginning of winter. I'm no expert, but isn't it likely to be a little cold up there? Not to mention dangerous. Wind, avalanches, rockslides, and other nuisances. You know."

"A sorcerer such as yerself ought to have no trouble whippin' up some spell or other to help us along. I hate to waste valuable time. Would ye rather spend the winter holed up in them rocks doin' nothin'?"

"No, I'd rather spend the winter in a nice, comfortable inn, thank you."

But Chesric seemed determined not to let something like a little cold and snow stop him.

As they ventured higher along the mountain path, the air grew thin and chill. Snow began to fall in soft, icy flakes. Even Chesric, with his quilted surcoat beneath his cloak (he'd packed his armor away for the climb), felt the cold.

Some situations call for very specialized spells. See appendix A for suggestions.

Sorcerers Almanac
Section Six: On the Successful Use of Magic

"I don't suppose ye can do anythin' about the weather, can ye?"

"You're the one who wanted to keep going in spite of the season. And, no, I can't do anything. They taught us to call up wind and rain, and to stop them again, but they didn't say anything about snow. There's not much I can do, short of melting the stuff. And that wouldn't do anything for the air itself. It'd still be freezing. Ice isn't much more comfortable than snow. Trust me."

"Aren't ye supposed to maybe *figure out* something?"

"Necessity is a bitch!" Erwyn groused, by way of an answer.

Nevertheless, if the weather got any colder, he would have to find a way to keep them warm. Preferably before they froze to death. Though his pack seemed virtually bottomless, Chesric could not seem to produce anything to keep out the cold.

That was suspicious, since he seemed to have everything else in there. Erwyn noticed that if the problem required a straightforward, easy spell, Chesric could come up with a more mundane way to solve it. But if it required something *new*, the old man had nothing to offer. Coincidence or planning?

Meanwhile, Erwyn studied the problem at hand in some depth. The increasing cold prodded him to find a speedy solution. Finally, teeth chattering, he determined to try some imaginative spellcasting. If it didn't work, either he'd be back where he started—freezing—or he wouldn't be around to care.

He started with the flame spell, concentrating it on his cloak.

Chesric took a cautious step backward.

"You have no faith in me," Erwyn commented, still working on his spell.

"It's not a question of faith; it's a question of good sense."

"Gee, thanks."

Before the fabric could ignite, Erwyn fused the foxfire

with the flame, weaving the two spells together by feel. Then he spread the combined effect throughout the material of the cloak.

It worked!

The results seemed to surprise Erwyn more than Chesric. The fabric felt warm to the touch, but not burning hot. As he ran a cautious hand over the cloth, his eyes widened with wonder.

The foxfire spell subdued the heat of the flame spell very nicely. Of course, the garment glowed slightly, but at least he would be warm.

Best of all, foxfire spells didn't fade. It would hold until dismissed or the energy of the spellcaster ran out . . . or he died. In which case, as Erwyn had stated earlier, he wouldn't be around to care.

Having verified that the young sorcerer could wear his cloak without risking personal injury, Chesric presented his cloak to be ensorcelled in like manner. They traveled the rest of the day in relative comfort. Relative, that is, because the hooded cloaks only fell to a point above their knees. While the glowing material kept their heads, arms, and torsos warm, their legs felt colder by comparison.

Erwyn resolved to try the same trick on his boots at the earliest available opportunity.

13

Any Port in a Storm

(Or, That's the Cold of the West)

When traveling through mountainous regions, remember
to take plenty of warm clothing.

Sorcerers Almanac
Section Two: On Weather and Its Effects

The rest of the trip through the mountains turned out to
be exactly what Erwyn expected a trip through the mountains to be: cold, wet, and occasionally downright difficult.

Snake Ridge resembled the Impassable Mountains, at
least in one respect. The path through the range was fairly
smooth, as mountain paths go. Still, sleeping on snow-covered rock wasn't Erwyn's idea of a good time. Their cloaks
kept them warm enough. So did their boots, once Erwyn got
around to bespelling them.

But there was still the matter of the space between the
bottom of their cloaks and the tops of their boots. Their
travel cloaks were *short*. And even if he went to the trouble of
fixing their trousers, it still wouldn't do anything about the
fact that the heat would melt the snow into the tops of their
boots. And melted snow was, well, *water*. Wet, cold water.

They reached the highest point in the pass, denoted by a

sign which read "It's all downhill from here!" scrawled on a convenient boulder. Erwyn found it when he walked into the edge of the rock. They also walked into the heaviest snows they'd seen yet.

Snowflakes swirled around them on the wind. A wind which had an annoying habit of occasionally playing with their cloaks, as well. A magic cloak doesn't do much good if it's flying behind you on the breeze instead of protecting your back.

As luck would have it—or maybe it was planning, Erwyn couldn't be certain—Chesric found a cave a few feet past the sign. A cave big enough for two travelers to stretch out comfortably, more or less.

Erwyn cast a sideways glance at Chesric. He got the impression the old man had been here before. He didn't have much time to follow that thought, though.

"It's a mite chilly in here, don't ye think?" Chesric puffed and rubbed his arms dramatically.

"Yeah, so?" He didn't feel up to falling into the old knight's traps.

"Well, how 'bout we put together a fire."

"Sure thing. You got any firewood left?"

"Nope."

"Of course not."

Erwyn buried his nose in his cloak. With his cloak and boots radiating their own warmth, he felt comfortable enough. But he didn't particularly want to sit up all night. And if he lay down, his cloak would slide off, letting his legs get cold.

Besides, he wouldn't get much sleep with Chesric huffing and puffing and swatting himself all night. But what could he do *this* time?

Maybe . . . he toyed with the idea for a moment. Couldn't hurt, could it? So he tried the cloak spell in reverse, more or less.

This time, he formed a foxfire ball and tried heating it up with the flame spell.

Chesric stopped puffing and watched while the flame ball formed in the center of the cave. Erwyn fed it until it grew large enough to keep the cave comfortable. A fire ball that fed on itself.

Without even a "thank you," the old man wrapped himself in his cloak, lay down beside the ball, and went to sleep. Snoring, as usual.

Erwyn just shook his head. Maybe someday he'd get used to the old man.

Chesric snorted loudly and rolled over.

Then again, Erwyn thought, maybe he wouldn't.

He rolled up in his cloak and stretched out. Moments later he, too, fell asleep.

Morning brought another day of slogging through the snow, followed by another night spent huddled against the cold. And so it went for days . . . and days . . . and days.

In spite of the discomfort, the two companions finally reached the other side of Snake Ridge just in time to bid farewell to winter. Or so they thought.

> *Winter in the plains can be as harsh as it is sudden.*
> *Sorcerers Almanac*
> *Section 2: On Weather and Its Effects*

As they left the mountains behind, the air grew warmer and the snow stopped. Erwyn considered removing the spells from their clothing, but he thought better of it. The nights were still cool, even though spring was on its way. They could always tie the cloaks to their packs during the day, if necessary.

Then morning dawn brought with it an icy wind and a few flurries of snow. Erwyn hugged his cloak closer about him, glad that he hadn't decided to return it to its normal state. As the day wore on, the flurries turned into a full-fledged snowstorm. They hadn't escaped the bad weather by leaving the mountains, he reflected. Winter followed them down.

By nightfall, weary and cold, they had still found no suitable place to make camp. There was nothing but an endless snow-covered plain stretching before them. No bushes, no trees, nothing.

Erwyn wrapped the edges of his cloak around his cold-reddened hands. He was warm and relatively dry from the top of his head to the soles of his boots, but that small comfort only seemed to make the cold worse on his exposed face and hands.

"Can't we just stop?" he whined for about the fortieth time since dusk.

"We need shelter," Chesric replied from the folds of his coverings. "We can't just stop in the middle of a field during a storm like this. We'd freeze to death.

"As long as we keep moving, we have a chance of surviving. Magical cloaks are nice, but I'm not sure how much help they'd be against three or four feet of snow. I 'magine they'd melt it just enough to leave us encased in a nice little mound of ice." He paused, as if thinking. "Of course, if ye've got some way of whipping up an inn or a hut or something . . ."

Erwyn sighed. "Not that I can think of offhand."

He thought about the sand castle. Wouldn't it be wonderful to sleep under an actual *roof* tonight, even if it was made of sand? If only he could reproduce it, life-size. If only there were some rocks or trees or something around here. If only he hadn't decided that magic was better than marriage . . .

No point in wishing for things you can't have, Erwyn thought. Besides, he found it highly annoying that he started thinking about marriage every time the going got tough.

He spent a few minutes blissfully wrapped up in mentally building a detailed sand castle to crawl inside and hole up in. That didn't last long. He didn't care much for empty wishes.

After that, he watched the swirling white blanket around

him. The snow reflected the pale glow from their cloaks, creating a circle of light. Erwyn stared at the flakes, fascinated, losing himself in the endless patterns they made while they danced about him.

He let the snow occupy his mind as he trudged through the night, following the light of Chesric's cloak. He tried to imagine what it was like to be a snowflake, swirling and spinning through the air, without thought or care. It helped him to stop thinking about sand castles and other forms of shelter.

He got so wrapped up in his reflections that he almost knocked Chesric down when the old man came to an abrupt halt.

"Merciful stars," the knight whispered, his breath turning to steam in the cold air.

Erwyn stared in the direction Chesric was pointing. Then he looked up, and the hood of his cloak slid back, allowing the snow to fall on his hair and down the back of his tunic.

In front of them, in the midst of all this snow, stood a castle. A full-size, regulation-style castle. Well, almost full-size.

But, no matter what its size, Erwyn didn't trust things that appeared in the middle of nowhere.

He craned his neck, looking as far up as the glow from their cloaks permitted. Walls stretched up into the snowy sky, merging into the snowflakes.

Curious, he freed his hands from his cloak and created a ball of foxfire in his palm. He gave the sphere of light all the power he could pack into the spell. It wasn't much. The ball ended up being palm-size, but it was big enough to illuminate the castle.

Holding his "lantern" aloft, Erwyn surveyed more of the wall.

In the light of the foxfire, the castle turned out to be only about twelve feet high. The steady fall of snow created an illusion of greater height.

The wall was smooth and featureless, except for the very

top. Crenellations atop the battlements, no higher than Erwyn's knee, took up two of the twelve feet.

Erwyn followed the line of the wall a few paces to his left. It made a sharp right turn only a short distance away. He turned around, heading toward the other side. Barely ten paces from the corner he'd just left, he found the other corner of the edifice.

There was something strange about the walls, though, if only Erwyn could place what.

"Let's see if we can find a door," came Chesric's practical suggestion.

Erwyn headed back to join his friend, and together they searched for an entrance to the castle. Tired as he was, even the thirty feet along one side of the castle seemed endless. The snow sucked at his boots, making his progress achingly slow.

Chesric fared no better. He trudged through the knee-deep blanket of snow, shoulders slumped, head bowed against the weather.

Frost rimmed the ends of his mustache where they stuck out from beneath the hood of his cloak. His normally long stride shortened as he pulled one foot out of the snow, only to have to sink it into the white, icy stuff a scant few inches away.

Willpower alone kept the two adventurers moving. Willpower and an innate dislike of freezing to death so close to possible shelter. They both needed rest and the familiar, friendly warmth of a roaring fire. Even enchanted cloaks had limits.

So, of course, they didn't find the door until they turned the third corner. They'd gone in exactly the wrong direction! Erwyn groaned softly. If they'd gone right instead of left in the first place, they'd have saved themselves the extra walk.

There, in the center of the last wall, they saw the faint outline of the doorway they sought. Hope flared inside Erwyn. Silently praying that the inhabitants would be friendly, he and Chesric approached.

When they got close enough to see the door clearly, they realized that they wouldn't have to deal with any inhabitants, after all.

14

People Who Live in Sand Castles

(Or, The Weather Outside Is Frightful. A Fire'd
Be So Delightful)

Never depend on a new and untried spell for survival.
Sorcerers Almanac
Section Six: On the Successful Use of Magic

Erwyn stared at the door, feeling his stomach sink to a
point near his toes. His palms itched furiously.

In the center of the last wall was the entrance to the
castle. The door.

Standing in front of that door, Erwyn felt the oddest feeling wash over him. It was as if he'd seen the castle before.
Which he had.

He knew now that no one lived in the building before
him. And why it stood there, in the middle of nowhere.
Right where he and Chesric would stumble upon it in the
middle of a raging blizzard, at night, in unknown territory.

He also knew why Chesric stood there, shivering in the
cold, staring wide-eyed in Erwyn's direction, mouth open,
and making no move to enter.

It was a sand castle. Not precisely the one he imagined.
This one was smaller. But it was large enough to accommo-

date two cold, tired travelers. Large enough to protect them from the worst of the storm. Assuming, of course, that it was hollow.

Well, no way to tell until he tried. Resettling the pack on his shoulders, he reached out and pushed. The door swung inward easily, throwing him off balance. He pitched forward onto the floor, which was, of course, sand.

Erwyn sat up, sputtering and spitting, trying to get rid of a mouthful of sand. The foxfire ball followed him inside. Chesric followed the foxfire.

Squinting against bright light meant to pierce the gloom of the blizzard, Erwyn turned to his surroundings, toning down his spell as he did so. Without a word, he accepted the wineskin Chesric handed him, then he took a long swallow and looked around the room.

Not a big room, as he'd expected. About twenty-four feet square, with the ceiling only seven feet above the sandy floor, scant inches above their heads. He did some mental calculations.

If the walls were twelve feet tall, including the two-foot crenellations, then the roof was . . . Erwyn gulped nervously . . . about three feet thick. How much did a twenty-four-foot-square slab of sand, three feet thick, weigh? He tried not to think about it.

Suddenly he wished he'd been more specific when he "conjured" his sand castle. But then, what could he expect on such short notice?

While Erwyn was admiring his own handiwork, Chesric busied himself with more practical matters. He laid out his bedroll and placed his pack neatly in a corner along with Erwyn's, which the young sorcerer had dropped while he was tasting the floor.

Then the old man began laying a fire, carefully placing small sticks in a hollow in the sand.

"Where did the wood come from?" Erwyn eyed Chesric suspiciously.

"Carried it in me pack," Chesric replied, not looking

away from his work. "Stuck some wood in there before we set out. Never know when ye might be needin' some."

" 'Set out' from where? In the mountains, you said you didn't have any firewood!"

Chesric shrugged. "I guess I was wrong. Didn't see it in there when I checked that night."

Not quite convinced, Erwyn rolled out his bed. Just how much stuff did Chesric cram into that thing, anyway? And how could he manage to *lose* a bundle of firewood in it?

Erwyn pulled his journal from his pack and settled himself onto his blanket. He hadn't made an entry in the book in *ages*.

He flipped it open to the last page and began reading the entry. He'd been reading for a couple of minutes when he realized that Chesric was staring at him again. He looked up into the old man's face.

"Yes?" he asked.

Chesric looked expectantly at the ceiling. "Won't do much good to start a fire, without no ventilation. D'ya suppose I could poke a hole in the top without bringin' the whole thing down atop us?"

Erwyn looked at the ceiling, too, very aware of the slab of sand kept in place overhead by a very tenuous spell over which he had little control. Not to mention all the snow building up on top of it. Was it his imagination, or did the edge to his right slip ever so slightly?

Gripping his journal to keep his hands from trembling, Erwyn moistened his lips and replied, "Chesric, I doubt that poking a hole in the ceiling would be a problem. Let us just hope that no one comes along to poke a hole in me!"

He laughed, hoping he sounded more cheerful than he felt. As long as he kept part of his attention on the castle, he reasoned, he didn't need to worry. And he could do that in his sleep—he thought.

Erwyn put his book back into his pack. The journal would have to wait a little longer. He didn't think he could concentrate on it, anyway.

Chesric used his sword to make a hole in the roof, and soon the fire crackled briskly. Flakes of snow drifted down through their makeshift chimney to melt, hissing, in the flames. They passed the rest of the evening in silence, the warmth of the fire helping to soothe tired muscles and aching joints.

They retired for the night, hoping the snow would stop and allow them to resume their journey the next day. It didn't.

They awoke the next morning cold and sore and half grumpy. Erwyn's half, anyway.

"I wish ye'd stop bein' such a wet blanket."

"*I* am not a wet blanket. *This* is a wet blanket." Erwyn peeled his cover off and turned it over. "I've reversed this thing five or six times, and it never seems to get completely dry. Maybe if I threw it into the fire . . ."

"Nah, as wet as that thing is, it'd just get steamed. Anyway," Chesric rushed on before Erwyn could comment, "we've got some time on our hands. You handled the edification, I'll handle the education. It's time fer sword practice."

"In here? With the fire?"

"You think you'd rather do it out there?" Chesric nodded toward the door and the blizzard behind it. "A little sword dance around the flame'll do ye some good. Teach you to think fast."

He was already thinking fast, but not fast enough to come up with an excuse not to practice, at least not one Chesric would accept. He could only hope the snow would clear soon and end his current misery.

The snow continued to fall for days. Chesric busied himself with trying to teach Erwyn to use the assortment of weapons and equipment in the old man's bottomless pack.

Erwyn mostly worried. He worried about the drifts of snow building up against a door made of sand. He worried about the piles of snow building up atop a roof made of sand. He worried about accidentally releasing the spell that held the castle together and waking up buried under a mountain of sand and ice. He worried too much.

One morning, no snow drifted through the hole in the ceiling, and Erwyn noticed a tiny shaft of sunlight bouncing off the soot-blackened ice that had formed around their chimney.

"Looks like we might be able to leave today," observed Chesric.

"With all that snow piled up against the door?" Erwyn's voice squeaked again. "Not to mention the ten- or twenty-foot drifts we'll have to trudge through to get across the valley?"

"No fear, we'll find a way through." Chesric chuckled. "We have to. We're out of firewood."

Chesric crossed the room that had been their home for the last few days and eased open the door.

Outside, bearing a perfect imprint of the door, was a wall of snow higher than the doorway. Erwyn nudged his way past his companion. At which point the entire wall of snow collapsed into the opening.

Erwyn jumped backward, yelping.

Too late. Snow covered his pants to the knees. Clumps of it melted into the tops of his boots faster than he could dig them out. He sat down on the floor, thoroughly soaked and miserable, glaring at Chesric from beneath a lock of hair grown too long to shove back on his forehead.

Chesric stood there with a smile poking from between his beard and mustache. Erwyn could see his friend's sides quivering. Chesric was laughing at him!

The boy's eyes narrowed in sudden anger. The old man shouldn't be laughing at him.

A good workman always selects tools that can be reused over a period of time. The same can be said of evil workmen.
                                        Sorcerers Almanac
                        Section Five: On Things to Watch Out For

That didn't make sense. Why was he so angry all of a sudden?

Words formed in his head; power gathered around him. He felt giddy, as though something pulled him outside himself, forcing him to be a spectator to his own actions.

That feeling he recognized! It felt just like the trip through the forest, right before he met . . .

Sparks collected at the tips of his fingers, building, ready to leap toward the unsuspecting man.

Horrified, Erwyn tried to stop himself, stop the completion of a spell he didn't know. But he couldn't. The spell's energy had built too high.

He had to direct it somewhere, or it would backfire. On him.

Still sitting in an undignified position on the floor, he swiveled toward the doorway at the moment the spell was unleashed.

Lightning crackled, blasting through the open doorway of the sand castle.

The backwash of the spell dried Erwyn's soaked clothing and scorched the sand in front of him. But outside . . . outside, the spell vaporized a path through the snow for more than half a mile!

"Well, that solves the problem of clearing a way out of here," Chesric observed casually. But his eyes told the truth. He knew that blast had been meant for him.

"Th-that wasn't me!" Erwyn shivered in the cool air. "I d-don't even *know* that spell. What happened?" He looked up at Chesric, his eyes wide with fear.

Chesric regarded his young friend for a long moment before answering. "I'm not sure, but I have an idea or two." He paused, considering. "This might be reaching a bit, but . . ."

Erwyn, in the middle of scrambling to his feet, stopped. "But what?"

"I was thinking about Sharilan."

"What about her?"

"Well, I've heard that she has this, well, *habit* of frying anyone who has the misfortune to anger her." Chesric paused again, stroking his mustache. "Your little—outburst—reminded me of a description I once heard of one of her tantrums."

"But how . . . why . . . could she really do that? Use me like that? Long distance?"

"Maybe. But I suspect she'd need some sort of help. A focus or something. You tell me. You're the sorcerer."

"The wand! She gave it to me." Erwyn finished standing up, then reached into the pocket where he kept the length of petrified wood.

"I don't think so," Chesric replied. "Too obvious. There must be something else."

The old man looked from Erwyn to the pack lying innocently in the corner.

"Did you ever get close to her? Less than an arm's length?"

Erwyn tried to remember his meeting with the sorceress, but it was like trying to remember a dream.

"I think so. I'm not sure, but I probably did get pretty close to her. It was a small clearing."

Something bothered him about that meeting, or at least his memory of it. He didn't usually have trouble remembering things. Important things. But the more he tried to remember of that brief encounter, the harder it became.

While Erwyn stood with his hands pressed to his temples, striving to clarify the memory, Chesric picked up the boy's pack. "Perhaps there's something in here." He handed the bag to Erwyn.

"I doubt it. It would probably have to be something I'd have near me all the time. Packs can get lost or be carried by someone else." He sighed. "Might as well have a look, though."

He sat down wearily and rummaged through his belongings. Flipping through his spellbook, he found nothing unusual among its yellowed pages or leather bindings.

A similar inspection of his journal revealed no more information than the spellbook.

Erwyn sighed, gazing at the journal. He was hopelessly behind on his accounts of his travels. But it probably didn't matter, since the accounts were just fiction. Real life seemed to be a little more interesting just now.

He finished his inspection of the pack's contents. Nothing there. The pack itself, though showing signs of wear, revealed nothing unusual, either.

"Ah, well. If it's here, we'll find it, sooner or later," Chesric said philosophically.

"Personally," Erwyn replied, "I'd rather find it sooner than later." He repacked his things and climbed to his feet. "I guess we'd better move. There's no telling how long the castle will last."

Chesric glanced apprehensively toward the ceiling, then gathered his own pack. They left the building and realized for the first time just how much shelter it had provided.

Outside the door, the wind raced across the drifts of snow, slipping icily across the path cut by Erwyn's blast.

Hugging his still-ensorcelled cloak about him, Erwyn turned to close the door to the castle.

The slab of solidified sand swung closed with a muffled thud, and the entire structure collapsed into a heap at Erwyn's feet.

The two adventurers stared at the sand dune, all that was left of what had been their home for the last several days.

"At least now we know how long the spell lasts," Chesric observed.

15

Check Your Bags
Before Leaving the Inn

(Or, We Don't Need No Stinking Beaches)

Sometimes it is easier to move the whole mountain than to reduce it to the size of a molehill.

Sorcerers Almanac
Section Six: On the Successful Use of Magic

"Yeah. As long as we need it, but not long enough."

"What do you mean?"

"I mean, I think I forgot something." Erwyn patted his pockets, trying to find the something.

"Nothing important, I hope."

"No. Just the wand."

"The wand!"

Erwyn tried to look apologetic. "I think I set it down while we were going through my pack."

"Could you have put it in the pack when you repacked it?"

Chesric turned from an appraisal of the mound of sand in front of him. His expression told Erwyn that the old knight didn't hold much hope of finding anything under the remains of the castle, much less a tiny branch ten inches long.

"I can look," Erwyn replied, "but I don't think it's there. I distinctly remember setting it on the ground. And I don't recall picking it up again." He sat down and began once more to unpack his stuff.

The sun overhead seemed pale in comparison to the warmth of summer, but it still melted some of the snow. It trickled onto the pathway, right where Erwyn was sitting. And melted snow was still water. His pants were soaked again.

To make matters worse, the wand was definitely not in the pack, or in Erwyn's pockets. Which left the sand. He looked up at Chesric.

"I don't suppose I could just leave it there?"

"Somehow, I can find it in me to doubt the wisdom of such a move." Chesric smiled grimly, crossing his arms over his chest. Erwyn took that as a sure sign that they—or at least he—would stay where they were until the wand was found.

He glared at the sand mound, then wearily rose to his feet and approached it.

"By the way," he said casually as he began sifting through the mound, "what happened to your accent?"

"My what?" Chesric joined the boy in his search with no outward reaction to Erwyn's question.

"Your accent. Up until a short time ago, you sounded like some uneducated wanderer most of the time, except for an uncanny knowledge of magic." Erwyn continued to sift through the sand, scooping up handfuls and depositing them in a pile behind him. "But since this morning, you seem to have acquired a bit more polish . . . ugh!"

At that moment, Erwyn struck water. Or, more precisely, mud. The sand where he was digging had fallen atop a drift of snow. Melted snow. And melted snow was . . . well, he'd covered that before. His hands were cold and wet, and covered with cold, wet sand.

He tried to wipe the sand off, but only succeeded in smearing it around. Now the front of his pants were covered with wet sand, instead of just wet water.

Erwyn stopped for a moment and examined his backside. As he suspected, he'd already gotten sand on the back of his trousers, too. Globs of the stuff.

Well, at least the front matched the back. Erwyn sighed and returned to his digging.

Chesric, without pausing, replied to Erwyn's question in a voice that came from somewhere at the top of his nasal passages. "Perhaps being in such close proximity to such an obviously educated gentleman as yourself has rubbed off on me a little, young master." He emphasized his statement with a bow and flourish, then returned to his work.

"Do you normally talk like that?"

"Nope."

"So, were you using your real voice earlier?"

"Nope."

"So, are you going to tell me what you *really* sound like?" Chesric smiled and kept digging. "Nope."

Erwyn sighed. Someday he'd find out.

The deeper they dug, the harder the digging became. Both of them were damp with sweat.

"Rats!" Erwyn tossed the edge of his cloak behind his shoulder for the fourth time.

"Problem?"

"I can't dig in this stuff with a wet, sand-coated cloak clinging to my arms."

"So, take it off."

"Right. Then I can just freeze to death. That wind is *cold*." He stopped complaining long enough to think about it. Would it really be that much colder without the cloak, as wet as it was?

"Or," Chesric added, digging into another mound of mud, "you could simplify this by rebuilding the castle."

Erwyn considered the idea for a moment before replying. "I doubt it. So far, I haven't managed to create one castle on purpose, remember? Then again, how do we know it isn't the wand that does the work? The damn thing collapsed when I closed the door, *and I didn't have the wand!*"

"Could be, could be. But still, isn't there some way we could get this done a little faster? At this rate, we'll be here for a week."

Erwyn had been digging furiously since he'd answered Chesric's question. Now his jabs at the sand got slower and slower.

"Maybe, just maybe . . ."

He stood, wiping his hands on his pants, feeling the weight and texture of the sand beneath his palms. He thought about what he would do, remembering the feel of the wand when he last held it. Carefully, he built his levitation spell, spreading it over the entire area of the sand mound.

With the size and weight of the wand in mind, he tried to filter it from the sand. Then he lifted the entire mound.

Before, levitation had been effortless, or mostly effortless. But lifting a mound of sand the size of a castle, even a small one, required real effort.

His neck muscles tensed, straining, as though he were actually lifting the sand himself. Which he was, in a way.

The mass of sand rose slowly, inch by weary inch.

He added more power to the spell. Sweat trickled into his eyes, running down the back of his neck in rivulets.

Erwyn fought the urge to reach up and wipe his eyes. He needed all his concentration.

When the sand cleared the ground by four feet or so, he risked a glance underneath. There was the wand, just two feet ahead of where they were digging. Two feet and five or six hours of work, the ordinary way.

Licking his lips, Erwyn said, "Chesric, you'll have to go under there and get it." His voice came out in a hoarse whisper. "I can't hold this spell and get the wand, too." He closed his eyes. He just couldn't bear to watch.

He heard Chesric's boots scrape across the ground, followed by grunting, as though the old man were lifting something heavy. Erwyn opened his eyes quickly. Not watching was worse than watching. His imagination conjured up worse things than reality.

Chesric, hunched over to avoid hitting the slab of sand overhead, inched toward the wand. Twice, he looked apprehensively from the sandy roof, to Erwyn, and back again. There was fear in his eyes, but he continued on. He reached the wand and grabbed it. Then he paused, holding it in both hands for a moment, as though praying.

"Hurry," Erwyn whispered, "I can't hold out much longer."

Chesric risked one more anxious look at the slab. Then he scrambled backward, away from the slice of sand.

Erwyn shook from the exertion. He didn't even notice when Chesric crawled out in front of him.

"Just one more minute, one more minute . . ."

"You lose this?" Chesric held out the wand.

Erwyn jumped. His concentration broken, the sand fell to earth, sending clouds of grit into the air.

"Yeah. Thanks heaps."

Coughing and only half conscious, Erwyn fell on top of the sand. His breathing was ragged, but he smiled and took the wand from Chesric.

"I sure hope this thing was worth all the trouble."

Chesric sat down, massaging Erwyn's neck. "All this and more, I suspect. All this and more."

16

Interruptions, Interruptions
(Or, Hold On While I Recharge My Batteries)

The easier the route, the more likely it is that someone else is using it, as well.

Sorcerers Almanac
Section One: On Getting the Lay of the Land

"So, where do we go from here?"

He had rested, eaten, and dried out, and now Erwyn felt ready to continue their trek across the gra—uh, snowfields.

Chesric indicated the slash through the snow, the walls of which were already turning to slush in the sunlight. "I thought we'd follow the path you so conveniently cut for us. After digging through all that sand, I'm not really in the mood to dig my way through the snow, as well."

"As I recall, *you* didn't do all that much digging. Besides, it goes in the wrong direction!"

"Is that my fault?" Chesric looked at Erwyn meaningfully. "Perhaps you would like to repeat your earlier performance in a different, more convenient, direction?"

Erwyn blushed. "Not really. I'm not sure I could, anyway." He shifted uncomfortably from one foot to the other. "I wish I knew how it happened, though."

"Try not to think about it, lad. If you do, it will sit in the pit of your stomach and gnaw at you. Quick way to go crazy, if you ask me."

Chesric put his arm around Erwyn's shoulders, no easy trick since he needed to snake it in between Erwyn's bony shoulder blades and his worn leather pack to do so.

"We'll figure out how it happened soon enough. Meanwhile," he continued, "isn't there something you can do to try to keep the incident from being repeated?"

Erwyn drew his cloak closer against the chill he suddenly felt. "I don't know, but I'll try to think of something."

He wasn't convinced it was possible, and wore a thoughtful frown as they started northward through the trench.

The walls of their path shortened the farther they walked from the remains of the sand castle. When they reached the end of the path, the snow was barely a foot deep. They wouldn't have to dig their way across the rest of the plain, after all.

Funny thing, though. The snow was deeper near the castle than it was just about everywhere else.

No, make that everywhere else. Not just about.

But why should the snow be deeper near the castle? Lots deeper. More than could be accounted for by ordinary drifts. As they turned west once more, they discovered that the snow was less than a foot deep in every direction. Except around the castle. Why? Did Sharilan have something to do with it? Or was it just the fact that he'd used magic to keep them warm and to shelter them. Magic attracts magic. . . .

Erwyn had no answers. Since he left the school, it seemed he had been inundated with questions for which he didn't know the answers. He had given up on listing them all.

Listing them all . . .

For the first time since the journey began, Erwyn realized he had a practical use for his journal besides writing fiction. He could use it to write down his questions.

Maybe that's what he was supposed to do in the first place. Erwyn had never given it much thought.

Situation normal. He'd received demerits more than once at school for the very same thing: not knowing (or caring) what to put into his journal.

Well, there was one consolation. He hadn't found much to write about most of the time. Of course, the exciting parts more than made up for the boring parts.

Erwyn shook himself from his reverie. They'd started out of the castle in early morning, spent too much time digging in the sand, and another small slice of forever levitating the same sand to recover the wand.

Then they'd rested and eaten. That meant that they actually started the trip fairly late in the day.

They had been walking through the snow for quite some time now, and even snow ten inches deep made walking difficult. Erwyn could tell because his legs felt like jelly.

He looked toward the sun, now low on the horizon. They had perhaps an hour or less before dark. He looked ahead for some place to camp, but saw nothing but snow glistening in the late afternoon sun.

Erwyn sighed. Was he going to have to try for another sand castle? He was worn out. He wasn't even sure he could maintain the spells on their clothing. There didn't seem much chance of him dredging up a castle tonight.

"That looks like a likely place." Chesric's abrupt comment startled Erwyn.

"What? Where?"

"Over there." Chesric pointed to the west, of course.

That was about the only direction Erwyn had traveled in since he'd started this whole adventure.

He looked in the direction Chesric indicated. A dark blot on the horizon marked possible shelter. A forest, maybe, or some boulders. Either one would be better than camping in the open. Of the two options, Erwyn preferred a forest. A fire would be nice, too.

Erwyn hugged his cloak closer. The evening was getting colder, and he felt the chill.

"At least it's in the right direction," he commented

lightly.

"What's that mean?"

"It's to the west."

"Why are you so set on heading west?"

"I'm not set on heading west. It just keeps getting in front of me."

Erwyn pulled his cloak tighter. It was definitely colder now.

Even Chesric held his cloak close to his body, as though trying to force more warmth from the fabric.

"Actually," Erwyn said, feeling he needed to explain himself a little better, "I decided to travel west because it seemed like the least difficult of all my choices at the time. Since then, I just always seem to end up going that direction.

"I was chased into the Western Wood, and the path through the wood ran roughly west. Then the path spilled into the valley where you said there was only one passable route through the mountains, which happened to also be to the west. And then . . ."

Erwyn stopped speaking when his brain finally registered what his body already knew.

"The cloaks have stopped working."

"You noticed that, did you?" Even Chesric sounded strained. "No matter. We're almost there now."

"There" was a small stand of trees directly in front of them. Erwyn breathed a sigh of relief. They would have firewood tonight. He couldn't possibly find the energy to re-spell the cloaks.

Wearily, they made camp beneath the leafless branches of some old oaks. While Chesric cleared away a few old, wet leaves and patches of snow, Erwyn gathered armloads of firewood. The snow beneath the trees was tight-packed, and the area showed signs of recent use. In minutes, they had a passable campsite and a roaring fire.

Too tired to prepare dinner, the companions sat staring into the fire, chewing on dried bits of venison that Chesric produced from his bottomless pack.

The fire hissed and crackled merrily, sparks dancing upward through the clearing in the trees and into a starless, cloudy sky. Erwyn allowed his mind to drift, trying to relax in the warmth of the fire.

Not surprisingly, he found himself thinking about the mysterious sand castles, trying to fathom their secret. He pulled the wand from its pocket and frowned thoughtfully at it. It was, he thought, the only clue he had.

Before he acquired the wand, he had never conjured castles of any kind. Only after Sharilan gave him the wand did the sand castles appear. But what caused them? What tied the appearances together?

Absently, he rubbed his thumb across the spiral carved on the side of the length of petrified wood. As he traced the design, he thought about his problem. It didn't help.

"This is getting me nowhere!" Erwyn almost hurled the stick into the fire. Instead, he took a few deep breaths and tried once more to relax. So many events in his life never seemed to turn out quite the way he planned them. He stared at the fire, continuing to trace the carving in the wood.

Golden sparks drifted up from the flames, twisting and spiraling into the sky. Like a shower of gold. A shower of gold . . .

* * * * *

"Betcha can't!" Brendan had teased him unmercifully, his violet eyes dancing in the torchlight as the two boys headed toward the apprentices' quarters.

"I'm not falling for it this time, Brendan. You're trying to get me into trouble." Erwyn stalked across the courtyard, fully intending to go straight to his room.

Behind him, Brendan sighed. "Oh, well. I suppose that just because Uriand did it doesn't mean just *anybody* can."

Erwyn stopped. "Uriand? *He* managed it?"

"Says he did."

That cinched it. Not only was Uriand the absolute worst student in their class, he was Erwyn's greatest rival, as well. The fact that he was the worst student simply made it easier for Erwyn to beat him at everything.

Ten minutes later, Erwyn had the lock open on the library door. Once inside the room, he slipped between the stacks, careful to avoid the squeaky floorboard. His foray shouldn't take too long, assuming no one already had the book he sought.

No one did. It lay on the huge reading table between a pile of history books and a box of bat wings. After quickly checking for alarm spells, Erwyn snatched the book from its stack. He ran his fingers along the worn red leather binding.

This was it, the book old Falwrickel had come for the night Erwyn had inadvertently swept the ceiling. *Master Level Spells, Volume 1*. He took a long, deep breath. Well, if Uriand could cast one, so could he.

He opened the book and flipped through its pages. Any spell would do, so long as it was harmless. But the more spectacular it was, the better. Aha!

He stopped at page thirteen, "The Shower of Gold." That ought to be good. Beneath the title was a short verse.

"If thou be of proper mold, cast thee then this shower of gold."

It seemed to have no connection to the spell itself. Since he didn't know what it meant, he ignored it.

Scanning the pages of instruction, he whistled. "Boy, the Master Level Spells sure are complicated!" But not impossible. And as long as he was there anyway, he might as well give it a shot.

What was the worst that could happen? Well, for starters, he could end up doing time as a statue in the courtyard. Or get blown up. Or worse, he could be assigned as Nasty Nazurski's lab assistant.

He paused to rethink. Maybe he shouldn't go through with this, after all.

But, no, he'd come too far to quit now.

He took a few minutes to familiarize himself with the spell. When he felt certain he had it, he cast, putting as much *oomph!* into it as he could.

He succeeded only in giving himself an ache in the back of his head. An ache that rapidly slewed around to a point in front of his eyeballs, then shot forward, toward the table, and up to the ceiling.

The roof exploded into a rain of golden, glittering particles. It fell in torrents from the beams. It drifted onto the books and nearly guttered the candles. In no time, the golden stuff was an inch deep on everything. And still it fell.

"I think I might have overdone it." Understatement of the year. How'd that dis-spell go again?

He tried to dis-spell the shower. It didn't work. He tried casting the spell again, like foxfire. The shower fell faster. There must be a counterspell.

Frantically, he flipped the pages of the book, searching.

The glitter dust kept falling, gathering in piles six inches high.

At last! The spell to halt the shower of gold. If only he could read it. Every time he stopped moving, the dust settled onto everything—clothes, pages, eyes.

Nearly a foot deep, now.

He tried holding the book upright. That did it. If he held it a couple inches from his face, he could just make out the instructions to the counterspell. It turned out to be a lot less complicated than the original.

Minutes later, the shower slowed to a trickle, then stopped. He looked around. All he had to do now was clean up the—too late.

The door burst open. Well, actually, it slid open slowly, pushing a mound of dust behind it. But the effect was the same. Erwyn froze, staring at the opening, heart pounding.

Master Gordrun stepped over the pile of glitter at the entrance and stood, hands on hips, shaking his head at the mess.

"This I gotta see." Master Nazurski poked his head through the doorway and whistled. "Very impressive." He waded into the room, followed by Masters Potterby and Hexis.

"I can't remember a Sixth Level Apprentice ever making such a mess before, especially using a Masters Spell."

"None ever has." Falwrickel joined them. "Not in the hundred and four years I've been here."

What was this? A convention? Erwyn stared at the crowd gathering around him. "You mean Uriand didn't—"

Falwrickel shook his head. "No. You're the first to try."

"But . . ." He didn't know what to say. Obviously, Brendan had tricked him.

Gordrun headed for the closet—the one where he kept his paddle.

Erwyn sighed. Great. The final humiliation. He'd probably be spending the rest of the semester standing up, if he was lucky. Shoulders slumped, he turned and cleared a spot on the table before setting the book down.

A hand on his shoulder made him jump. "Okay, Apprentice." Gordrun shoved a broom into Erwyn's hands. "You made the mess; you clean it up. And when you're done, maybe we can teach you not to be so sloppy next time."

Erwyn almost collapsed with relief. Until he realized exactly how much mess there was.

"But what do I do with all this gold dust?"

"Throw it in the trash. It's just glitter. Worthless."

"Then why is the spell listed in the book?"

"Any spell has a potential for being useful. You never know when a little glitter might come in handy."

A *little?*

"Now get to work. And don't try any more spells. At least for today."

"Yes, sir." Erwyn leaned into his broom.

"You might use this, too." Falwrickel handed him a feather duster. "And remember, even a young sorcerer needs to be—molded." The old man patted Erwyn's shoulder and shuffled out the door.

Erwyn nodded and continued sweeping. Even a young sorcerer needs to be molded . . . the proper mold . . . mold . . .

* * * * *

A mold! Erwyn sat up suddenly. Every time a sand castle appeared, he'd been thinking about castles, constructing them in his head. The rest of the time, he'd just stared at the ground, willing a castle to appear. Maybe the castles worked more like the glitter spell.

With the shower of gold in mind, he stared at the ground by his feet. Mentally, he built up the image of a castle, like a candle mold. Then he "poured" the sand into the mold.

As the sand in his mental picture fell into the mold, so the castle appeared in front of him. First the foundation, then the walls, roof, and turrets.

He did it! A perfect replica of the castle, exactly as he imagined.

Preoccupied with the castle, Erwyn didn't notice anything amiss until too late. He heard a soft footstep behind him and started to turn. His concentration broken, the tiny castle fell to ruins, but he didn't notice.

A flash of color, the impression of a hand beside his head, and pain came in that order. His head seemed to explode in a shower of sparks.

Well, at least I'll get a chance to sleep, he thought as the darkness of unconsciousness claimed him.

17

If You Have to Be Kidnapped . . .

(Or, Pardon Me, Lady, Your Bronze Is Showing)

Sorcery is an old and honorable career. There are those, however, who aren't very impressed with it.

Sorcerers Almanac
Section Three: On People and Their Influence

Sunlight filtered through Erwyn's closed eyelids. His eyes felt as if they were glued shut. He moved, trying to shift into a more comfortable position. Somewhere inside his head a hammer was having a very loud argument with an anvil.

To make things worse, someone started moaning loudly nearby. It took Erwyn a couple of minutes to discover that the moaning was his own. His stomach was turning flip-flops, too. Not good.

He heard movement next to him and realized he wasn't alone. Someone—or some*thing*—was leaning over him. Tensing, he mentally ran through the list of possible monsters in this part of the world and tried to think of spells to defend against them. As usual, nothing appropriate came to mind.

Oh, well. Better to see what I'm up against than to die

ignorant, he thought. Then he carefully opened his eyes.

For a few seconds, Erwyn couldn't focus. When his eyes finally decided to work properly, he found himself looking at his own reflection in a polished steel chest plate. Only the plate had a couple more bumps on it than he was accustomed to.

Slowly, he raised his eyes.

His captor was tall and muscular, with long red hair bound by a twist of gold wire. Blue-green eyes watched him from a face whose features were both strong and determined. And most definitely female.

Ignoring the throbbing in his head, Erwyn tried to twist into a better position to see the woman.

In addition to the chest plate, she wore matching polished steel greaves and a kilt made of strips of the same material with a leather backing. Well-worn leather boots with steel toes covered her feet. She wore an arm guard extending from her right wrist to her shoulder, also made of steel overlaid on leather. The top of a hunting bow slanted up from her left shoulder. She also held the point of a large, and apparently sharp, sword at Erwyn's throat.

Erwyn closed his eyes and scanned her, using his steel location spell.

In addition to the bow and sword, he located a pair of throwing knives in her boots, two steel pins in her hair, another knife (or was it a short sword? He never could keep them straight) in a sheath at her belt, and a half-dozen throwing stars in various other hiding places, not to mention the dozen or so steel-tipped arrows in the quiver beside the bow. All in all, she was heavily armored—and heavily armed.

He sighed. Sometimes the steel location spell could be more a hindrance than a help. Now that he knew about all her weapons, he was more nervous than he might have been otherwise.

Having given her captive time to size up his situation, the woman prodded Erwyn with the toe of her boot. "Come on, get up. You've had plenty of time to sleep."

"Easy for you to say," he muttered as he rose unsteadily to his feet.

The pain in his head intensified, and he clutched at his temple, swaying. He remembered thinking about getting some sleep just before he got clobbered.

Sleep, hah! Never again would he equate unconsciousness with rest.

Before his head had time to settle, the woman grabbed him roughly and pushed him through the flap of a tent. Apparently, they weren't too worried about him escaping, or they would have stashed him in something more substantial than a tent. They hadn't even tied his hands.

Erwyn wasn't sure whether to be frightened or insulted. Either they thought they had enough steel, and warriors to use it, to keep him from escaping, or they didn't give him credit for being able to escape on his own. Or they didn't care. Of the three, Erwyn preferred the first option. It made him feel less incompetent.

They stepped from the shade of the tent and into the sunlight. He held his hand up to protect his eyes, squinting as he glanced across the compound. Everywhere he looked, he saw women in armor.

"Searching" again with the steel location spell, he saw that each woman carried as much weaponry as his guard did. Somehow, he got the impression that they didn't like strangers, or maybe it was magic-users they didn't care for. And whatever had happened to Chesric? He would be right at home in a place like this.

"So, do you do much wizard hunting around here?" Erwyn remarked casually to his escort. He was probably taking a big risk, but maybe he could shock the guard into giving him some information.

"What do you mean?" The guard halted abruptly, watching him with cautious interest.

Erwyn stopped, too, matching the woman stare for stare. "Well, you're armed to the teeth with all sorts of steel.

Either you don't like magic, or you don't like intruders. Or both." Or maybe it was something else entirely.

He'd heard a story once, a long time ago, about a sect of female warriors. But he thought they lived quite some distance away. The description fit, though. Mostly.

He took a shot. "You're Marlian warriors, aren't you?"

"None of your damn business, *man*." The woman made a curse of the word. "You won't be alive long enough for it to matter, in any case." She punctuated her statement with another shove.

"I'm not trying to pry or anything. It's just that . . ."

"What?"

"I don't understand. From what I'd heard, I thought Marlian warriors fought alongside their men. Where are they?"

"Never mind that. You'll be given all the explanation you need in a few minutes."

Erwyn decided to try a different tactic. "In case you're interested, steel isn't really much help against wizards and stuff."

She didn't look convinced. And the change in subject hadn't improved her mood any.

"Don't tell me you *believe* all that hogwash about steel being proof against magic? It doesn't really work, you know."

"You'll speak when you're spoken to." The woman gave him another shove in the direction they had been heading, sending the boy sprawling to the dirt.

"I just thought you might want to know," he mumbled.

It occurred to Erwyn that she'd never answered his questions, either.

Then again, maybe she had.

After a moment, he got to his feet. His head seemed to have started throbbing again.

They continued to walk, weaving back and forth between the tents. Erwyn took the time to look around.

It was a big camp. Cooking pots hung suspended above

crackling fires in front of some of the tents. Female warriors
in various states of battle dress stood in front of others.

Very conspicuous, Erwyn thought.

About the third or fourth time they passed the same
blonde washing her shirt, Erwyn figured out they were trying to trick him.

Really! He might be a man, but he wasn't *that* stupid.
Of course, it wasn't a bad ploy, if he stopped to think about
it. A lot of people might have been too preoccupied to
notice.

"You seem to have quite a large force encamped here."
He placed a slight emphasis on the word "seem." The
woman only grunted, but Erwyn noticed that her grip on
his arm tightened.

Smiling to himself, Erwyn changed tactics. "Do you
have a name?"

"I said no talking!" She shoved him again, causing his
head to complain once more.

Erwyn decided to be quiet.

After a while, he heard a voice behind him say, "Lariyn."

"Huh?" Erwyn stumbled, but caught himself.

"My name is Lariyn." The woman's voice softened to
almost, but not quite, friendly.

"Mine's Erwyn," he replied. "For a few more minutes,
anyway."

He wanted to turn to look at the woman, at Lariyn, but
he really had no desire to renew his acquaintance with the
ground. No point in pushing his luck.

They continued in silence. Erwyn was not sure how far,
or for how long, they had walked, but he felt fairly certain
they had almost reached their goal, whatever that was.

In the first place, they were approaching a large clearing
in the tents. Possibly the meeting area of the camp, he
thought. Second, and to Erwyn most important, a group of
heavily armed and apparently irate women milled about in
the center of the clearing.

He stretched on tiptoes, straining to learn what, exactly,

they were clustering around. Whatever it was, he couldn't see it.

He did notice, however, one very important thing lacking in the crowd. Men. He'd already pointed out to Lariyn that he didn't see any males of any age in the camp. He'd hoped they'd be wherever Lariyn was taking him, but there weren't any to be seen.

Erwyn and his guard approached the crowd of spectators. Beneath the openly hostile stares of the women, he felt himself blushing. Once more he wondered where Chesric had disappeared to. He could use some moral support.

The crowd parted in front of Erwyn, leaving him a wide aisle to the center of the gathering. There he found answers to two of his questions.

Chesric stood on a low platform, surrounded by four women. Each held a large sword pointed straight at the old knight, who seemed to be enjoying himself immensely. The old man stood on the platform, rocking back and forth on the heels of his boots like a child at the fair.

When they'd started their walk, Erwyn had wondered whether or not to be insulted by the lack of guards and restraints. Now he knew.

Chesric had four guards, Erwyn had one. They obviously thought Chesric to be the more formidable opponent.

The idea rankled. Surely a sorcerer ought to be counted as an opponent to be reckoned with. Briefly, he considered the odds. One journeyman sorcerer with thirteen spells, fourteen if he counted a useless glitter spell. Uh-huh.

Come to think of it, they were probably right, and Erwyn felt no desire to prove them wrong. Not any time soon.

Lariyn prodded him, and Erwyn stepped onto the platform. Chesric simply smiled, as though this sort of thing happened every day.

"Hi there, young fella." Chesric's accent was back in place. Erwyn smiled, remembering that Chesric had never answered his question about the changing accent.

"Together again." The guard pushed Erwyn into place beside Chesric. "Some fun, huh?"

"Wouldn't miss it fer the world, boy." The old man chuckled. "Adventure is the spice of life."

"I think I'd prefer my life a little on the bland side, thank you."

The crowd became quiet suddenly. Erwyn and Chesric turned to see, coming up the aisle Erwyn had just traveled, another of the female warriors. This one was different, though.

She held her head high, almost regally, as she strode purposefully down the pathway. Her armor looked similar to the other women's, except for the short leather cape swirling behind her. She stood half a head taller than most of the women and seemed to Erwyn to be broader in the shoulders as well.

As the newcomer mounted the platform, Erwyn took a good look at her face. Her dark brown hair, held in place by a twist of silver wire, hung down to slightly below her shoulders. She had high cheekbones, a straight nose, and a wide, expressive mouth.

By Erwyn's standards, she might have been the most beautiful woman in the world. Except for two things.

One: She was frowning, and the look she gave Erwyn made him feel like an intruder, in spite of the fact that it wasn't his idea to be standing on top of a platform with a bunch of women holding their swords at his back.

And two: She seemed to be in charge of the women who were currently holding their swords at his back.

Considering that he was completely innocent of anything and everything, at least up to this point, her words as she addressed her people took Erwyn somewhat by surprise.

"Warriors of Marli!" Her voice rang out across the gathering. "We are met to decide the fate of these two male intruders—"

"Intruders! We didn't . . . oof!" An elbow landed in the

middle of Erwyn's stomach.

The woman continued, "We must decide now what manner of death is most appropriate."

Erwyn looked at Chesric. It was going to be one of those days.

18

Sweet-Talkin' Guy

(Or, Start the Execution Without Me)

*When faced with overt hostility, remain calm. The last
thing you should do is let the enemy know you're frightened.*
                                        Sorcerers Almanac
                            Section Three: On People and Their Influence

Shouts went up from the crowd of women around the
platform. Cheers, jeers, and catcalls assailed them from all
sides.

"Now's the time, boy." Chesric nudged Erwyn in the ribs.

"Time for what?"

"To do yer stuff. You know. Dazzle 'em with a little of
that there magic. Or baffle 'em with bullshit. Whatever."

"Anything in particular? I mean, I could maybe whip up
a nice little foxfire ball and shed some light on the proceed-
ings. Only it's broad daylight, and nobody would notice.

"Or maybe I should make a campfire, or heat their
cloaks, or levitate myself and fly around the camp singing
sea chanteys. That'd really impress 'em. Just what the hell
do you think I should do?"

"Calm down, son. Don't get excited. Beet red ain't yer
color."

"Calm down? I'm standing here surrounded by a few dozen women with very sharp swords who are in the process of trying to decide what's the best way to kill me, and you want me to calm down?"

"Well, it's just that ye'd attract a little less attention that way."

Erwyn looked around. The women were staring at him. And it wasn't because of his looks. "Too loud, huh?"

"Just a mite," Chesric replied. "Now that ye've got their attention, why don't ye see if ye can't get us out of this here per-dicament."

Chesric spoke a moment too late. The woman who seemed to be the leader of the Marlians glared at Erwyn. Or, more precisely, at Erwyn's chest.

"The boy's a magic-user."

Though barely above a whisper, her voice carried to the entire crowd. Angry murmurs rippled through the clearing. It was bad enough he was male. Now they knew he was a sorcerer as well. Double trouble.

"Burn him! Burn them both!"

Great! Erwyn wondered if his refrigeration spell would help. Except that it was intended to preserve steak, not people.

"Burning's too good for them. Throw them off the cliffs."

"Draw and quarter them."

"Cut off his head and hang it from the captain's tent. That's the way to deal with wizards!"

Erwyn felt chills run up his spine. This was getting a little out of hand.

"Better do it soon." Chesric still looked confident.

Erwyn took a step backward as the crowd edged forward. "Do what?"

"Whatever comes natural!" Chesric's voice rose ever so slightly in pitch. It seemed even Chesric could be shaken.

Erwyn understood why, since he had been panicking since he got here.

The spectators surged toward the platform. The guards,

who had moments before been keeping watch on Erwyn and
Chesric, now turned to protect the two captives. But five
swords against an army . . .

"Stop!"

The captain's voice rang out over the hostile crowd. She
shouted only once, and only one word, but it worked. The
angry muttering died down.

"Your behavior is unforgivable. You are warriors of Marli.
Do not forget that."

The women were mostly quiet now.

Erwyn gazed at the captain with new interest.

Here was no sticky-sweet damsel seeking an unsuspecting bachelor to drag into marriage. This woman com-
manded the loyalty of an army of well-trained fighters.

The only trouble he could see was the fact that she was a
Marlian, and he was a man. Since all of the women in atten-
dance seemed to feel that men were a couple of steps lower
than gor-worms, that might prove to be something of an
obstacle.

Of course, that was just an unsubstantiated observation,
one Erwyn felt inclined to believe, from the comments he'd
heard from the crowd.

Then, too, there remained the little matter of avoiding a
lynching—or worse. Well, you can't fail until you try, or
something to that effect.

"Excuse me, Captain." Erwyn tried to keep his voice
steady as the guards turned their swords back toward the
captives.

The captain looked at Erwyn in surprise. She might have
been less surprised if a gor-worm had spoken instead. Erwyn
stood a little straighter.

"You have something to say?"

He tried to pretend she was just one of his instructors
during finals. Maybe he could bluff his way out of this.

"It seems to me . . ." Erwyn paused as the angry rumble
resumed.

The Marlian captain raised her hand, and once more

silence reigned.

"It seems to me," Erwyn tried again, "that the two of us might have something to say on the subject of death. Ours, that is."

The captain raised one eyebrow at the boy.

Erwyn swallowed and pressed on. Now that he had her attention, he found he could think of plenty to say.

"I mean, where the hell do you people get off deciding to kill us? We didn't do anything to you. There we were, minding our own business, when someone comes up and clobbers us over the head—uh, heads—and drags us away from our campsite."

As he warmed to the subject, Erwyn's voice rose in both pitch and volume.

"Then I wake up in a musty old tent, with little men playing with hammers inside my head and someone pointing a sword at my throat. Why? We weren't bothering you. Why did you kidnap us in the first place?"

Erwyn realized he was yelling and stopped. He glared at the woman defiantly. If they were going to kill him anyway, he might as well have his say first. What could they do? Kill him twice?

"We have been persecuted since we entered this land." Her voice had become soft, almost reasonable. "And you say you have done nothing to us?"

"I, personally, didn't have anything to do with it. Couldn't you at least go kidnap the people who were actually responsible?"

Erwyn's guard leaned over and whispered something to the captain. The captain nodded, looking thoughtful, then turned back toward her captives.

She moved closer to Erwyn, towering over him. The boy looked up into a pair of determined gray eyes.

"The men here fear and hate women in general, and women with swords in particular. You are a magic-user. A man of power. The worst kind. Can you honestly say that you're an exception?"

"As a matter of fact, I can't, not at this moment. But then, it's sort of hard not to fear a woman with a sword when she has it pointed at various important parts of one's anatomy. I'd be afraid of a robin right now if it had a sword pointed at my—uh—middle."

Erwyn looked nervously at the guards flanking the woman, their swords aimed at an area just below his waist.

"Under ordinary circumstances, though," he continued, "I don't think armed women would bother me much."

"If so," the captain replied, "you are either a fool or a very extraordinary man."

"I've been called both, mostly a fool."

"Who is it that calls you extraordinary, then?"

Erwyn shrugged, embarrassed. "My mother."

For a moment, Erwyn thought he'd made a serious mistake.

The Marlian captain looked at him, a strange expression on her face. Then she laughed. She had a beautiful laugh, especially since it meant they might get to live a few minutes longer.

"Come," she said, motioning them forward. "We will talk. Let's see if you can convince me of your—differences."

She turned and walked away. The crowd parted to allow her through.

The young sorcerer glanced at his companion.

Chesric smiled and shrugged.

"You sure weren't much help," Erwyn remonstrated. "She could have decided to kill us right here. Diplomacy isn't my strong suit."

"Never a doubt."

"Oh? Is that why your voice was squeaky a few minutes ago?"

"Me? Squeak under pressure? Never. I keep my armor well oiled at all times."

Lariyn poked Erwyn in the ribs. "Get going."

"Must be a different suit of armor than the one you were wearing when we met." Grumbling, Erwyn hurried to catch up with the captain, with Chesric only a step behind.

They followed Lariyn to the captain's tent. It had to be the captain's because it was about three times the size of any other tent in the area. Besides, it also sported a huge sign that read "Captain's Quarters."

The outside flaps of the tent were adorned with hunting scenes. Nice stuff. There were horses, lions, gryphons, brave victors, and fallen heroes.

Erwyn noticed there were no men . . . on either end of the sword.

By the time they entered the tent, the captain had removed her cloak and armor, leaving only a leather under-kilt and cloth tunic. She sat facing them across a small wooden table upon which she laid her sword. An unmistakable message.

The inside of the tent was decorated like the outside, but with battle scenes in which Marlian warriors fought with vaguely masculine forms. There were no distinct figures other than the women, except in one panel.

Behind the captain was the only recognizable male form he had yet seen, on or off the canvas.

The masculine figure wore a black cloak edged in silver, his hood pulled up so that little of his face showed. In his hand he held a small golden pyramid that seemed to glow in the flickering light of the tent's single torch. There was something about that figure, something familiar, if he could just place it. . . .

Erwyn shook his head to clear it. Taking the seat offered him, he tried to smile confidently at the captain.

"If we're just going to have a friendly little chat, we should introduce ourselves."

She didn't look like she was there for a "friendly little chat," but Erwyn rushed on anyway.

"My name is Erwyn, and this is my friend, Chesric." He kicked the old man, who stood gaping at the panel behind the captain.

"Uh—pleased to meet ye." Chesric glared at Erwyn.

"I am Kerissa, First Captain of the Marlian guard," the captain said formally. "Now that we have the amenities over with, tell me what makes you two different from any other men around here. I hope your answer is a good one. Your lives depend on it."

19

I'd Rather Be Selling Carriages

(Or, Can You Say *Sucker?*)

When handling delicate negotiations, always keep your goal firmly in mind and never let your opponent get the upper hand.

> *Sorcerers Almanac*
> *Section Three: On People and Their Influence*

Kerissa sat with one hand resting casually across the hilt of her sword. As though she had all the time in the world, the Marlian captain watched Erwyn shift about uncomfortably in his seat. She seemed to be enjoying her advantage. Her expression reminded the boy of one of the cats back home in the barn, watching the mice.

Erwyn looked to Chesric for help, but the old man offered only a brief smile of encouragement. Then he crossed his arms and rested his chin on his chest.

Erwyn waited for the inevitable sound effects. Fortunately, the old man had the grace not to snore in the face of the enemy.

Finally, Erwyn cleared his throat, trying to think of where to begin. "Well, uh . . ."

"Can ye tell us just why it is that ye don't get along with

members of the male persuasion?" Chesric jumped in before Erwyn could get started. He didn't even open his eyes.

Erwyn squirmed. They were supposed to convince Kerissa to let them live, not ask tactless, embarrassing, and possibly fatal questions.

After a few moments, the captain replied, "You already know we are warriors of Marli. If you know that much, you must know more."

Erwyn tried to appear unconcerned. "I heard once about a group of women who called themselves Marlian warriors, worshipers of the goddess Marli. A story told to frighten little boys, that's all."

"You don't appear to be very frightened. Are you?"

"Scared to death."

"You must be a very accomplished actor."

"Required course. Acting Superior 101. 'How to Appear Calm, Cool, and Collected When the World Is Disintegrating All Around You'."

She sighed. "Okay. Let's try again. I'll assume you know nothing about us or what's going on." She didn't sound convinced. In fact, she sounded as if she expected them to lie to her.

The captain clasped her hands on the table in front of her. After a moment, she continued in the kind of voice one used to lecture very young, very stupid children. The kind of voice Erwyn's father used to state the obvious to someone who insisted upon being ignorant. Erwyn had been the recipient of more than one of those lectures.

"We come from Senderlaan in Terregonia. We worship Marli, the Enlightened One. Only a woman can enter the temple of Marli. Therefore, Marlian warriors are all women, and strange stories have been told about us. Many of them untrue. For nearly a century, we have fought alongside our men in times of war. As equals.

"Now, we have entered this strange new land where the customs are different, alien to us. We have come against a wall of male prejudice. It's bad enough being in a strange land, without being treated like we were less important than cattle!"

Kerissa glanced from Erwyn to Chesric and back again.

Erwyn gave her his best blank look, which wasn't difficult, since he had no idea what she was talking about.

The captain looked at them in confusion. "You're not from around here?"

"No," Erwyn replied. "In fact . . ."

"And you don't know anything about this?"

"No, but . . ."

"You mean to tell me you've just been blundering blindly around without knowing anything about what's going on in the neighborhood?"

"Well . . ."

"Then you really are a fool. It's dangerous enough trying to survive when you know the territory."

"Now wait just a minute! I'm only a journeyman sorcerer. What do you expect? They send us out without much of anything in the way of supplies *or* information." Same old defense. He wondered what it would be like when he became an old man and still used inexperience as an excuse.

"If I hadn't run into Chesric here, I'd very likely have to spend the next four years mostly alone and virtually defenseless."

"If you're a sorcerer, you're not exactly what I would call defenseless."

"I said 'virtually,' and that's the way it feels. Does the phrase 'I'm making it up as I go' mean anything to you?

"Of course, if what Chesric tells me is anywhere near the truth, I couldn't actually be alone if I wanted to be. I never know just who or what I'm going to run into. Or whether the spells I have are truly adequate for the job.

"So far, I've been chased, picked on, bewitched, tricked, and spied upon, not to mention being kidnapped by a bunch of heavily armed women who seem to be intent on killing me just because I had the misfortune to have been born male! Speaking of which—" Erwyn took a deep breath

and brought the conversation back to its original subject—
"what did you mean, 'less important than cattle?' Less
important to whom?"

"The men who live here."

"Where here? You're camped in the middle of a field."

Kerissa glared at him. "I mean in Perbellum. It's a town a
short distance from here."

"Wait a minute! You mean the women there are treated
like—" Erwyn paused, shocked "—like *property?*"

"That's basically correct."

"But how can they *do* that?"

Erwyn rose indignantly and suddenly found himself surrounded by several very sharp knives that seemed to appear
out of nowhere.

"Oops." He sat down, fast.

The knives disappeared. Erwyn noticed a half-dozen
women milling about the tent. Funny, they hadn't been
there before.

Erwyn was beginning to feel a little like a mushroom—
very much in the dark. "I don't get it. You can't be recruit-
ing. I mean, cattle don't usually grow up to become warriors.
And it doesn't sound like a good place to settle down. What
are you doing *here?*"

"I thought you'd never ask." She wore that cat-and-
mouse expression again.

Kerissa smiled and gestured to someone behind Erwyn.
The room emptied as the rest of the women vanished out
the door. Leaning back in her chair, the captain relaxed.

Somehow, Erwyn didn't feel any safer.

"A few months ago, a sacred talisman, the Tetraliad, was
stolen from the Temple of Marli at Senderlaan. All of the
guards were killed save one." Kerissa leaned forward, toying
with the hilt of her sword. "I was that guard. I have pledged
my life to finding the talisman and returning it to its right-
ful place."

"So you've just been chasing across the country looking
for the person who took it?"

"That's right."

"Do you know who it was?"

"Yes. We even know where he is."

"I have a feeling I'm going to hate myself for asking this but, why haven't you recovered it yet?"

Kerissa smiled again.

Erwyn began to develop an intense dislike for that smile.

"Because the slime-ball who has it is holed up in the town of Perbellum, that's why."

"So where *is* Perbellum?"

"Not far. About two miles west of here."

"And you can't get the talisman out."

"Uh-uh."

Erwyn sighed. He was being led, and he didn't like it even a little.

"Okay, let's cut to the punch line. The men of Perbellum hold an extremely . . . unflattering . . . opinion of women, and they won't cooperate with you because you're all women. Right?"

"Right on the first try. They don't particularly want the creep who stole the talisman around, but they're not about to let us have him. The last time we tried to haul him out, I lost three warriors. They lost four. Stalemate. Fortunately, they don't seem inclined to carry the battle too far outside the city walls." She paused. "Or maybe that's not so fortunate. It is, at best, difficult to fight anywhere near the city."

Erwyn resisted the urge to ask why. Instead, he muttered to himself, "Here we go again," and threw a quick glance at Chesric. He hated volunteering for anything, especially when someone else forced him into it.

The old man didn't move. As far as anyone could tell, he was asleep.

Taking a deep breath, Erwyn asked, "So, uh, Captain, would you like some help in retrieving this, um, talisman?"

"I thought you'd never ask." That was the second time she'd said that.

The captain looked immensely pleased with herself.

Erwyn felt a little sick.

"Let me get this straight." Erwyn looked cautiously around before leaving his seat. He stared at the painting behind Kerissa for a while before continuing. "In order to save our lives, Chesric and I have to walk into a hostile town where you've already lost three perfectly good warriors, and force the townspeople to turn this guy over to us." Erwyn turned to face the Marlian. "What's to keep us from continuing out the other side of town?"

"Well, first of all, there is only one way into or out of Perbellum. And second, it won't be you *and* Chesric. Just you."

He missed the chair on the way down.

* * * * *

A couple hours later, Erwyn paced the floor of the tent they'd been given. He just wanted to get the job over with. But Kerissa insisted that it was too late in the day to get started. So, in spite of Erwyn's protests, the companions were fed well and told to rest.

After dinner, Chesric, as usual, had dropped into a sound sleep instantly. After a while, Erwyn gave up pacing and lay awake on his bedroll staring at the ceiling of the tent.

If a troop of heavily armed warriors, regardless of their sex, couldn't drag the thief out of Perbellum, what could one man do? He couldn't think of a thing.

As dawn broke through the morning haze, Erwyn still hadn't come up with a workable plan. Chesric lay snoring happily on the opposite side of the tent.

A rustle at the entrance brought Erwyn out of his reverie. He sat up to see Lariyn enter with a platter of cold meat, cheese and fruit.

"Ah, breakfast!"

Erwyn turned to his tent mate and found Chesric wide awake, nose twitching. He could sleep through anything but mealtime.

The old man rose and helped Lariyn settle the plate onto a small table that had been tucked away in a corner. "Won't ye join us?"

Lariyn shook her head. "I have work to attend to."

Before Chesric could insist, she disappeared through the entry. The two adventurers fell to eating. That is, Chesric did. Erwyn wasn't very hungry.

After breakfast, Lariyn returned to take them to the edge of the camp, where Kerissa, in full battle dress, awaited their arrival.

Erwyn wondered who she was trying to impress.

"So, the moment of truth is at hand." Kerissa watched the young sorcerer with interest.

"Uh, could you tell me just how you expect me to accomplish this, er, task."

"The manner is entirely up to you," the captain replied. "It should be simple for a man of your—qualifications. Especially considering the price for failure."

"You make it sound so easy. Frankly, it makes me a little nervous to think that our lives ride on whether I can talk a bunch of belligerent bullies into turning the guy over. They can't help but know that I'll just give him to you after I leave."

"Then you'll have to *persuade* them."

"Right. Persuade them. Sure thing. No problem." Shaking his head, Erwyn turned in the direction Kerissa said Perbellum lay. He had two whole miles to figure out a plan. And he had to walk the whole distance.

20

You Can't Tell a Book by Its Cover

(Or a Latrine By Its Smell)

Personality-altering spells can have a nasty effect on everyone and everything in the vicinity.

Sorcerers Almanac
Section Three: On People and Their Influence

While he walked, Erwyn savored the scent of the first wildflowers of spring. He hadn't realized how long he'd been on his journey. More than half a year.

Unfortunately, the journey wouldn't last much longer if he didn't figure out what to do about the Marlian's thief.

He was still trying to decide what to do when he caught his first sight of the town of Perbellum. In the golden glow of the early afternoon sun, the town seemed, well, downright dismal.

Small, compared to the rambling cities Erwyn knew, Perbellum was squashed uncomfortably in the valley formed by three smallish mountains. Or perhaps they were largish hills. He couldn't honestly remember what the difference was.

The houses and buildings were surrounded by a high stone wall that crowded them together. From his vantage point across the valley, Erwyn could see only one main gate facing him. If there were any other gates, they must be crammed right into the face of the hills. Or else they opened out onto the river that wound between the hills. Neither option was very helpful.

The stone of the walls was gray and dirty, with here and there a block gone like a missing tooth. Perbellum sat hunched over its badly tilled fields like a bully waiting for someone to fight.

Well, no help for it. He slowly trudged toward the gate, picking his way carefully through the brambles that crowded straggly patches of wheat and barley. There was no love lost on this land, he decided.

The wildflowers were left behind, and so was their scent. Instead, the enticing aroma of raw sewage drifted toward him.

As the young sorcerer approached the gate, he discovered that the town wasn't in the terrible state he had first thought. It was worse. Much worse.

The gate sagged on its hinges, ready to fall at the slightest touch. Fortunately for Erwyn, it was already open, so he didn't have to touch it. He'd already decided that levitation was out. He had no intention of advertising his tendencies in the magic department unless, and until, it was absolutely necessary. Adjusting his cloak to cover his Guild patch, he stepped through the gateway.

"Oh, no!" The moan escaped from Erwyn's mouth before he could stop it.

And he had thought the *outside* was bad! Nowhere could Erwyn see the inhabitants of the town, but evidence of their existence assaulted him.

Refuse littered the streets and sidewalks. The houses slumped on their foundations, as though the stench was too much for the old stonework to bear. Erwyn brought a hand up to cover his nose.

"'Ere now. 'Oo's this?" The voice didn't sound particularly friendly, in Erwyn's humble estimation. "Wot you doin' 'ere, mister?"

Erwyn turned to the source of the question. Younger than Chesric, but not by much, the owner of the voice was a grizzled old man who hadn't shaved in weeks . . . or bathed for even longer.

Erwyn's nose wrinkled in disgust. The man's odor was stronger than the garbage in the street.

"I-I'm here to speak to your mayor, or king, or whatever." He couldn't help backing away from the man.

"Oh, you are, are you?" The man smiled, showing rows of rotting teeth in swollen gums. He took a couple of steps toward the boy.

Erwyn gulped, but stood his ground.

"Wot you want to see the Lord Mayor for, eh? You think you got business with 'is Worship?"

"Yes, as a m-matter of fact. It's a matter of utmost urgency."

"Ow, listen to the fancy words. I reckon 'is Lordship might want to see you, seein' as 'ow you're new to the town, an' all. All alone in a strange city. Might want to educate you on our ways and customs, 'e might."

The man laughed, not a pleasant sound. Then he headed up the nearest street toward the middle of town without even a backward glance. Apparently he expected Erwyn to follow him.

As he hurried to keep up, Erwyn noticed that the town did indeed have people enough to account for the massive amounts of trash clogging the streets. From behind shutters and half-closed doors, he was being watched.

He caught glimpses of the people behind the doors before those doors slammed shut. Of those few he saw, all were just as dirty and scraggly as his guide. Erwyn shuddered. It gave him the willies to think there might be hundreds more like the man he was following.

His guide turned a corner unexpectedly, and Erwyn hastened to catch up with him. He wasn't certain, but he got the distinct impression that he was not wanted. His best course of action would be to get this job over with as soon as possible.

He rounded the corner, nearly walking into his aromatic "friend." Swerving to avoid the collision, Erwyn found himself ankle-deep in a puddle of vivid green muck. It seeped into the leather of his boots and spattered his pants up to the knees.

"There. You look right at 'ome now."

"Terrific." Maybe levitation wasn't such a bad idea, after all.

Rounding another corner, Erwyn found himself fronting the most impressive edifice he had yet seen. That is to say, the building before him still had all its walls in a more or less vertical position. Otherwise, it was just as dirty and dingy as the rest of the town. Maybe more so.

"This 'ere's the town 'all," Erwyn's guide volunteered.

"Wonderful."

Erwyn surveyed the rotting timber of the door. It must have been a magnificent piece of work, about a hundred years ago. As it was, the only things holding it together were the massive iron hinges. Sagging doorways seemed to be the norm around here.

"If anyone asks," the man added, "my name's Urik. In case anyone wants to know 'oo brung you 'ere."

He smiled, making Erwyn wonder exactly *why* Urik would want anyone to know who brought him. Or why anyone would want to know.

Half afraid it would collapse on him, Erwyn carefully pushed the door open. The interior of the town hall was in better repair than it seemed from the street.

Surprised, he took a cautious step inside.

The door opened onto a long hallway. The floors were of marble, the walls of polished wood. As Erwyn walked slowly down the passage, he discovered that the walls were covered with portraits. Every few feet, he found himself confronted by stern men in well-made, though long out-of-date, doublets, who stared at him from aging canvasses.

Passing through the double line of pictures of obviously wealthy and well-bred gentlemen, Erwyn had difficulty connecting them with the people he had seen outside in the town itself. There was no recognizable resemblance.

"Great, another mystery," Erwyn groaned.

The hall ended at a large door that was made of solid wood, instead of the spongy variety that seemed to be the favorite outside. As he reached the door, it swung silently inward, revealing a richly appointed, wood-paneled courtroom. The courtroom was full.

Seated on large wooden benches, milling about on the marbled floors, and sprawled in various corners were numerous representatives of the populace of Perbellum, each and every one a prime example of the dregs of humanity. And all of them were watching Erwyn as he was hustled into the room by two muscle-bound, hairy men who had appeared out of nowhere.

In a large, ornately carved chair behind a huge desk sat a man who could easily have bested Urik in a contest for the worst body odor in recorded history. This was the Lord Mayor, Erwyn surmised.

"I am the Lord Mayor Phamstall," the man declared, vigorously pounding with his gavel on the desktop. "You may address me as Lord Mayor, Your Lordship, or any other appropriate title of respect you might think of." His voice dropped to a more threatening tone. "But you better make it very, very good."

He smiled at the young man in front of him. He had fewer teeth than Urik, too.

"State your business in this, our lovely town of Perbellum."

Silently, Erwyn wished for an army at his back. Preferably one with a few hundred buckets of water and some soap. It was getting hard to breathe in here. He wasn't sure which was worse, the odor of unwashed bodies, or the fumes from their mouths.

Trying to resist the urge to cover his nose with his cloak,

Erwyn addressed the assemblage at large, and the Lord Mayor in particular. "Your, uh, Lordship, I have come to ask about a certain thief, who is supposed to be hiding here in your, ah, beautiful town."

He suspected that honesty was not the best policy in this case, but he couldn't think of anything else. The Lord Mayor exchanged meaningful glances with another man, whom Erwyn supposed was the bailiff, or some such.

"And who might this thief be?" He smiled again.

Erwyn was learning not to trust people who smile too much.

"He, uh, stole a talisman from a temple, Your Lordship. I have been sent to retrieve him, or at least to retrieve the talisman."

"And you think he's here?"

"He was seen entering your gates, yes."

"I think we can *accommodate* you." The Lord Mayor laughed. A very unpleasant sound. "These men will escort you to the . . . thief."

The same two hairy apes who had dragged him into the courtroom appeared at Erwyn's elbows.

Lords, what now? Erwyn asked himself.

It was too easy. One man, unarmed, simply couldn't walk in, ask for something an entire army had failed to recover, and expect to get it. Life didn't work that way, not in his experience.

He had a feeling they weren't going to let him walk out the gates with the man or the talisman. And if he somehow managed to leave Perbellum, without the man and/or the Tetraliad, the Marlians would be certain to kill both him and Chesric.

On the other hand, the Perbellans were probably going to kill him, and then the Marlians would kill Chesric. They were dead either way.

In any case, he wasn't completely certain of his ability to get out of town, since the man probably wouldn't want to leave the dubious safety of Perbellum in the first place.

So matters stood when Erwyn's guards reached a small iron door with an even smaller window on it. A window with bars.

"What the . . . ?"

One of the guards quickly produced a key and opened the door while the other unceremoniously shoved Erwyn through it.

"There he is." One of the guards nodded toward the corner of the cell. "Talk all you like."

Then he stepped back through the doorway, and the door clanged shut behind him. Erwyn heard the rasp of the key in the lock. He was trapped, at least for the moment.

There was movement in the corner, and Erwyn turned, pressing his back to the door.

"Welcome to the hospitality of Perbellum." The newcomer or, more appropriately, the earlier resident, spoke in a soft drawl. "I think you will find it somewhat less than satisfactory." He moved into the light afforded by the room's one window.

He was young, not much older than Erwyn. Light brown hair fell to his collar around an oval, boyish face, a face which currently bore signs of a recent run-in with someone's fist.

He wore a green tunic, once well tailored, but now torn in places. His pants were brown rags whose ends were tucked into a pair of scuffed leather boots.

Around his waist was a belt of some kind, with what looked like a scabbard attached to it. The remains of his tunic bore a threadbare diagonal stripe, as though another belt or something had been worn there. Another sword? For once, Erwyn wished he'd learned more about weapons.

"You're the thief I've been looking for?" Erwyn could not believe this soft-spoken man could be responsible for the deaths of a half-dozen Marlian warriors.

"At your service." Doffing an imaginary cap, he gave a low, sweeping bow. "My name is Devydd, swordsman, lover, thief, entrepreneur. Not necessarily in that order." He smiled, straightening. "And you are . . . ?"

"I'm Erwyn. I have been sent by the captain of the Marlian guard to take you out of Perbellum and"—Erwyn took a deep breath—"to see that you are brought to justice for the theft of their talisman."

21

Strolling Past the Cesspool

(Or, Could You Just Wait for a Spell?)

*In case the need arises to affect a quick escape from some-
where, it is wise to pay close attention to how you got there.*
                                                    Sorcerers Almanac
                            Section One: On Getting the Lay of the Land

"Are you crazy?"

"Huh?"

"Well, unless you are a most accomplished escape artist
and a sorcerer to boot, I think you'll have some difficulty
escaping from this box. I have. That's why I'm still here. It's
tougher than it looks."

Erwyn smiled and calmly threw the edge of his cape over
his shoulder. The patch on his chest seemed to glow in the
dim light. He watched as first surprise, then amusement
registered on Devydd's features.

The young thief might not know the meaning of the
patch itself, but the symbol of the Sorcerer's Guild was uni-
versal.

"Getting out of this cell won't be much of a problem,"
Erwyn informed Devydd, wishing he felt as confident as he
sounded. "The real trouble will be to get out of the city.

Intact. I suspect that they didn't lock me in this cell just to prevent *you* from escaping. I got the impression they don't like strangers much around here."

"All that from a first meeting? Wait until you get to know them better." Devydd's tone changed from flippant to serious. "The people of Perbellum would happily boil you down and use your body fat to fuel their oil lamps, if they thought they could get away with it."

"Well, then," Erwyn replied as cheerfully as he could, "I guess it behooves us to get the hell out of here as fast as we can. Before they run out of oil."

Without waiting for an answer, Erwyn turned his attention to the all-important matter of getting out of the cell. He knelt to examine the lock while he mentally ran through his stock of spells. The lock was too complicated to be picked as he had the lock on Gordrun's library. Besides, he didn't have anything to pick it with. The Marlians had kept his knife.

"Could you, perhaps, speed this up a little? My stomach tells me it's almost time for the guards to bring dinner."

"You mean you can tell by how hungry you are?"

"Nope, I can tell by how nauseated I am. The food here is worse than the hospitality."

"You sound like you're actually looking forward to facing the Marlians."

"Believe me, it's better than the current alternative."

"Well, here goes nothing."

Using his scry spell, Erwyn peered intently at the inside of the lock. One by one, he levitated each tumbler into position. There were five of them.

By the time he had the fifth in place, Erwyn was trembling from the exertion. It took a lot of energy to control a scry spell and levitate five tumblers into different positions at once.

As the last tumbler clicked into position, Erwyn leaned against the door. To his relief, it swung open easily.

"Ow! Damn!" Bereft of the support of the door, Erwyn

fell to the floor with an audible *thump!* When would he ever learn not to lean on things that move?

Devydd hurried out the door, swinging it closed behind him. The lock clicked loudly, informing Erwyn that his concentration had been broken in his fall. Big surprise. Well, he had lasted long enough.

"I hate to bring this up, my friend, but if we don't get out of the area soon, we'll have to take up residence here again. Know what I mean?" Devydd helped Erwyn to his feet.

"Right. Um . . ." Erwyn looked around him in confusion. He didn't quite know how to ask his next question.

"'Um' what?"

"Well . . . I don't suppose you know how to get out of here, do you?"

"You came in here to rescue me, but you don't know the way out?"

"I didn't say I came to rescue you. I said I came to take you out. I had hoped to get a little more cooperation from the natives, as it were."

"Is everyone in your profession this naive?"

"I'm not naive!" Erwyn felt his temper rising again. "It's just that I'm inexperienced."

"Not to mention uninformed."

Erwyn glared at him. "They didn't give me much of a choice."

"They?"

"The people who sent me."

"The Marlian guard? Big, mean women, with lots of sharp, pointy things waving about?"

"Uh-huh."

"Maybe they get their jollies out of sending people off to do an impossible job with a minimum of information. We still need to decide which way to go."

Heavy footsteps sounded down the corridor to their left.

"I guess that takes some of the guesswork out." Devydd grabbed Erwyn's elbow. "It's this way or nothing." So saying, the young thief ran to the right, pulling Erwyn along behind.

Either luck was with them, or the Perbellans weren't used to their captives escaping. They saw no one during the first few minutes of their flight down the hallway.

Devydd chose random directions at each intersection, sometimes turning left, sometimes right, sometimes going straight, until Erwyn was dizzy from all the zigzagging around.

Finally, the thief must have felt they had left pursuit far enough behind, for he slowed down to a trot.

Erwyn didn't mention that they were still *inside* the town hall. He was too tired to complain any more.

They turned another corner and Devydd stopped short. "Uh-oh."

Such descriptive warnings Erwyn could do without. In this case, the warning applied to three rather husky men, dressed in what passed for guard uniforms in Perbellum, who were loudly arguing about something as they stalked in the fugitives' direction.

Fortunately, the guards were too busy yelling at each other to look where they were going.

Devydd and Erwyn hurriedly ducked back around the corner.

"What do we do now?" Devydd asked, as if their predicament were all Erwyn's fault.

"Start by getting out of their way!" he replied. "Follow me."

He turned and ran back to the last intersection. And stopped.

"What are you doing?" Devydd's voice squeaked, just like Erwyn's did when he was terrified.

"Shhh!" Erwyn stood in the center of the intersection, turning slowly to face each of the hallways in turn as he cast his spell. "I'm trying to find . . . there! This way."

He dashed down one of the halls. A moment later, Devydd followed.

"What the hell were you doing back there?"

"Scry spell."

Erwyn couldn't waste much breath on his answer. He had too little left. He turned at another intersection, with Devydd on his heels.

It's got to be here somewhere, he thought furiously. I know it is.

They heard shouts behind them as they turned another corner. Erwyn had the distinct feeling they had been going around in circles. The building couldn't be *that* big. Then he stopped again.

"Holy cow!" Devydd exclaimed, skidding to a stop beside Erwyn. "Hey, kid. They're right behind us. Let's get outta here!"

"We *are* getting out of here," Erwyn panted as he stared at the window in front of him. He stopped to glare at his companion, adding, "And don't call me 'kid.' I know a particularly nasty spell I've been dying to try on someone. Don't tempt me." He was bluffing, but Devydd couldn't know that.

"Okay, okay. Whatever you say. Just get us out of here. And hurry."

"Certainly," Erwyn replied. A moment later, the bars on the window tore loose from the casement. "Here, hold this." He levitated the bars, frame and all, into Devydd's hands. Then he climbed into the window opening, releasing the levitation spell at the same time. The bars landed on Devydd's toes.

"Ow! You whoring son of a . . ."

"Temper, temper!" Erwyn shook his finger at the thief. "And you better keep your voice down, or our 'friends' will find us."

"You didn't have to drop it like that."

"I don't like being rushed. You coming, or staying?"

The shouts were closer. Much closer.

"I'm coming. Get out of the way."

They dropped to the ground outside the window. Devydd

kept watch for undesirables while Erwyn put the bars back in place.

"It won't stand up to a close examination. I broke one of the stones. But it'll slow them down." Dusting his hands, Erwyn turned to check the street.

The window opened onto a back alley between the town hall and the sewer entrance. He could tell it was a sewer because it looked cleaner than the streets. Maybe they didn't use it.

The walls of the building next to them cast a cool shadow on the alley. The smell of the street was less noticeable here, almost bearable.

The alley stretched for some distance in either direction, and Erwyn couldn't tell exactly where it led. One direction was as good as another at this point.

"It's clear. Let's get out of this dump." Devydd started up the alley.

"'Dump' is too nice a word for this place," Erwyn muttered as he caught up with the thief.

> *Springtime in the lowlands can be somewhat warm. A bathing suit is recommended.*
>
> Sorcerers Almanac
> Section Two: On Weather and Its Effects

Moments later, they reached the end of the alley and stepped out into the warmth and sunlight. Too warm, Erwyn decided as they were hit by a wall of stench from the sewage-strewn street.

He'd thought the smell was bad that morning. In the afternoon sun, it was almost overpowering.

Devydd had gone on ahead. After taking a second to catch his breath, Erwyn turned to follow. That's when he heard Devydd's warning.

"Uh-oh."

"Can't you be a little more informative?" Erwyn was at the end of his patience.

Devydd pointed to the end of the street. "Look."

Erwyn looked. "Uh-oh."

He checked the other direction. They were trapped. Two or three dozen of Perbellum's finest were closing in on the two fugitives. And the smell didn't seem to bother *them*.

22

Garbage In, Garbage Out

(Or, Get Your Tentacles Out of My Face!)

Always test the water before taking a swim.
                              Sorcerers Almanac
               Section Four: On How to Have a Safe Trip

"Quick! Back the way we came!" Erwyn tugged on Devydd's elbow before racing back to the alley they had just left.

Footsteps thudded behind him, which Erwyn prayed belonged to Devydd. He skidded to a halt beside the sewer entrance and knelt, trying to pry the cover off.

"What are you doing?" Devydd asked anxiously. "You're not going to go down *there*, are you?"

"You got a better idea?" Damn! The cover wouldn't budge.

"I guess not." Devydd sounded dubious.

More footsteps sounded in the alley, heavier, slower, and at both ends. The guards could afford to take their time. Their quarry was trapped. Theoretically.

Devydd tried to help Erwyn with the cover. It still didn't budge.

"I'll just have to levitate it, then."

"Great. But make it quick, will you?"

"I'll try." Erwyn tried to relax as he stared at the iron lid.

"Come on, come on," Devydd muttered, softly this time, aware that their lives depended on Erwyn's concentration.

The footsteps were getting closer, making concentration more and more difficult.

Calm down, Erwyn thought. You can do it.

Sweat trickled down his forehead, dripping into his eyes. He couldn't seem to stop thinking about the guards. Why didn't they just hurry and get it over with? The alley wasn't that long.

Devydd moved closer behind Erwyn. A moment later, the thief's hands closed over his ears. The footsteps became muffled.

Erwyn closed his eyes and tried again to relax. He reached out with his mind and . . . the grate moved!

In the end, Erwyn leaned over to push on the grate. He was too exhausted to continue the spell. Devydd added his strength to Erwyn's, and the cover slid out of the way just as . . .

"Halt!" The voice sounded as if it expected to be obeyed, but Erwyn and Devydd ignored it. The young thief dropped into the sewer first. Erwyn all but fell in after him.

He really had planned to replace the cover. That was before he discovered that the reason the streets were sewers was because the sewers were full.

Eight feet below street level, Erwyn found himself plunging into a river of the vilest, most disgusting sludge he had ever had the misfortune to go swimming in.

"Shit!" That was a mistake. Now he had the noxious stuff inside his mouth as well.

As thick as the sludge appeared, a strong current bore him, coughing and sputtering, out of sight of the entrance and into darkness.

Ahead, Erwyn heard a moan, followed by a bout of coughing and muffled curses. Devydd had made the same mistake as Erwyn.

And the moral of this story is, Erwyn thought, "When

you're floating in a sea of excrement, never, never, *never* open your mouth!" He almost laughed.

The garbage streamed swiftly and, Erwyn guessed, somewhat in the direction of the backside of the city. The smell was overpowering, and the taste was enough to make him retch. Fortunately, he didn't.

Under the circumstances, it was understandable that Erwyn didn't think to light their way until they had gone quite some distance. Then, just as he was about to summon a ball of foxfire, he landed with an "Umph!" on something solid.

The something moved. And swore.

"Back off, you stupid . . ."

The rest of Devydd's words were lost as he sank beneath the slime. Erwyn reached under the surface and dragged him up.

The thief coughed and wheezed for a while before launching his complaint again. "Next time someone comes along to rescue me from jail, I think I'll just stay in my nice, cozy little cell, thank you. What the hell did you think you were doing, anyway?"

"Those guys looked like they wanted to carve us up for supper. I figured the sewer had to go someplace. The garbage goes in; it has to come out."

"Yeah, it goes someplace, all right. An iron grille."

"An iron grille?" Erwyn shoved his way past Devydd.

Pale gray light filtered through from the far end of the tunnel. Enough for him to see that they'd found a door with iron bars three inches apart set into it. The river of sewage rushed between the bars without letting up. Erwyn found himself washed against the grille, along with a lot of other junk. The junk stayed on his side of the grille. So did the muck.

He took a deep breath, clamping his teeth against his protesting stomach. Was it his imagination? No. There was a definite touch of fresh air on the other side of the door. Experimentally, he tugged, then shoved, at the gate. It didn't budge.

"Now what?"

"As I suspected," Erwyn said in his most supercilious manner, "the sewer had to go somewhere."

"Well, what are you waiting for? Open it up."

Erwyn turned on Devydd, though he couldn't actually see him. "Look, *friend*, sorcery takes energy, and I'm just about tapped. You're supposed to be a thief. Why don't you see if *you* can open it."

"Hmmm. Okay, I will." Devydd shouldered past the sorcerer, and Erwyn could hear him examining the gate with his hands.

"Would you like some more light?"

"No, thank you. It's bad enough I have to smell this gook. I don't think I have the stamina to look at it too closely. I'll do this one by touch, if you don't mind."

"Okay."

"It's a simple latch, anyway. No problem."

"If you say so."

"It *is* locked, though."

"That figures."

"And slimy."

Devydd fumbled in the gloom for a few seconds. Erwyn busied himself with looking at the dull light glinting off the rivulets of slime on the tunnel walls. Then the sorcerer heard a muffled *thud!* as Devydd's hand hit the grillework.

"Damn! It's stuck, too."

"I thought you said it was easy. You sure you don't want some light?"

"I'm sure."

"Have it your way." Erwyn would have liked a little more illumination, as he thought he saw something else moving along the tunnel wall. It couldn't be water or slime. For one thing, it was going up. He watched the dark blob until it disappeared through the gate, about three inches from Devydd's head.

"Damn!"

"You're cer—"

"No light!"

"Okay."

"Damn!"

"You—"

"*No light!*"

Finally, something clicked, but the grille stayed closed.

Erwyn sloshed forward to peer over Devydd's shoulder and nearly tripped over a board that was stuck in the mud. After wiggling it free, he peered at it in the half-light.

"You know, I believe this gate marks the edge of Perbellum."

"Oh, really?" Devydd grunted as he strained to open the grate. "What makes you think that?"

"This." Erwyn shoved the board in front of Devydd's face. The sign was dripping with muck, but they could just make out the words "Sewer Egress, Perbellum City Limits."

"That's nice." He strained against the door again. "I don't suppose you have anything on you to help me pry this open, do you? I seem to have left my sword in my other cell."

"Not really."

"Great! Grab my waist, will you?"

"Your waist? What for?"

"So you can add your weight when I try to open this thing."

"Oh." Erwyn grabbed the thief by the waist and pulled.

"Ouch! Could you wait till I *tell* you to pull? You damn near jerked my fingers off!"

"Sorry." Erwyn loosened his grip while Devydd grabbed the door again.

"Okay, now *pull!*"

They pulled. And pulled. And . . .

"Oops!"

That was the last Erwyn heard from Devydd as the current sucked them through the opening and onward to— wherever the tunnel led. The door clicked shut behind them.

The water flowed faster on this side of the gate. They

flashed past the source of the dim light—a hole set in the ceiling of the tunnel—and on into more darkness.

Erwyn struggled to keep his head up. Flailing his arms, he tried to find anything to grab on to.

His groping hands finally found something. A thick, wet, slimy something, with soft, bowl-shaped things attached to it. It curled around his waist, lifting him above the water.

Lights snapped on overhead. Two of them. With pupils.

23

Creature Comfort

(Or, Up the Creek Without a Boat)

Cities fortunate enough to have a working sewer also tend to have something living in it.

Sorcerers Almanac
Section Five: On Things to Watch Out For

Erwyn was saved the trouble of screaming by Devydd's strained "Uh-oh." At a guess, Devydd was caught, too.

"Y-You want some light now, or do you want to die not knowing what ate you?"

"L-Let there be light!"

And there was light, a ball light the size of Erwyn's head, which was dwarfed by the head right next to it.

"Cripes!" The eyes snapped shut, and the tentacle holding Erwyn quivered. "Did you have to do that?" The monster blinked rapidly. "I mean, you could have warned me, you know."

"Uh, sorry. I really didn't . . ."

"It's okay. I'll live." The creature peered at its captives.

Erwyn twisted in the creature's hold. It didn't seem to mean them any harm. Yet. Maybe he could reason with it. "Could you please set us down now?"

"Oh. Certainly."

It placed them carefully on the ledge that paralleled the river, then it peered at them, as if not knowing what to do next.

Erwyn leaned back, trying to get the full picture.

The creature was roughly the size of a house, with a huge oval head, large eyes, no visible mouth, and bright blue skin. It heaved itself onto the ledge beside them. That is, it heaved most of itself onto the ledge. Some of it still trailed in the water.

"What are you?"

"The official, scientific name is triskadekapus, which means a creature with thirteen feet, or, in this case, tentacles. But my name's Felix. Welcome to my home."

He reached out a tentacle for Erwyn to shake—the tentacle he was using to hold himself on the ledge. Without that one support, he fell *kersplat!* into the stream. Water and sludge flew everywhere.

"Thirteen? Isn't that supposed to be unlucky?"

"I don't know about unlucky" —Felix hauled himself, dripping and sputtering, out of the water— "but it certainly is inconvenient. I never can get a grip on that odd tentacle." His face turned a deep purple.

Erwyn stared. Was the monster actually *blushing?*

Felix didn't stay embarrassed long. "Oh, no!" He surveyed the damage from his inadvertent swim.

Erwyn followed his gaze. Felix's home was a cavern, big enough to accommodate at least two Felixes, maybe three. Stone ledges ran along either side of the cave, confining the stream of sewage and providing display space for Felix's belongings, all of which were now covered with filth, from the braided rug, to the pink lamp with the beaded fringe, to the lace doilies scattered on the rocks. Even the overstuffed white chair next to Erwyn hadn't escaped.

Looking closer, the boy decided that maybe the spots on the chair belonged there. It looked like some sort of cowhide.

He eyed the triskadekapus warily. Had the creature bought the chair, or found it, or—Erwyn gulped—killed the cow himself? What, exactly, did a triskadekapus eat?

Felix had retrieved a pair of brown-spotted rags from the nearest rock and stared at them in dismay. "My doilies!" He swished them in the water, but only succeeded in smearing the slime around. "They're ruined." He looked like he was going to cry.

"If you'll excuse us," —Erwyn edged toward the other end of the tunnel and freedom— "we'll just be going, now." He nudged Devydd, and the two of them headed away from the monster.

"Not so fast!" A slippery rope grabbed Erwyn around the waist again. Another had Devydd in a bind. A third wagged in the sorcerer's face. "You two aren't going anywhere until you clean up this mess. Lords know when the garbage pixie will come by again."

"Garbage pixie?"

"Don't they have garbage pixies where you're from?"

Erwyn shook his head. So did Devydd.

"Trash monsters? Litter basilisks? Sewer sprites?"

Erwyn shook his head again. "No, we just chuck everything out to the compost creep."

"Well, a garbage pixie cleans the sewers and gutters, and maintains the filter spell on the grate. But ours has been on strike since Lord Mayor Pain-in-the-Ass insulted him. Hasn't been back for at least two months now. Since I can't be certain he'll be back at all, you boys will just have to clean up your mess."

"I think that's your cue, kid." The thief eyed the grunge on Felix's lace.

"*My* cue? How come it's my problem? You made some of the mess."

"Because the sooner we get out of here, the better. And magic works faster than elbow grease."

"You've got a point."

With the door closed again, the filter spell kept at least

some of the gunk out, so the water in the channel was relatively clean. Most of the filth that had come past the grill
with them had flowed down the tunnel and out with the
water. So, all that remained was the ledges and furniture.
And, of course, the doilies.

"Anyone mind getting wet?"

Erwyn smiled at Devydd's glare. He and the thief were
already soaked to the skin and caked with slime. A little
more water would be an improvement. And Felix lived in
the sewer.

The only answer he could see to the problem was a nice
rainstorm, a real gully washer—or doily washer, as the case
may be.

"Hold on to something. This may be a little hairy."

He meant the warning for Devydd, but Felix wrapped his
tentacles around the nearest thing he could reach. Which
happened to be Erwyn.

The young sorcerer squirmed, gasping, "Do you mind? If
I can't breathe, I can't cast the spell!"

"Oops! Sorry." The tentacles relaxed.

"Sure, no problem." Erwyn took several deep breaths to
make sure his lungs could still expand.

"Do you really think this will work?" Felix asked with
some agitation.

Erwyn shrugged. No way to know for certain until he
tried.

In minutes, the rain had scoured clean everything in
sight.

"You want me to dry everything, too?"

Felix flicked the water from the tip of one tentacle, then
gingerly picked up one of the doilies. "No, thanks. It would
probably ruin my upholstery. You boys run along. And
mind you, watch out for my friend Oscar on your way out.
He's nice, once you get to know him, but sometimes he can
be a real grouch."

"Uh, yeah. Thanks."

Felix started hanging his lace up to dry, and the two fugitives headed for the gray light at the end of the tunnel.

"If this sort of thing is going to happen very often," Erwyn remarked as they left Felix's cavern, "I'll have to fine-tune my rain spell."

"What for?"

"I'll need different power levels for cottons, linens, wash and wear, and delicate fabrics. Maybe I could come up with a way to clean leather without getting it wet. Sort of a dry clean."

"Personally," Devydd responded, "I think I'd rather stick to doing my laundry the old-fashioned way, if you don't mind, kid."

Minutes later, they found the end of the sewer. Light streamed into the tunnel through a screen of trees and bushes. Unfortunately, all the muck they'd let in through the grate had piled up at the tunnel mouth. The aroma of standing sewage gave Erwyn a new appreciation for a fast trip through the tunnels.

The smell was unbearable. At least the air was moving in the tunnels. Here, it just hovered over the gunk, strong enough to melt nose hair. It also lay between them and the exit. And the ledge didn't extend that far.

Undaunted, Devydd plowed through the muck toward the opening. Grimacing, Erwyn followed, stopping abruptly as the thief halted at the edge.

"Why don't you go on through?" he asked as he sloshed up beside the thief.

"Because of them." Devydd nodded toward the opening.

Erwyn looked through the screen of vegetation. Outside, a river flowed serenely past the sewer opening. And there, on the riverbank, pounding assorted bits of clothing on the rocks, were—women.

"I was beginning to wonder where they kept them," Erwyn commented. "From the description I was given, I almost expected them to be kept in cages."

"They probably are, when they're not working," Devydd replied seriously. "Say, kid, are we going to just stand here dripping, or are we going to get out of this pit?" He eyed the river wistfully.

Looking down at his legs, now knee deep in slime, Erwyn commented, "Lords, I could use a bath." But he wasn't sure it was a smart idea to try with the women so close.

Especially since the women had ventured that far up-river at some point in time. The sewer opening was partially blocked by a very carefully constructed dam of stones and mud. The same sort of stones the women were using to do their laundry.

"What's the point of building a dam, when you've got a filter spell to clean the water and a garbage pixie to handle everything else?"

There was a loud splash ahead of him, and Erwyn realized he had been talking to the air. Forgetting about the dam, he plunged into the water after the young thief. Together, they swam a short way upstream and around a bend in the river.

It felt so good to get completely clean again! He had never particularly liked water for the purpose of drinking, but his experience in the sewer gave him a new appreciation of water as a beverage. He rinsed his mouth, then gulped some of the cool liquid.

Finally, Erwyn stood in a shallow spot in the river, letting the water flow past him. After removing his cloak and tunic, he washed them carefully. Then, barefoot, wearing only his trousers, he dug his toes into the soft sand. It was wonderful, reminding him of the springs back home.

Not far away, Devydd had washed himself and the remains of his clothing. Now he sat in the shallows, just staring up into the sky, watching puffs of clouds float past.

"How long were you locked up in there?" Erwyn asked as he waded closer.

"Five, maybe six weeks."

Strange. Erwyn had gotten the impression from the Marlians that their thief had only been holed up in Perbellum for a few days. Maybe he was wrong. Then again . . .

Shouts sounded from downstream. Angry shouts. And

they were getting closer!

Erwyn ran onto the sand, with Devydd close behind. He looked around for somewhere to hide. He was out of luck. A screen of brush protected them from being sighted immediately, but there was nothing that would serve as a hiding place. And nowhere to run.

Finally, their pursuers stormed through the bushes. Fifteen or twenty of them. And all of them very, very angry.

24

Escaping's a Drag

(Or, No Apron Strings Attached)

*When leaving the area, be sure you've remembered to pack
everything you brought.*

Sorcerers Almanac
Section Four: On How to Have a Safe Trip

"What do you mean by polluting our river?" The first
woman was taller than Erwyn, and weighed more than he
and Devydd together. "Why the hell do you think we
blocked off that damn sewer, anyway?"

"I was wondering that, myself." Erwyn backed up a little,
just to be on the safe side. "Especially since you've got a filter spell at the end of the tunnels."

"True. But ever since the menfolk pissed off Carruthers,
the garbage pixie, we've had to take extra precautions."

"They're not from 'bellum, Mommy." That was from a
little girl, maybe seven or eight years old, who peeked out
from behind the large woman's apron. She had big blue eyes,
curly red hair, and a dirty finger in her mouth.

"No, we're not." Erwyn smiled. He had forgotten little
girls could be cute. Even when they were dirty and wearing
crude gray shifts, instead of silks and satins.

"Where you boys from?" A thin older woman with three youngsters clinging to her stepped out of the crowd.

"I'm from the Kingdom of Veridan, milady." Erwyn gave the woman a slight bow. "It's across the mountains, to the east."

A loud murmur rose from the group. For a moment, Erwyn was worried. Then the large woman spoke again.

"You don't talk as though you come from around here. No *man* would talk like that to a woman, if he lived around here. Not these days." She made a curse of the word "man," just like Kerissa's crew had.

"I heard how the men here treat their women, but I didn't really believe it. I mean . . ." Erwyn paused. "Well, women are people, too."

Several of the younger women were watching him. And Devydd. Erwyn suddenly became aware of how he was dressed—or rather, not dressed.

"They don't look much like the men from around here, either. They're *clean*."

"Uh, yeah." Erwyn felt himself blushing. "That's how we got your river dirty. We were bathing."

"Where'd you come from that you got that dirty?"

"Well . . ." Erwyn looked toward Devydd.

"You're doing fine, kid. Keep it up."

The thief wasn't much help. He sounded like Chesric. The same rousing, but completely ineffective, pep talks.

"We sort of escaped from your jail." Erwyn backed up a little more, preparing to run, if necessary.

"You *escaped?* How?"

"We, uh, jumped into the sewer and just floated out of town."

For a moment, her expression was unreadable. Then . . .

"What are you laughing at?"

She wasn't the only one. It made Erwyn a little nervous, after the incident at the sand castle when he'd nearly broiled Chesric. But, fortunately, nothing happened.

"I wish I'd been there to see their faces. Their precious,

impregnable, escape-proof jail. Phamstall must have been livid."

"Phamstall? That's the Lord Mayor, right?"

"Right. Lord Mayor, Chief Judge, Executioner, and Head Slimeball. He's also my husband."

"Your husband!"

"Yeah. Disgusting, isn't it?"

"How do you stand it? Why do you stay?"

"Where would we go? Perbellum is our home."

"But the men here treat you like property, at least that's what I've been told. The streets are as bad as the sewers. Worse, maybe. The houses are decrepit. And the men are pigs. No offense intended."

"None taken."

"But you're all clean and fairly neat. Sure, you don't wear fancy clothes and jewelry, but you seem to have some pride in your appearance. I don't understand. What's the deal?"

"We don't know," she replied sadly.

"You don't . . ." Erwyn paused, confused. He seemed to get that way a lot these days.

"That's right. It hasn't been that way long, only for two or three months. Every male over seven years of age. Poof! Instant slob. Started treating us like doormats. So, we moved outside the wall next to the river. Built ourselves some huts downstream of here to wait and see what would develop."

"It was right after that she-devil come a-visiting," put in an old woman in a ragged brown shawl.

"What she-devil?" Erwyn had a bad feeling about this.

"Her name was Sharilan."

"Sharilan? What was *she* . . ."

"They're coming! They're coming upstream!" A young girl came running around the bend past the screen of bushes. She was out of breath, and her ill-fitting dress had slid halfway down her shoulders. The large woman turned to her.

"You mean the men are coming?" The girl nodded. "Well, it took them long enough to figure it out." The woman turned to Erwyn. "We've got to get you out of here."

"You'll help us? Why?"

"Can't help wanting to frustrate that man of mine! It passes the time."

"But you don't even know us."

She stuck her hand out. "Hi, my name is Lucilla. What's yours?"

"Uh, I'm Erwyn and that's Devydd."

"Okay, now we've been introduced. Let's get moving."

"But—but won't this get you into trouble?"

"Nothing we can't handle, boy. Here, put this on."

"But this is a dress!"

"Very good. Best place to hide is in plain sight. They'll never think to look for you there."

"But . . ."

"Shut up, quit arguing, and get dressed! You haven't much time."

"Yes, ma'am."

The women made a protective circle around Erwyn and Devydd as they hurriedly donned the dresses. Someone produced a pair of scarves and tied them in place to hide the boys' hair. Or lack thereof. Then two wicker baskets appeared in front of them, and they plopped their wet clothing inside.

Once more, they heard angry shouting from around the bend in the river. Only this time the voices were pitched lower.

"All right, woman, where are they?" Phamstall was in the lead. He approached his wife, glowering.

"Where are who?" How a woman as large as Lucilla could look girlish and innocent was beyond Erwyn. But somehow she managed. "Whatever do you mean, husband?" She turned to the knot of women. "You girls go on upriver. I'll take care of this."

Protected by their living female fence, Erwyn and Devydd headed upstream. Behind them, Phamstall and Lucilla launched into a loud argument about everything from escaped captives to the weather.

It wasn't too long before they would turn the corner of the city wall and be out of sight. They almost made it, too, but Devydd stopped suddenly.

"Uh-oh."

"I hate it when you say that! What now?"

"I think I left my belt back there."

"You left what?"

"My sword belt, the one for my . . ."

"You must be kidding. I can't believe you—oh, hell!" Erwyn cast a furtive glance behind them. "Hurry up. Maybe we can make it around the corner before . . ."

Too late. "There they are!" They'd been spotted.

"Run!" Without stopping to see if Devydd had listened, Erwyn hitched up his skirts and ran.

The wall rambled approximately eastward, but not particularly straight. Erwyn occasionally caught an enticing glimpse of the valley that spread out in front of the gates. Fortunately, this stretch of wall wasn't very long, and the young sorcerer soon reached the end of it.

Not for the first time during his travels, Erwyn wished he had some form of transportation other than his feet. It would certainly make these fast getaways easier. Especially now.

Erwyn slowed to a walk. Before him stretched the fields through which he'd hiked only that morning. But now they seemed to go on forever. What had been only a morning stroll when he was relatively rested was now a real pain in the neck, as well as other parts of his anatomy.

"Come on, speed up. We've got to keep moving." Devydd caught up with him. "You slow down, you die."

"I—" Erwyn tried to catch his breath. "I don't think I can make it. It's too far."

"Those wonderful ladies back there are doing their level best to delay their menfolk. Considering what their menfolk are like, I wouldn't want to be in their place for anything. The least we can do is not be here when those menfolk finally get past them."

"Sheesh! You would put it that way. I just wish there were some way to *keep* them from following us—*permanently*."

Erwyn took a couple more breaths, then poured his last few ounces of energy into a mad dash across the field. His mind was racing nearly as fast as the rest of him. There must be some way to stop those guys, preferably without actually hurting them.

> *Investing too much energy into a spell can have disastrous effects.*
>
> Sorcerers Almanac
> Section Six: On the Successful Use of Magic

There was a nice patch of sand back by the river, near the wall they'd just passed. What if he could manage to build a castle from that sand? Maybe the men of Perbellum would be more interested in the castle than the two escapees. Or maybe they'd fall into the hole it left.

He allowed himself a moment to fantasize about the scenario.

"Uh-oh!" Devydd stopped again.

"Stop saying that! Every time you say that, you stop moving."

"Sorry, kid. But it looks like we've got some more company." He pointed to the top of the hill they were headed toward.

Erwyn looked. There was a flash of reflected sunlight. Swords probably. And armor. But who . . . ? Oh, yeah.

Without explaining, Erwyn raced up the hillside. Kerissa, Chesric, and Lariyn met them halfway. They were all on horseback. Chesric leaned down in his saddle to talk to Erwyn.

"What's yer hurry?" Chesric was unruffled, as usual.

"All our troubles are behind us," Erwyn managed between gasps, "and I'd like to keep them that way!"

"What are you talking about?" Kerissa looked across the valley.

It can also prove fortuitous, upon occasion.
                                        Sorcerers Almanac
                        Section Six: On the Successful Use of Magic

Erwyn turned to stare in the direction from which they had just come. The valley was empty . . . of people, anyway. The angry mob, which *should* have been behind them, wasn't. There was, however, a very large hole in the field, just about the size of—Erwyn gulped—of the sand castle at the top of the southernmost hill.

25

You Can Please Some of the People

(Or, Mistaken Indemnity)

When engaging the services of a local expert, it is always wise to check his credentials.

Sorcerers Almanac
Section Three: On People and Their Influence

"What's the matter?" Chesric had dismounted and now stood with Erwyn as he stared across the valley.

"Nothing much. It's just . . ." Erwyn shrugged. "That castle."

"What about it? You pulled it off right in the nick o' time."

"I'm just wondering *how* I did it."

"You mean you didn't do it on *purpose?*"

"Nope. And there's something else, too."

"What?"

"That hole. I think that's where the sand came from."

"That makes sense. What about it?"

"I never thought about it before. I mean, it never even occurred to me that it actually had to *come* from somewhere." Erwyn turned to look at Chesric. "Makes you kind of wonder, doesn't it?"

" 'Bout what?" Chesric looked perplexed.

"Remember the snowstorm? Where'd the sand come from for *that* castle, huh? I mean, it would have left an awfully big hole. I sure hope no one fell in it."

There was some satisfaction in seeing Chesric's worried expression. But as the group left Perbellum, Erwyn couldn't stop thinking about that hole.

If the sand had to exist somewhere, was it possible to control exactly *where* it came from? Erwyn didn't know. He still had a long way to go before he learned to control where it *went*, much less where it came from.

He was still thinking about it when he ran right into Kerissa.

"All right, *sorcerer's apprentice*, where's that thief? You were sent to bring him back."

"I'm not an apprentice. I'm a journeyman."

"Just tell me where he is." She placed her hand on the hilt of her dagger.

"He—he's right over there." Erwyn nodded to where Devydd was in earnest conversation with one of Kerissa's warriors. The next thing he knew, he was flat on his back, staring up at Kerissa.

"Don't toy with me, *sorcerer*. That's not the man I sent you into Perbellum after. Where is he?"

"It's hard to talk effectively with a dagger at my throat."

He glared at Kerissa. She moved the point back an inch or two, a major triumph as far as Erwyn was concerned.

"You sent me in to find a thief. He's the only one I found. If he's not the right one, it's not my fault. It's not like you gave me a description or anything!"

Kerissa seemed to consider for a moment, then she sheathed her knife.

"Follow me." She walked over toward Devydd.

"Easy for you to say," Erwyn muttered as he got slowly to his feet, dusting himself off and checking for additional bruises. He hurried to catch up with the Marlian captain.

Stopping only for a quick word with one of her women,

Kerissa went directly up to Devydd. "So you're the thief they had stashed in the Perbellum jail."

Devydd stopped in midsentence, his mouth hanging open for a second before he answered. "That's me. At your service."

He bowed, once more flourishing his nonexistent hat. He scanned her from head to ankles, evidently liking what he saw.

Erwyn felt a brief flare of jealousy, followed by confusion. Why should he be jealous?

Kerissa continued her inquiry. "Have you ever heard of the Marlian Tetraliad?"

"The Tetraliad?" Devydd was confused. "Yeah. I've heard about it. I, uh, spent some time in Senderlaan. The talisman's supposed to be fabulously beautiful and priceless. But I've also heard that it would require a wizard to get to it." His eyes grew round with wonder. "You don't want me to try to steal it, do you? That would be suicide."

"You don't have to. Someone already did."

"Who? How? More to the point, why? He couldn't sell it for the gold, and it would take a master magician to use it."

"I don't know. We traced the thief as far as Perbellum, but the *good* people of Perbellum wouldn't let us near him. Our sorcerer friend here," she said, waving a hand in Erwyn's general direction, "was sent to drag him out of town. He brought you instead."

Devydd glanced at Erwyn. "Is that the talisman you were talking about? The Tetraliad?"

Erwyn nodded. Devydd, for once, was at a loss for words.

"How come you know so much about the Tetraliad?" Kerissa's tone was still belligerent.

"Professional interest. It pays to know what to steal, and what not to steal. The Tetraliad comes under the latter category." Devydd looked thoughtful for a moment. "How long ago did your thief enter Perbellum?"

"Two weeks. Why?"

"There was a man in Perbellum a short while ago, I'm

not sure how long. I heard the guards talking about another
thief. I thought I was going to have company in my cell, but
they never brought him. As near as I can figure, they smug-
gled him out of town."

"They *helped* him?"

"They said something about taking him to see someone.
But I never heard a name."

Kerissa's hand tightened on the hilt of her sword. "I'll
tear down that stinking hellhole! I'll take it apart brick by
brick." She stalked over to her horse and swung herself into
the saddle.

"Wait!" Erwyn ran to catch up with Kerissa. "Wait a
minute. There's no point in destroying the town."

"What do you mean? Why not?" She glared down at
him.

"Have you ever heard of a woman called Sharilan?"

"She's an evil sorceress, but her domain is far to the east."

"Not anymore. According to the women of Perbellum,
everything started to go to hell a couple of months ago, after
the town had a visit—from a woman named Sharilan."

"What difference does that make?"

"Don't you see? The Tetraliad was stolen a few weeks earlier. The thief brought it to Perbellum, and I'll bet the men
helped get him out. There was a second thief incarcerated in
the jail at the same time." He turned to Devydd and asked,
"Why were you in that jail, anyway?"

"I'm not sure. I think it was for walking on the wrong
side of the slimepits, or something like that."

"Not for stealing anything?"

"Nope."

"How'd they find out you were a thief?" Seeing the
expression on Devydd's face, Erwyn wasn't sure he wanted to
know.

Finally, Devydd admitted, "I told them."

"You what?"

"I didn't mean to, kid. It's just that . . ."

"What are you getting at?" Kerissa apparently wasn't in

the mood to wait.

"The men of Perbellum are under some kind of spell. That's why the thief came here, that's why the men helped him, and that's why you shouldn't destroy the town. Sharilan's at the bottom of this."

"So you think it's Sharilan I should be after."

"I'm positive. Well, almost positive."

"And just how am I supposed to find her?"

"Well, you could hang around with me." Erwyn winced as he thought of spending the rest of his journey with the entire Marlian army tagging along. He wasn't even certain he was right.

"That will help me find the sorceress? How?"

"She's sort of following me around."

Kerissa's eyes narrowed with suspicion. "Why would she be following you?"

"Well, it's like this." Erwyn launched into a narrative of the adventures he'd had since leaving Sorcerer's Apprentice School, with frequent interruptions from Chesric, whose addition to the group had somehow gone unnoticed.

"So you see," Erwyn concluded, "I'm fairly certain she'll turn up again. Unfortunately."

Kerissa sat silent for a moment. Then she dismounted, yelling for her lieutenants at the same time.

"Pack my bags. Saddle two other horses and outfit a packhorse. Have them and Gallerian ready and waiting in half an hour." She patted her horse affectionately, then turned to Erwyn and Chesric. "Come with me."

They followed the Marlian captain back to her tent. This time there was no sword on the table. That was encouraging—unless, of course, the sword wasn't on the table because it was going to be used.

Kerissa excused herself and left. After several minutes, Erwyn found himself shifting nervously from one foot to the other. Chesric was unperturbed, as usual. He stretched out on a convenient chair, arms crossed, chin on his chest, for a short snooze.

Couldn't he work up a little sweat just once? Waiting was murder.

"What do you suppose we're waiting for?" Devydd's voice behind him almost made Erwyn jump.

He hoped it didn't show.

"What's the matter, kid? Nervous?"

It showed.

"Just a bit." Erwyn managed to smile. "They sent me to get a thief. They said they would kill us if I didn't. I got the wrong one. Therefore . . ."

"So you think they're just going to off all of us and that's it, huh?"

Erwyn winced. "Something like that."

"Do the Marlians know you're a sorcerer?"

"Yes."

"Do they have any idea just how much magic you can work?"

"I don't know. I don't think so." He looked to the old man for support, but Chesric didn't move from his chair.

"So tell me, if you captured some strange sorcerer and you had no idea how powerful he was, would you just up and try to kill him without gauging his powers first?"

"Well . . ."

"Especially if he just freed an inmate from a supposedly impregnable jail?"

"But . . ."

"In a town where several of your warriors had been killed trying to do the same thing?"

"He's got a point, ye know." Chesric couldn't resist any longer. He had to stick his nose into the conversation.

"I would, if I could do it without him having a chance to zap me first." Erwyn glared at the two of them as he finally got a word in edgewise.

"And if you couldn't, would you try to kill him, anyway?"

"I guess not."

"Then relax, kid. You've got nothing to worry about."

"Right. Sure." Erwyn wasn't quite convinced.

"Besides, didn't you just tell the lady with the big sword that you could lead her to this Sharilan broad? If she wants the Tetraliad as badly as it seems, she'll probably want to keep you alive."

Erwyn relaxed a little. "True."

Devydd smiled wickedly and added, "Even if it's in an iron cage."

"Thanks ever so much for the comfort and encouragement. I don't know what I'd do without you. But I'd like to try."

Devydd looked as though he was about to reply when Kerissa returned. She still carried her sword and her other usual pointy objects. But she had also added a bow and arrows to her arsenal.

Chesric bounced to his feet expectantly.

"What's going on?" As if Erwyn didn't already know. Devydd had just told him.

"I'm going with you," Kerissa replied, as though daring him to argue the point.

It happened that he was in an arguing mood. The fact that he had practically told Kerissa to follow him in the first place didn't matter at all.

"Just what are you going with me for? To find Sharilan?" Erwyn marched up to the Marlian. This time, no one shoved a sword in his face. "And what are you going to do when you find her? As I told Lariyn, steel and iron are no protection against magic, no matter what the old wives' tales say. How do you plan to get your talisman back?"

"I'm not. I'm going with you to make sure you stay alive long enough to get it for me."

26

Five's a Crowd

(Or, A Rolling Stone Probably Got Kicked at Some Point)

There are times when being a Good Samaritan is not a good idea. Learn to know the difference.

Sorcerers Almanac
Section Four: On How to Have a Safe Trip

Kerissa gave orders to her lieutenants to take the rest of the troop home. "Tell Queen Ireda that I will find the Tetraliad, or die trying."

The three of them, Chesric, Kerissa, and Erwyn, headed out of the tent and toward the horses. Erwyn eyed his mount suspiciously. He never had gotten along well with horses. He fervently hoped that this one was better tempered than the ones back home.

Oh, well. Might as well get it over with. He started to swing himself into the saddle.

"You don't think you're going without me, do you?" Devydd stood with hands on his hips. "I've got an interest in this expedition, too, you know. If your theory is right, this sorceress of yours is responsible for me spending several miserable weeks in that rotten jail cell. I'm coming with you."

"Me, too." Lariyn already had her horse saddled and ready. "With your permission, Captain. I thought you might need an extra sword."

Kerissa nodded curtly. "As you wish." Then, glaring at Devydd, she said, "Have a horse readied for the thief, as well. And hurry."

"That's just great!" Erwyn, with one foot in the horse's stirrup, groaned. It wasn't bad enough he was traveling with an eccentric knight. Now he had to deal with two man-hating female warriors and a thief of doubtful qualifications.

His horse gave him a reproachful look as he hung there by one stirrup. Self-consciously, Erwyn finished mounting the beast. The horse took a deep breath, then expelled it loudly, reminding Erwyn of his father during a particularly disappointing round of lessons.

"His name is Bandal." Lariyn caught him off-guard.

"Huh?" Very intelligent.

"Your horse. His name is Bandal."

"Oh. Uh, thanks." He watched Bandal suspiciously for hostile movements. The horse just waited patiently for things to get started. Erwyn never knew a horse could look so bored.

One of Kerissa's warriors arrived, leading a horse for Devydd. Erwyn noticed as the thief swung into the saddle that everyone else seemed to be right at home on horseback. He began to regret the hours spent avoiding the lessons his father had tried to cram into him. One more regret among many.

The entire camp had gathered to watch the group ride off. Erwyn rode hunched over his saddle. He knew what he'd said to Kerissa was true. Sharilan probably *would* be looking for him. But if his party got much bigger, he might as well start waving a flag and shouting, "Here I am. Come and get me!"

"Why so glum, my friend?"

Erwyn hadn't been very talkative in the days since they left the Marlian encampment. Chesric's sudden question brought him out of his reverie. But not out of his depression.

He was finally ready to talk about the problem, though. "I don't get it, Chesric. All I wanted was to stay out of trouble for the next four years and see the sights. Alone." He glanced at the old man. "No offense."

Chesric smiled indulgently.

Erwyn continued. "But trouble seems to be following me. I know you said that it's part of being a journeyman sorcerer, but, well, what's with all the people gathering around? I mean"—Erwyn shrugged, having no better way to express his exasperation—"here we are, traveling with two Marlian warriors who, under the circumstances, should have killed us outright, especially since I'm a magic-user. Instead, they've decided to travel with us, and provide us with horses, and supplies, *and* weapons. It doesn't make sense."

"Well . . ."

"And another thing. Why is this sorceress picking on *me?* What did I do to her? I just don't get it."

"Well . . ."

"And how did the Marlians just *happen* to find *us* to capture, instead of some other poor dupes? I mean, why us?"

"Well . . ."

"And while I'm on the subject, what about you? How did you just *happen* to stumble on to me in the middle of a forest which, supposedly, no human ever goes near? And why didn't you ever answer me about your missing—or rather changing—accents?"

"Well . . ."

"And another thing . . ."

"Hold on there a minute, Erwyn! I can't answer all of your questions at once. I can't answer half of them at all."

Erwyn stopped talking. It was the first time he'd ever heard Chesric raise his voice.

"First of all, as I understand it, it isn't just *journeymen* sorcerers who attract these situations. It's magic-users in general.

"It's got something to do with the flow of magical energy. Magic attracts adventure, for want of a better description. Good magics attract evil magics and vice versa. Nature just jumps in to provide the opportunity for both sides to meet.

"Journeymen attract trouble more than others. Teachers protect the apprentices, and Masters know how to keep the balance, so they don't run into the unexpected.

"As for why it's you caught in the middle of all this, it could be that you are the only person in this area that the energies have to focus on. Or maybe there's something special about you, something important. I don't know. You'll find that out in due time. I *do* know that you will have to see it through. You have no choice."

"Why?"

"It's like rolling down a long, smooth hill. The only way to stop is to make it to the bottom. Or die trying."

"That's *so* comforting."

"Cheer up. That's why they send you young journeymen out unarmed and unprotected. So you'll have to use magic to survive. The magical energy you expend attracts adventures and you're forced to learn new tricks, or die."

"Who are you?" It was becoming more and more important that Erwyn find some answers about Chesric. He hated being in the dark. "And why do you know so much about magic?"

Chesric laughed, but it was laughter without humor. "That, my young friend, is one of those questions I can't answer. Not to your satisfaction, anyway." He paused, looking thoughtful. "I'm just an old soldier traveling in search of a lost dragon, adding his sword to the fight when needed, giving a few words of advice where possible, helping the poor and infirm and unfortunate . . ."

Erwyn thought he heard violins playing in the background.

". . . giving aid and comfort where it will help, providing dry firewood on cold nights, defending the right, punishing evil, and battling for truth, justice, poetry, and the right to drink beer with dinner on weekends."

Erwyn looked at Chesric for a moment. "You're right. It's not a satisfactory answer." He sighed. "But I guess it'll have to do, since you're not going to give me another. Come on, let's catch up with the others."

"You're learning, young Erwyn, you're learning."

"And you might as well slip your accent back into place, before the wrong person starts asking about it."

"Ye've got a point, boy." He grinned, the ends of his mustache nearly touching the corners of his eyes.

The rest of the party had ridden well ahead while Erwyn and Chesric talked. Now the two companions kicked their horses into a trot to catch up. As they crested the hill, they could see the others at the top of the next rise.

Kerissa turned in her saddle and waved. Erwyn waved back and continued down the slope as the captain and the others disappeared behind the hill.

Suddenly, Erwyn reined in his horse. "Did you hear that?"

"Hear what?" Chesric leaned forward, listening.

"That." It was barely audible, but Erwyn felt sure it wasn't his imagination.

He was certain he heard a tiny voice yelling, "Help!"

It seemed to be coming from a clump of bushes to Erwyn's left. He dismounted and approached the bushes cautiously.

"Help! Save me!" The voice was nearer now, almost directly below Erwyn.

Erwyn looked down. There, half-hidden by long strands of horse-grass, was a tiny woman with gossamer wings folded against her back. She couldn't have been much larger than Erwyn's little finger.

She wore a delicate shift of shimmering spider-silk decorated with tiny pink flower petals that were partially obscured by cascades of light blonde hair. Her feet were clad in miniature slippers of the same silk as her shift. She was tiny, beautiful, and in trouble.

She shrank against the stone behind her, biting her finger to keep from screaming again. A dragon was stalking her. A dragon perhaps six inches high, with transparent wings.

The creature hissed and spat tiny bursts of flame, his wings fanning the air behind him. Closer and closer he came.

Erwyn wondered why the girl didn't just fly away. Then he discovered the reason. Her ankle was pinned beneath a pebble. A pebble the size of a large boulder, from her perspective.

Wasting no more time, Erwyn reached forward and batted the dragon away. Then he flicked the pebble off the girl's ankle.

"My hero! You've saved me! I'm yours forever." She flew straight into Erwyn's face, showering him with little kisses. "Oh, you wonderful human, you! How can I ever repay you?" She flew around his head a few times, then rained another shower of kisses on the hapless lad.

"Come on, cut that out!" Erwyn ducked a third wave of kisses, resisting the urge to swat the tiny woman. "Is that really necessary?"

"Of course it is," she replied sweetly. "My name is Viona. I'm a damselfly."

27

Damsels, Damsels Everywhere

(Or, And Not a One Can Think)

*Magic has a magnetic effect on the world around you.
Don't be surprised if you attract attention, some good, some
bad, some merely annoying.*

Sorcerers Almanac
Section Six: On the Successful Use of Magic

"Please! Tell me you're joking." He just wasn't up to damsels today, even little ones.

"Why would I joke about a thing like tha—"

"Help! Save us!" A tiny chorus of cries sounded from a tree stump ahead.

Chesric walked over to the stump.

"No, Chesric, don't—" Too late.

Chesric removed the stone on the top of the stump, and suddenly the world was filled with damselflies.

Cries of "Our heroes!" and "You saved us!" filled the air as the miniature maidens fluttered about, bathing them with caresses.

Erwyn leaped astride Bandal, shouting to Chesric at the same time. "Mount and ride! We've got to get out of here!" Then he kicked the horse into a gallop and raced as though demons were on his trail.

Behind him, Erwyn heard the hoofbeats of Chesric's horse as they left the startled damselflies behind. He didn't slow down until they came within sight of the rest of the group.

Kerissa turned in her saddle, pulling back on the reins. "What is it now, Erwyn?"

"N-Nothing." Erwyn gasped for breath. "Just trying to avoid a terrible fate."

"What was that?"

"Death by smooching."

"I resent that!" A familiar voice said from the vicinity of Erwyn's collar. Viona had somehow managed to get tangled in Erwyn's hair and had thus remained with him during his ride.

After carefully removing strands of hair from her wings, Viona got out of Erwyn's hair, at least in the literal sense, and hovered near the boy's face.

"What are you doing here?" Erwyn noticed his voice was squeaking again.

"You didn't mean what you said, did you? You weren't really trying to avoid me, were you?" Her lower lip trembled. Tears glistened on her eyelashes.

Just like Sharilan, that voice in the back of Erwyn's head warned him. *But this was different. Wasn't it?*

While his mind wrestled with the problem, his mouth stammered on without him. "Well, uh, no. Not exactly. It's just that . . ."

"Oh, I knew you wouldn't be so mean and cruel as to desert me in my hour of need!" Viona fluttered up to his ear, grabbing it to plant a particularly spectacular kiss on his earlobe.

"Come on, stop that!" Erwyn tried to jerk his head away from her.

It didn't work. Viona had a tight grip on his ear.

"If you are quite finished, shouldn't we be resuming our trip?" Kerissa seized an opportunity to jump into the conversation.

To Erwyn's relief and surprise, she wasn't laughing.

"Where are we going?" Viona squealed like a school-girl . . . or a princess . . . or some other feminine mutant. She flew around to stare at Erwyn, her eyes round with wonder.

"What do you mean 'we,' Viona? You aren't coming with us." Erwyn looked to his companions for help.

Kerissa might have managed to not laugh at him, but Devydd and Chesric were grinning from ear to ear. Lariyn was pointedly looking in another direction. He was on his own.

"Of course I'm going with you, silly. After all, you saved my life. I can't let you go traipsing off alone without trying to pay you back at least a little bit."

"But I'm not alone! As far as I can tell, I'll never be alone again."

"Come, come. Don't get yourself all upset. It's bad for the digestion, you know." She simpered prettily, patted his cheek, then alit softly on his shoulder. "Shall we go?"

Erwyn shook his head and lightly kicked his horse. There was no point arguing with her. He recognized the symptoms. Talking wouldn't change her mind, but maybe actions could.

They rode together in relative silence, Kerissa and Lariyn in front, Chesric and Devydd next, with Erwyn and, unfortunately, Viona bringing up the rear. Erwyn had no idea where the Marlians were headed and, frankly, didn't care. By the time the group made camp, the young sorcerer had worked himself back into a beautiful depression.

He helped with the normal chores involved in setting up camp. Then, after wolfing down his dinner, Erwyn took his journal from his pack and found a nice quiet tree where he could be alone. It had been some time since his last entry, so he quickly brought his notes up to date.

. . . then, summoning the dregs of my failing energy, I turned on the scoundrels from Perbellum and cast my spell. The entire male

population of the city fell into the gigantic hole I had conjured. The thief and I were free at last.

We returned to the Marlian warriors victorious, but the Tetraliad was no longer in the hands of the thief I had rescued. Captain Kerissa and her people begged me to help them recover their lost talisman. They have provided us with mounts, weapons, and supplies.

I have decided we should take Devydd with us. He may prove useful should we ever locate the hiding place of the Tetraliad.

After leaving Perbellum, I was forced to perform one more good deed before being allowed the rest to which I was entitled. A beautiful damsel was caught beneath an avalanche of rock. Worse, a huge, fire-breathing dragon was stalking her, obviously intending to eat her.

In spite of my extreme distaste for damsels in distress, I waded into the fray and soon routed the beast. The lady was so happy to be safely delivered from so untimely a death that she swore to remain with me forever. It's tough being a hero, but someone's . . .

"What are you doing, Erwyn, my love?" Viona flitted over to where Erwyn sat.

Erwyn looked up, startled, and slammed the book closed. "N-Nothing important. I'm supposed to keep a journal of my adventures."

"Oooh! Can I see?"

"No! That is, we're not supposed to let anyone see it."

"Oh. Well, that's all right. I can't read anyway." She frowned that pretty frown of hers. "They don't make books small enough, so I never learned."

"That's good. . . . I mean, that's too bad." Erwyn hesitated. "I guess you can look at mine." He opened the journal, while Viona fluttered over to his shoulder to get a comfortable seat.

"Oooh! That's pretty."

"What is?"

"All those cute little curves and squiggles. Do you think you could teach me to make curves and squiggles?" She flew around to hover in front of his nose.

"Sure thing. Catch me sometime when I haven't got anything else to do."

"How about now? Do you have anything to do now?"

"Uh, yeah." Erwyn quickly produced a yawn and stood up. "I think it's past my bedtime."

"Oh." Viona looked disappointed.

"Maybe another time," Erwyn said gently as he headed for his bedroll.

"Okay." She smiled. "I'll remind you."

"Great."

"Can I help you get your bed ready?"

"No, thanks. I can handle it."

"You sure?"

"I've been doing it by myself for a long time, thank you." He opened his bedroll and laid it out on the ground.

"Well, okay, if you say so."

"I say so."

After removing his boots, Erwyn snuggled into his bedroll. He closed his eyes and tried to relax. As an afterthought, he decided to set the wards. He'd almost forgotten about them. There hadn't been any need to set them in the Marlian encampment with so many armed women about. Who would attack them? Besides the men from Perbellum, that is.

"Good night, Erwyn."

Erwyn's eyes popped open. There was the damselfly, already half asleep, tucked comfortably in a fold of his bedroll. Erwyn sighed and closed his eyes again. As he drifted off, he wondered if he could be accused of murder if he rolled over on her in his sleep.

28

Sticky Help Is Better Than No Help

(Or, Spring Preening)

A good leader knows how to make the best use of his men.
                                        Sorcerers Almanac
                    Section Three: On People and Their Influence

"Erwyn, honey, wake up. We've got company."

Erwyn rolled over, moaning and pulling the covers over his head. His neck and back muscles were tight and sore, and his left arm was asleep. He needed five more minutes of sack time.

Seconds later, something tugged at his bedroll.

"Come on, sweetie. It's time to rise and shine. It's a beautiful morning."

He cracked one eye open and glared at the damselfly, mumbling. "Funny, I don't remember asking for a wakeup call." The other eye flew open as he realized that the damselfly in front of him had red hair, not blonde.

"Hey, Viona! I think he's awake," the redhead called to a point above Erwyn's covers.

Another tiny damsel flew in front of his face. This one was a blonde.

"Good morning, sweetie-pie."

"Uh, yeah. G' morning, Viona." Erwyn groaned as he carefully rolled onto his back and started to inch his way out of his bedroll.

"Hi, handsome," came a call from the tree above Erwyn.

"I thought we'd never catch up with you. You sure rode fast." Another shout came from somewhere near the foot of Erwyn's bedroll.

He sat bolt upright, wincing as the circulation started in his left arm again. Rubbing his arm, he stared around the clearing.

They were surrounded . . . sort of. The entire population of damselflies, as near as Erwyn could determine, hovered, perched, flitted, or flew around their camp. And all of them seemed to be talking. The noise was, well, not precisely deafening, but loud and sort of—itchy. Like being at a cricket convention.

He glanced over to where Chesric had placed his bedroll. The old knight sat on his blankets, his chin cupped in his hand. But he wasn't alone. Damselflies perched on his head and arms. Others lay on his covers or swung from his mustache.

Devydd seemed unperturbed. Actually, amused would be a better description. But then, there were fewer of the pretty pests swooping around him.

"This is not to be borne!" Kerissa strode into the area where the men had bedded for the night. Apparently, the damselflies had never seen a woman in armor before.

Five or six of the tiny ladies fluttered in and out through the chinks in Kerissa's armor. From beneath the breastplate came soft "pings," as though little hands rapped on the metal from the inside. The captain's expression was haunted. Or maybe her suit was. At any rate, she wasn't happy.

Lariyn stood a pace behind her captain. The cloud of tiny women, all "oooing" and "aaahing" over their armor, didn't seem to bother her much. She just looked a little uncomfortable. Erwyn's opinion of the lieutenant went up a notch.

Kerissa glared at Erwyn and Chesric. "Do something!"

"What do you suggest?" Short of mass murder, he could think of nothing.

"I don't know. Just get rid of them!"

"Hey, kid, can I borrow a couple of your—friends?" Devydd watched the damselflies, his expression cryptic.

"I can't give them away. They don't exactly *belong* to me. Anyway, why would you want one?"

"They could be useful for my work. You know, polishing tiny crevices, sneaking into locked rooms, slipping through small openings, steal—er, *carrying* small objects, gathering information and scouting around . . ."

Erwyn stared at the thief, a slow smile coming to his lips as the idea formed in his head. "That's perfect."

"What's perfect?" Chesric had finally extricated himself from his blanket of beauties.

"Devydd's suggestion."

Devydd looked at Chesric and back to Erwyn. "What suggestion?"

Erwyn didn't answer. Instead, he turned to the damselfly population at large. "Ladies, could I have your attention?"

The damselflies got quiet. Well, almost. They looked at him expectantly.

Erwyn cleared his voice nervously. He wasn't much good at public speaking, even if most of the audience was only three inches tall. This could be worse than the interview with Kerissa.

"Um, have any of you ever heard anything about a castle somewhere around here?" Erwyn tried to keep his voice from squeaking. "A big stone one, surrounded by a high wall of thorns and guarded by a dragon?"

"Not a word . . ." "Nothing . . ." "Nope . . ." "Not around here . . ." "Uh-uh."

They didn't quite answer all at once, but they came close. When the round of answers stopped several minutes later, Erwyn continued.

"Do you really want to repay us for releasing you from the stump?"

"Of course . . ." "Always . . ." "Certainly . . ." "Yeah . . ."
"Uh-huh."

"Well, how about finding it for me?"

"But how will that help repay you?"

"I have to find that castle. If you will all separate into small groups, say, two or three at a time, and look around, I'd be able to find it sooner."

The damselflies coalesced into a huge, seething, buzzing ball for a minute or two. Finally, they separated.

"Is it important? We'd much rather stay with you."

"Very important. Extremely important. A matter of life and death, as it were."

"Okay."

Then they disappeared. Or at least they flew away so fast they seemed to disappear.

"What happens if they find this castle?" Lariyn asked the question Erwyn didn't really want to consider. "How do they find us? We're not going to wait here until they come back, are we?"

"Uh . . ."

"Don't worry," Viona interrupted Erwyn, who nearly jumped into the nearest tree. He'd hoped Viona would go with the rest of the crowd, er, flock, whatever. "As long as I'm with you, they'll be able to find you wherever you go."

"Great. That's *so* reassuring."

Erwyn's sarcasm was wasted on Viona.

"I'm so glad. It makes me feel wonderful to be able to repay you, even in so small a way, for saving my life. You have *no* idea how frightened I was when that mean old dragonfly landed. And there I was, helpless and alone. I'm so happy someone as brave and kind and cute as you came along in time to save me."

Erwyn wasn't quite as happy about it as Viona. She looked as though she might go into another kissing fit at any moment. Quickly, he turned to the others.

"Shouldn't we get started? *Soon.*"

They packed their gear and headed out, still continuing

to travel west, for lack of a better direction to take.

The rest of the group was in good spirits for the remainder of the day. Erwyn's spirits, however, dropped drastically. The others didn't have any damselflies to contend with, while Viona acted perfectly damselish throughout the morning and most of the afternoon.

She darted here and there on her gossamer wings, examining each flower and bush with exclamations of "Oh! How pretty!" and "I must get one of these for my very own!" and "Wouldn't that make a perfectly *lovely* gown for the next damselfly ball!"

Erwyn was so thoroughly disgusted by the time they made camp that he couldn't even eat his supper. He just crawled into his bedroll and tried vainly to ignore Viona's queries about his health.

The next several days were pretty much the same. Erwyn lost track of how far they had come, or what the scenery was like. He wasn't even sure what they were doing anymore. His head buzzed from Viona's incessant chatter.

Finally, he'd had enough. They were setting up camp in a nice grove of trees, and Viona had been giving a running commentary for about an hour on how nice the trees were and how much nicer they'd be if someone would just move them a *little* to the left.

"Viona, I don't mean to be rude, but could you leave me alone? Just for a little while?" he yelled, a little louder than he'd planned.

Not waiting for an answer, Erwyn stalked off into the trees. For once, the damselfly didn't follow. She stayed at camp, probably sulking.

He felt just awful about yelling at Viona that way, but he needed to have some time to himself once in a while or he'd explode. Like he just had.

After a few minutes' walk, he found a nice, comfortable spot beneath a tree and sat down.

Ah! Peace and quiet at last. He leaned against the tree, eyes closed, listening to the rustle of the leaves and the sounds of the birds who made the tree their home.

Regretfully, he hauled his mind back to the present. It had been a long time since he'd practiced his lessons, much less worked on learning more about the sand castles. He'd been more than a little afraid to let his conscious mind start muddling things up, anyway. His subconscious seemed to handle the castles so easily.

First, there had been the tiny castle which had appeared when he was trying to figure out the wand. Then there was the castle that sprang out of nowhere in the midst of a blizzard. Right when and where he'd needed it most.

And the business at Perbellum. Not only did the castle appear at an extremely opportune moment, but the sand itself came from the perfect location. In fact, it wasn't the castle which was important that time. It was the hole. Erwyn sometimes wondered about his subconscious.

But there had to be a way to control it. He couldn't depend on his subconscious forever. And he had done it consciously once. Just before Kerissa and her crew clobbered him.

Trying to remember how he'd done it that time, Erwyn concentrated on building another miniature castle.

This time it was easy. Well, relatively easy.

He imagined a tiny castle-shaped mold on the ground at his feet. He felt a tingling around him as the magical energies built, then he pictured sand pouring into the mold.

And there it was. A perfect replica of the castle at Dunaara, Veridan's capital.

He sat back against the tree feeling very satisfied. He still didn't know where the sand had come from, but that shouldn't be a problem. The amount of sand in this castle wasn't enough to cause trouble, and he could figure out how to control his source later, anyway.

Erwyn tried maintaining the castle in the back of his mind as he looked about him. Before, the castles created by his subconscious had only lasted as long as he needed them. Really needed them. He had to learn to maintain them indefinitely.

He needed a distraction . . .

"Thou art summoned, young master," a bass voice sounded from deep within the trees.

"Huh?" It was the most intelligent response Erwyn could think of. This wasn't quite what he had in mind.

A large black robe with a hood on it emerged from the shadows. It appeared to be occupied. At least, it had one bony hand, which was currently pointed at Erwyn.

29

So Much To Do, So Little Time

(Or, Wake Me When It's Over)

Always leave your campsite the way you found it. Cover your fire, pick up the trash, and fill in any holes you made.
                                    Sorcerers Almanac
                        Section Four: On How to Have a Safe Trip

"Thy talents are needed," the voice inside the robe intoned. Then it began to chant:

> *"Fire and earth, wind and wave,*
> *Seek to build a gruesome grave.*
> *Sorcerer's power by sunlight blessed*
> *Is summoned now to fill this quest.*
> *Come to us by . . ."*

"Now wait just a doggone minute," Erwyn interrupted. "I know you're trying to tell me something, but do you really have to use bad poetry get the message across? I mean, couldn't you just ask?"

"Uh, sure." The voice rose in pitch for a second, then resumed its intonation. "Thou art summoned to aid my master in his holy quest."

"Uh-uh. No way."

"What?" The voice was up in the stratosphere again.

"Just what I said. I'm busy." Erwyn held up his hand as he counted out his current preoccupations. "I've got to rescue an unknown damsel in distress, who may or may not exist, help some Marlian warriors find their stolen talisman, solve the problem of the enchanted town of Perbellum, find some way to get rid of a few hundred damselflies, figure out what the Sorceress Sharilan is up to, and learn how to make decent sand castles. All in the next four years. I'm swamped." He paused. "By the way, how'd you find me?"

"The Sorcerer's Apprentice School mailing list, graduate placement program."

"You're a little premature. I haven't graduated yet."

"Oh. Okay." The voice hesitated. "You don't happen to know where I can find another sorcerer in the area, do you? A cheap one?"

"Nope. I'm the only one around here that I know of. Unless you'd like an *evil* sorcerer. Sorce*ress*, actually. There just happens to be one following me right now. Maybe you'd like to recruit her."

"Uh . . . no. Thanks anyway." The robe shuffled back toward the trees, muttering as it went. "Boy! The trouble you have to go to just to find decent help these days . . ."

Erwyn watched the robe as it disappeared into the forest. He *had* wanted a distraction, after all. . . .

Oh, dear!

Anxiously, he looked down by his feet. This time he really surprised himself. His castle was intact. He still wondered about the sand, though.

"Ouch! Damn potholes!" came a muffled curse from the direction the robe had taken.

I wonder if . . . thought Erwyn as he gazed pensively toward the sound. Naaah!

He shook his head and turned his attention back to the sand castle.

By the time Chesric came looking for him, Erwyn had a

miniature city spread out beneath the trees. The royal capital of Caldoria was there nestled among the toadstools. The old castle that currently served as the Sorcerer's Apprentice School stood proudly about six inches high in the shelter of a fallen branch. Various rocks, stumps, and leaf piles also sported assorted castles from Erwyn's own designs.

Picking out a fairly clear spot, Erwyn settled back to start another variation.

"Erwyn!" Chesric's bellow could be heard throughout the forest. "Have you been practicing at sand castles again?" He crashed through the brush into the young sorcerer's current domain.

"Yes. Why?" Erwyn asked reasonably, looking up as the old man limped up beside him.

Chesric stared at Erwyn's handiwork. "Thought you might be. There seem to be a lot of new potholes in the area all of a sudden. You know what I mean?"

Erwyn grinned mischievously. "I was thinking of trying a full-sized one now. Want to watch?"

"Uh . . . no, thanks. If you don't mind, I'd prefer to do my watching from a league or three away. I don't fancy accidentally falling into any castle-size holes any time in the near future."

"You know, that *is* a bit of a problem." Erwyn frowned down at his sand-castle town. "I'll have to work on it. See if I can learn to control that part."

"Not right now, you won't. We need you back at the camp."

"What for?" Erwyn couldn't quite guess Chesric's meaning from his expression.

"You'll see."

Still wondering, Erwyn followed the old knight back through the trees.

It didn't take long for him to discover the answer to his question. In fact, he heard the answer before he actually saw it. It was a pretty loud answer.

Stepping out from under the trees, Erwyn faced the

assemblage gathered there.

"Oooh! There he is. . . ." "Isn't he cute, for a sorcerer, I mean? . . ." "Hiya, Erwie! . . ." "Hey, handsome, how about doin' time with me for good behavior?"

The damselflies were back.

Erwyn wasn't sure whether to be glad about their quick return or not. On the one hand, the fact that they were back ought to mean that they'd found something. On the other hand, he wasn't sure he wanted anything to be found.

Well, no use crying over spilled mango juice, or something to that effect. He smiled, trying to cover the sinking feeling in his stomach.

"You have something to tell me?"

"Yup . . ." "Sure do . . ." "Uh-huh . . ." "You betcha!"

"Just for the sake of saving time," Erwyn interjected as the answers died down, "could you just pick *one*, er, damsel to tell me the news? I could die of old age waiting for all of you to finish."

"Sure thing, sweetie." That was Viona. The designated speaker for the damselfly contingent fluttered up from Erwyn's bedroll. "The rest of the girls just flew and flew and flew looking for news of this castle of yours.

"It was just awful. I mean, the wind and the rain mussing everyone's hair and just *drenching* their gowns." She bounced up and down in excitement.

"Clotilda's just *ruined* her slippers, and Lyla Mae's beautiful hair's all matted, and . . ."

"Hold on a sec. Could you just give me the important part?" Erwyn pleaded.

Then, noting Viona's glare, he added, "I promise I'll write down the whole story in my journal later."

"Humph!" Viona patted her hair, which Erwyn now recognized as a sign that the damselfly was miffed. "Well, if that's really what you want . . . Anyway, they found it."

The abrupt change in narrative style startled him.

"Huh?"

"I said they found it. Your castle."

"They found it? Are you certain?"

"You said it was a large stone castle, with a wall of thorns around it, and a dragon guarding it, and a moat, and everything, didn't you?"

"Well, I didn't say anything about a moat, but that's essentially it. Where is it?"

"Same direction we've been going. If we keep going west, we'll run into it. Figuratively speaking, of course."

"Yes, but how *far* is it?"

"About four day's flight from here."

That meant he was almost done with this stupid quest. *If* he could get inside the castle. *If* he could free its prisoner. *If* he could get back out alive. *If* he could avoid running into Sharilan in the process. No sweat.

Then another thought occurred to him.

"Uh, Viona?"

"Yes, Erwyn, dear?"

"Um . . . how far is that in horse-time, since the rest of us can't fly?"

Viona hovered in front of him, tapping her finger thoughtfully against her cheek.

"A couple of weeks."

30

Yet Another Thorny Problem

(Or, Once More, off to the Beach, Dear Friends)

Magically grown vegetation has long been used for fencing around enchanted castles. A wand made from this vegetation can be invaluable for penetrating it.

Sorcerers Almanac
Section Six: On the Successful Use of Magic

Actually, it turned out to be a month before the entire group, damselflies and all, gathered in front of the gates of the castle. Or more precisely, in front of the thornbushes in front of the gates of the castle. A month of sticky, sugary sweetness. A month of simpering and petty bickering. A month of sniping and waterworks.

The damselflies hadn't been able to decide between them who got to ride with, or on, whom. And there wasn't enough surface area between the five of them, and their horses, and their packhorses, for the diminutive damsels to all ride at once.

Then, there was the fact that Kerissa didn't want them riding on *her* at all. In fact, she preferred to leave them all behind. *That* comment caused so much whining and boohooing that Erwyn wasn't sure he'd ever get them mollified.

Likewise, the advent of summer seemed to call for a complete wardrobe change as far as damselfly etiquette was concerned. Kerissa told them what they could do with their wardrobe, and the crying started again.

Finally, they had gotten their respective acts together and reached the castle.

Kerissa, Chesric, and Lariyn were currently engaged in a discussion on the best way to get through the living wall. So far, they were divided about whether to burn the whole wall, or try the old hack-and-slash method. There seemed to be some doubt as to whether the latter would work, and they weren't certain they could accomplish the former without burning the contents of the castle, as well.

Besides, by the time they'd reached the castle, summer had settled in firmly. Everyone and everything had already started to wilt, and no one was really interested in being part of a bonfire.

Devydd was busily examining the wall up close, but was having little or no luck. There were no openings big enough for a full-sized person, no locks to pick or windows to climb through.

The damselflies tried flying through chinks in the thorny fence. But each time they found an opening, the vines would move into the hole, batting the tiny intruders out of the way. It was as if the plants were alive—and aware of their presence.

Erwyn himself was engaged in what he considered to be his most important activity for the moment. He was resting.

"Ain't you goin' to join us?" Chesric punctuated his question by prodding Erwyn's foot.

The boy looked up from where he sat cross-legged in the shade of the thornbushes. "I'm resting."

"We could use some help."

"What do you need my help for? There are forty billion of you over there poking at the bushes already."

"Seems to me ye'd want to get this thing over with quick."

"I'd love to, but they're going about it the wrong way."

"What do ye mean?"

"I mean, this castle positively *reeks* of magic. And I suspect it'll take magic to get into it."

"Then we definitely need you."

"*I* don't know how to get in. I don't have enough information about the castle or why Sharilan sent me here." He paused, tapping his chin thoughtfully. "But maybe I can find out. Viona, dear," he called out in his most enticing voice.

"Yes, Erwyn, sweetie?" The damselfly fluttered up to rest on his shoulder.

"When your, uh, friends were looking for the castle, did they happen to learn anything about it? Besides its location, I mean?"

"Why, certainly. How do you think they found out where the castle was, silly boy? They just listened to all the big people talking about it."

"You mean they didn't actually come all the way to the castle?"

"No, silly. As soon as they learned where it was, they rushed back to tell us."

"What did they find out? Where did it come from? Who put it here? How long has it been here?"

"One question at a time, honeybunch. As far as the girls could determine, the castle just appeared, thornbushes and all, a couple or three months ago. And guess what?" Viona paused dramatically. "The person who put it there was— Sharilan!"

"Oh, great!" Erwyn moaned, putting his hands to his head. "I knew she had more to do with this than she admitted. I bet this Fenoria girl doesn't even exist."

"You mean the princess who's locked up in the castle?"

"Princess?" Erwyn felt his stomach sinking again. "Nobody told me she was a princess."

"Of course she is. Why else would she be locked up in a castle? Honestly, Erwyn, sometimes you sorcerers can be *so*

weird." She flew off to join her friends in their inspection of
the thorns.

Now all that remained for Erwyn to do was decide if he
really wanted to get into the castle and, if so, how. Of
course, he *could* leave Sharilan's little task unfinished and go
off somewhere where he could wait out his four, that is,
three and something years in comparative peace.

But what if Fenoria really *needed* to be rescued, whatever
Sharilan's reasons were. He couldn't just leave her there.
Could he?

Phooey! Here he was, sitting outside a fairytale castle,
with one of the strangest groups of adventurers ever collected in one place, and he didn't know whether he was
coming or going.

Erwyn got up and stalked over to examine the thornbushes himself. Hands on hips, he surveyed the twisted
greenery, looking for anything that might give him a clue to
its secret. Nothing. The only thing he knew for certain was
that the bushes were grown magically.

He looked closer. There was something about those
bushes, something familiar. . . .

Erwyn turned to the others to ask if they'd found anything. Halfway around, one of the thorns caught his tunic.

"Look!" Chesric shouted, pointing behind Erwyn.

The boy whirled about, to be confronted by the same
impenetrable wall of spines.

"Damn!" Erwyn plucked at the hole in his tunic.

The thorn had ripped right through the pocket, and the
wand was slipping out. He retrieved the rod and turned
again to his comrades. For some reason, they were all looking at him.

"What's going on here?" he demanded, waving his arms
for emphasis.

The entire group caught its collective breath. Erwyn
froze, his arms still extended. They weren't actually watching *him,* not specifically.

Slowly he turned his head. Then his breath caught, too.

His left hand, the one holding the wand, was in the thorn-bush. Actually, it was *between* the bushes. The vines and branches had separated on either side.

Out of curiosity, Erwyn carefully withdrew his hand. The thorns settled once more into a thick wall.

He put his empty hand out toward the mass of vegetation. Nothing happened.

He tried again with the wand in hand. The plants moved out of the way.

"I think we've found the way in!"

"Excuse me fer mentionin' this, but ain't that hole a trifle small fer us all to squeeze through?"

Leave it to Chesric to point out the faults in Erwyn's logic.

"Don't worry. I can solve that problem. I think."

Erwyn moved his hand, and consequently the wand, in a circle. A slow circle, in case his idea didn't work. The plants gave way before the rod.

When the hole was about a foot across, Erwyn pulled his hand out. The plants began to seal the hole again.

"See," Erwyn told the rest of the group, "I'll just open a hole wide enough to walk through, and we've got it made."

Kerissa looked doubtful. "Yeah, well, someone's got to stay here with the horses. We need a lookout on the outside, in case something happens." She glanced toward Lariyn.

The lieutenant hesitated, as though she wanted to refuse the implied order. Instead, she answered, "I'll stay, Captain."

"I'll stay, too." Devydd stepped to Lariyn's side.

Erwyn looked at the two of them, wondering why Devydd would want to volunteer for guard duty. Lariyn seemed perfectly capable of handling it herself. He shrugged. The thief must have his reasons.

A few minutes and a short discussion on strategy later, Chesric, Kerissa, and Erwyn, plus a few dozen damselflies, approached the wall of thorns. Those who had weapons held them ready.

Erwyn, in front, opened a large hole in the wall and stood

waiting for the last of the expedition to go through. Then he followed them.

Once through the thornbushes, they stood in a clear space in front of the castle gates. The gates themselves were huge, which went without saying, since they could be seen over a fourteen-foot wall of thorns. They were made of iron and looked very, very heavy.

The castle towered above the doors. Giant stone blocks, set with great precision, formed its walls. Turrets and towers stretched toward the skies. The structure was large enough to hold the entire city of Dunaara, with room to spare. But something was wrong.

For some reason, the sunlight didn't seem as bright inside the wall of thorns. The drab quality of the light made an otherwise extremely impressive castle appear dull and gloomy.

"There's no moat."

"What?" Chesric seemed confused.

"There's no moat," Erwyn repeated. "Viona said there was supposed to be a moat."

"Well, I for one am kinda glad about that. Makes gettin' into the place a mite easier."

"Really? You have any ideas about how to get through those doors?"

"Not really. But ye might try that there wand of yers."

"I don't know. That seems a little too easy."

Erwyn extended the wand toward the gates. He didn't expect it to work. But it did.

The iron barrier swung slowly inward, groaning in protest as it went. The companions entered just as slowly.

Erwyn felt the hairs rise on the back of his neck. He stuck his hands into his pockets to hide the fact that they were shaking violently. There was something terribly wrong with this. It *was* too easy.

The doors gave entrance to a short, unlit passage, which in turn led to the central court. The group traveled the length of the passage as quietly as they could, expecting at any moment to be attacked by forces unknown.

At the end of the hallway, they emerged into the sunlight. Not the dingy stuff on the other side of the gates. The light here was dazzling in its brilliance.

As his eyes became accustomed to the brightness, Erwyn looked around him. They stood in a huge courtyard, almost like a receiving area, if you happen to receive armies. Big ones.

Instead of bare, well-kept dirt, the yard was a tangle of flowers and summer-dead grass, once carefully cultivated, but now growing with wild abandon. Except for a small section in the middle. Erwyn wondered about that.

"Piece of cake." Chesric slammed his sword back into his sheath.

"If you say so."

The walls were covered with vines and flowers, and there was no visible sign of a door leading to the rest of the castle. Together, they set about examining the walls for exits. They had not gotten far when . . .

"What puny mortals dare to invade my glorious domain?" a voice boomed from behind the back wall. It was followed by the loud beating of enormous leathern wings.

31

Games People Play

(Or, More Fun Than a Barrel of Man-eating Lizards)

Contrary to popular belief, dragons are very reasonable, likable creatures. Except when they're hungry or under contract.

Sorcerers Almanac
Section Five: On Things to Watch Out For

Erwyn felt his blood run cold. At least, he thought it was running cold. It certainly wasn't keeping him warm anymore.

No one moved a muscle—the voluntary kind, anyway—except the dragon. He flew over the back wall and glided into the courtyard.

The courtyard, which, as Erwyn had noted earlier, was big enough to hold an army, barely contained the dragon as he settled comfortably to the ground. The huge wings spread almost from one wall to the other. There was a little space left over, and into this the three explorers huddled. The damselflies seemed to have vanished.

Once settled, the dragon folded his wings across his back. To Erwyn, he actually looked smaller that way. In fact, he was. Wings take up a lot of space. No wonder he'd managed to hide behind the wall without being seen.

The dragon was still a little on the large side, though, and most of him seemed to be muscle, from Erwyn's point of view. He stood right below the creature's chest.

A long serpentine neck supported a large, square head, which, in turn, supported two large, wicked-looking horns. Heavily muscled legs ended in claws with six-inch talons. He also had claws, like a third set of hands, at the tips of his wings.

The wings themselves were translucent blue. Scales of a deeper blue-green covered him from the top of his head to the tip of his tail. As the dragon moved, rainbow shimmers rippled across the scales. He was beautiful, and at the moment, dangerous.

"Who art thou and what dost thou seek in this, my home?" The dragon's voice was no longer booming, but it was still pretty loud. The echo didn't help much, either.

Putting his hands to his ears, Erwyn shouted, "Could you tone it down some? You'll deafen somebody. Probably us."

"Gee, I'm sorry. I didn't mean to." The dragon sounded as if he meant it. "It's just that, well, it's my job. Chapter three, paragraph one of the Dragon Charter states that 'The initial challenge to intruders must be made at such a volume as to prevent the misinterpretation of the guard dragon's intent.' " He lay down in front of the young sorcerer and rested his head on his claws. "So, what brings you folks here?"

"Nothing much," Erwyn lied. "I don't suppose you could tell me if there's a girl locked up in here somewhere."

"Yup. Sure is. What do you think I'm here for?"

"You could be on vacation," Erwyn offered.

"Ri-i-ight." The dragon smiled indulgently. He had a lot of teeth.

Erwyn was feeling perversely dense just then. After all, how was he going to learn anything if he didn't ask questions? Even stupid ones.

"Uh, why exactly are you here?"

"I told you," the dragon growled. Erwyn took an involuntary step backward—right into the wall. "It's my job."

"That's some job."

"It beats the hell out of burning villages. The pay's terrible, the hours are lousy, and the only bonuses you get are the odd occasional virgin or two. Some of them are pretty odd, and some are only occasional virgins."

"Yeah, I can see how that could be a problem."

Erwyn paused, thinking. Then curiosity got the better of him.

"Tell me, Master Dragon . . . um . . . can you actually tell the difference between virgins and, uh, nonvirgins?"

"Of course I can. It's like the difference between . . . say, kid, you aren't a vegetarian or anything, are you?" He looked at Erwyn through one slightly bloodshot eye.

"No. I have a real weakness for steak. Makes it difficult to be a vegetarian."

"Good. Well, the difference between virgins and nonvirgins is kind of like the difference between fresh beef and aged beef. Some people like it fresh, some like it aged, some like it both ways. The point is, it's edible either way. It's a matter of personal preference."

"Y-You actually eat them?"

"That's what they're there for."

"Wh-what about boys, er, male virgins?"

"Depends. Farm boys, blacksmiths, guys who *work* for a living, are too tough. Now, magic-users and nobility—there's good material for a nice snack. Mmmm." He smiled wistfully, his eyes half closed. "Tasty."

The dragon opened his eyes. Erwyn suddenly realized how a bowl of candied cherries felt. Then the huge beast heaved an equally huge sigh.

"Unfortunately, I *am* a vegetarian. Poor digestion. Humans give me gas."

Erwyn wilted against the wall.

"M-Master Dragon . . ."

"Call me Virgil."

"Okay, um, Virgil. I'm Erwyn."

"Pleased to meet you." The dragon extended a talon for Erwyn to clasp.

"Uh, yeah." Gingerly, he shook the dragon's claw. "Anyway . . . do you mind if we just have a look at this princess of yours?"

"Sorry, can't do that."

"Why?"

"I told you. It's the job." The dragon sounded just like some of Erwyn's old instructors. "Chapter two, paragraph seven. 'The guard dragon shall, under no circumstances, allow anyone to pass unless and until he/she/it fulfills the qualifications for said passage.' I'm supposed to guard the princess. I'm *not* supposed to let anyone see her."

"How come?"

Before Virgil could answer, a shadow passed over the courtyard and a chill wind sprang up from nowhere. Erwyn shivered.

> *It is important to remember that there may be more than one person in the world whose goals conflict with your own.*
> Sorcerers Almanac
> Section Three: On People and Their Influence

The dragon sat up, looking ruefully at the sky and flexing his wings.

"Uh-oh. Back to work."

"Huh?"

Then Erwyn wished he hadn't asked that last question. Virgil sent a great gout of flame into the sky, accompanied by an earsplitting roar. Wings extended, neck arched, he towered over the young sorcerer. His eyes glowed.

"No man may set eyes on yon damsel, lest he first pass the Test of the Dragon." Virgil had his voice set on "boom" again. "Dost thou wish to challenge the dragon?"

With his eyes glued to the claws flexing just above his head, Erwyn started to stammer some sort of reply. Then the

sunlight returned and with it the warmth. Virgil settled
back down to earth.

"Stupid witch," Virgil hissed. "A dragon's work is never
done."

"What's going on? What was that?"

"You mean the cloud and the icy wind?" Virgil shrugged,
accidentally knocking some of the masonry off the courtyard
wall with the tips of his wings. "That was the broad who
put me here. There are certain things one is supposed to do
when one guards a princess. Miss Priss up there likes to
check up on her *employees* once in a while, to make sure
they're not shirking or anything."

"You mean she doesn't trust you?"

"That's right."

"Why don't you quit?"

"Mostly because I'm more or less stuck here."

"I thought you said it was a job."

"Yes, but the witch who put me here didn't exactly ask
me if I wanted the job. She just dumped me here. And to
make sure I stay, she's put a spell on me."

"Um, what kind of spell?"

"Nothing special. If I try to leave, I'll be changed into a
damselfly."

"Ugh!" It gave Erwyn the shivers just thinking about it.

"I heard that," Viona called from one of the vines overhead.

"Sorry."

Erwyn turned his attention back on the dragon. This
whole setup sounded fishy. "I'll probably regret asking this,
but . . . the name of that witch is Sharilan, right?"

Virgil looked at Erwyn for a moment, his expression
unreadable. "Nope."

"Good." Erwyn breathed a sigh of relief.

"It's her sister, Fenoria."

"Well, that's a relief. For a minute there I was . . . did you
say *Fenoria?*"

"Yup."

"But I thought Fenoria was the princess who's locked up in the castle."

"She is."

"But you just said she's the witch who dumped you here to guard the princess."

"Uh-huh."

"But how can it be the same person?"

"It isn't."

Erwyn did a double take. "Come again?"

"I see they haven't improved the hearing in your species. I said, it isn't."

"But I don't . . ."

"Look, Erwyn. You aren't the only human in the world named Erwyn, are you?"

"No, I guess not."

"And I, personally, have both an uncle *and* a cousin named Virgil. So why is it so hard to believe there are two women named Fenoria?"

"It just never occurred to me, that's all." Erwyn sat down, thinking furiously.

So, Sharilan hadn't been lying to him. Not exactly. She had just bent the truth a little. Question was, what should he do now?

"Why did the witch Fenoria imprison the princess Fenoria in this castle?"

"Don't ask me. I just work here."

"So in order to see Princess Fenoria, one of us has to take the—what did you call it? The Test of the Dragon."

"Correctamundo. But not just *any* one of you. It has to be the leader. I guess that's you."

"I don't suppose we could just leave the way we came and forget the whole thing."

"Nope. Chapter two, paragraph eight. 'Anyone entering the guard dragon's territory must submit to a qualification check before either entering or withdrawing from the field.' If you try to escape, I'm supposed to toast your buns, as it were."

"Um . . . what exactly is the Test of the Dragon?"

"Nothing elaborate, really. You have to join me for a game of three-handed poker."

"That doesn't sound too difficult."

Virgil watched Erwyn very closely as he added, "I get to play two of the hands. You have to beat both of them." Somehow the dragon managed to look sympathetic.

"Uh, I probably don't want to know, but . . . what happens if I lose?"

"I'm supposed to eat you." He didn't look happy about it, either.

32

To Beat, or Not to Beat

(Or, Indigestion on the Hoof)

The loyalty of dragons cannot be forced.

Sorcerers Almanac
Section Five: On Things to Watch Out For

"But you don't eat humans! You said they give you problems with your digestion."

"Ah, yes. Therein lies the problem. I'm supposed to prevent you from getting to the princess. But if I prevent you from getting to the princess the way I'm supposed to, I'm going to have tummy trouble for the next six months or so."

"Why six months?"

"Don't they teach you humans *anything?* It takes at least six months for a dragon to digest meat. That's another reason for becoming a vegetarian."

"I guess they skipped that part of my education. We don't see too many dragons where I come from."

Erwyn cupped his chin in his hand and stared at the dragon for a few moments. "So, what it boils down to is this: You're in trouble whether you win or lose."

"True."

"So why did Fen . . . um . . . the witch keep you here? It

seems to me she should have let you go the first time she
found out."

"To tell you the truth, she doesn't know."

"What?"

"She doesn't know I'm a vegetarian. The subject never
came up. She never asked. And I never volunteered the
information. She didn't seem to be the sympathetic type,
you know. And you're the first human I've seen come
through that door since I got here."

"How long ago was that?"

"Only a couple of months. There I was, minding my
own . . ."

At that moment, the wind picked up once more. Fenoria
Two was spying again.

"I guess we'd better get on with this," Virgil sighed
mournfully.

He produced a deck of cards from somewhere and started
shuffling.

"Aren't those cards kind of *large?*"

"Not if you have claws a big as mine."

"But I don't!"

"I know." Virgil sighed again. "Those are the rules. Chapter one, paragraph one. 'The customer's always right.' I play
two hands, simultaneously. Plus, I can swap cards between
hands. You get one hand, and you have to lay yours on the
ground. Face up, so I can see 'em. Cute, huh? Fenoria's not
too big on fair play."

"I really wish I knew more about what's going on."
Erwyn sat down cross-legged in front of the dragon.

It occurred to him that he hadn't heard from the rest of
the group since he'd started talking to Virgil. He looked
around for his companions, but Chesric and Kerissa seemed
to have disappeared, just like the damselflies.

Erwyn suspected they'd found a door into the rest of the
castle and gone exploring, but decided that now would be a
bad time to mention it to the dragon. Virgil was in enough
trouble right now. But then, so was Erwyn.

Virgil finished shuffling the cards and dealt them.

"The game's five card draw, unicorns wild. We both know the stakes." The dragon stopped. "What are you looking at?"

"You." Actually, Erwyn wasn't looking at Virgil himself so much as his aura. "Didn't you say there was a spell on you?"

"Yes. Why?"

"What would you do if the spell were removed?"

"Removed? How?"

"Well, um, I'm a sorcerer."

"Do you think you *can* remove the spell?"

"Not unless I can find it. And so far, I haven't had any . . . wait! There it is. And I think I can unravel it. I can try, anyway."

"Well, go ahead. Do it!"

"And if I do?"

"I'll let you go, of course. It's not like I'm getting paid to do this lousy job. That spell's the only thing holding me here. The only thing I know of."

"But if you're not under contract to do this, why do you keep quoting rules to me?"

Virgil looked at him sideways. "Chapter one, paragraph two. 'Always do the best job you can, no matter what the circumstances.'"

"Oh." Just his luck. An ethical dragon. "Okay, but you'd better act like you're still playing the game. Just in case your ladyfriend comes back." He took a deep breath. "Here goes nothing."

While Virgil kept up appearances, Erwyn tried to get a fix on the spell. He knew it was possible to break an enchantment cast by someone else. They'd practiced it at school. But this one was a lot more complicated than any of Brendan's, and he wasn't sure he could do it. He forced himself to concentrate.

The spell was like an onion. Several layers of spells were fused to one another. The first few were easy. Those he stripped away with no problem.

It reminded him of the time he and Brendan were practicing spell removal. He'd managed to strip away five layers of spells that Brendan had put together. When he removed the sixth, he found out the hard way that his friend had tucked a thunderstorm in the center. Erwyn had gotten soaked and his leather boots had shrunk. He didn't speak to Brendan for a month.

As Erwyn progressed through the spell on Virgil, the layers got progressively more difficult to undo.

It was hard work. Erwyn's head began to feel light. He began to feel dizzy. Blood pounded in his ears. With a sickening feeling, he realized that he'd experienced this before. . . .

Sharilan! He'd felt like this that time he nearly fried Chesric. He had almost forgotten about that episode. She'd probably used him at other times, too. Like a spy or something.

Now, she was using him again. Suddenly, Erwyn realized exactly why Sharilan had recruited him. She needed a fledgling magic-user to work through. He was certain now that rescuing Princess Fenoria was a bad idea. But why did Sharilan want her?

He had to get loose somehow. But this time he couldn't. Sharilan was too strong.

"Hey, Erwyn. You doing all right? You look a little strange, even for a human." Virgil snaked his head around until he could look Erwyn in the eye. But Erwyn couldn't answer.

Against his will, Erwyn continued stripping away the spell. Or rather, his mind provided the means. The sorceress provided the methods. Sharilan was using him to undo Fenoria's enchantment, and he doubted she was doing it for purely philanthropic reasons.

In spite of himself, Erwyn was fascinated by the process. Sharilan was doing exactly what he had been trying to do himself. Only faster and better.

Then it was over. Except Erwyn was still locked in that faraway place to which Sharilan had exiled him. She wasn't through yet.

Power flowed into him, building somewhere behind his eyes. His arms and hands began to itch. He couldn't move, except . . .

"Erwyn, sweetie, what's wrong?" Viona's voice came from a long way off. "What's the matter, can't you . . . Ouch! That hurt."

Erwyn was distantly aware of movement on his lap. Then everything came back into focus. The power buildup fizzled out, leaving him drained, with a still-aching head. He looked down to see what had happened.

Viona fluttered just above his lap, holding a small silver pin in one hand. She was rubbing her cute little behind with the other hand, and looking very indignant.

"Where'd you get that?"

"It was stuck in the hem of your cloak. I accidentally sat on it! Don't you know better than to keep straight pins in your clothes?"

"I didn't put it there." He reached down and took the pin from the damselfly.

As soon as he touched it, Erwyn knew the pin was the mysterious link between him and Sharilan. He almost threw it into the mass of vines across from him, but thought better of it. Sharilan's pin might actually be used against her.

"Hey, Erwyn! Get up off yer duff and come on. We've found that princess of yours."

"That's nice." Erwyn answered. He stood slowly, looking thoughtfully at the sliver of metal he held. What should he do with it?

"What's going on?"

"This." Erwyn handed Chesric the pin.

"What is it?"

"I believe it is Sharilan's connection to me."

"Then get rid of it afore she uses it again!"

"Nope." Erwyn shook his head, taking the pin from the old man. He stared at it for a few minutes, getting the spell right, then put it into his tunic pocket. "I think I may have a better use for it."

"But won't she be able to use it against ye again?"

"I don't think so." He smiled again, hoping he looked confident. "She uses the pin as a focus for her spells. If she can't connect with the pin, she can't do anything. Theoretically."

"How are ye going to keep her from, uh, connecting with the pin?"

"The refrigeration spell I learned in school. It includes an insulator so you can carry a refrigerated object without getting cold. I stripped off the cooling spell and just used the insulator part. Hopefully it will keep her from being able to use it against me."

"You sure?"

"No, but there's no way to test it. What did you say about the princess?"

"We've found her. We need you to come get her."

"What do you need me for?"

"She's asleep."

"Well, wake her."

"We can't."

"It should be a simple, straightforward storybook spell. Just kiss her."

"Well, uh . . ."

Erwyn suddenly realized what the old man was trying *not* to say. "You want *me* to do it?" The mere thought made his stomach turn flip-flops. He still wasn't sure he should wake her up at all.

Chesric just gave the boy an apologetic look.

"Oh, all right, but I don't have to like it."

Erwyn started to follow Chesric, but he was stopped in his tracks by the large clawed paw which suddenly appeared in his path.

"Now wait just a second. You can't just run off like that.

We haven't even finished our game yet. You're such a pleasant guy to talk to and everything that I'd really hate to have to roast you alive. Burnt hair smells just dreadful, you know."

33

Mission Accomplished

(Or, Damsels Come in All Sizes)

Enemies aren't the only ones who set traps. Sometimes it's your allies.

Sorcerers Almanac
Section Five: On Things to Watch Out For

"But I thought you were going to let us go if I removed Fenoria's spell."

"And I will, too. Just as soon as you get . . . you mean it's done? That's it? It's over?"

"Uh-huh. All gone. Care to try it out?"

Virgil didn't need to be asked twice. Without stopping to say good-bye, he launched himself straight up and was soon level with the highest turret. It was a beautiful sight . . . for as long as it lasted.

As he passed the turret, the sky flashed blue, then red, then yellow, then green. Thunder rolled across the castle grounds, shaking the walls and knocking masonry loose.

And the dragon disappeared.

Seconds later, a tiny figure hurtled toward them with a cry that sounded like a gnat screaming, "Oh, shi-i-i-t!"

"Oops!" Erwyn could think of nothing else to say.

Before Virgil could crash, the young sorcerer "caught" him with a levitation spell, then lowered him carefully to the ground.

The dragon had survived his transition reasonably well. His fall had been caused by the sudden loss of size, coupled with the equally sudden addition of a second pair of wings. Gender shock could have accounted for some of the problem, as well. Damselflies were, by definition, female.

He made a beautiful one, though. Long, wavy jet black hair flowed over an iridescent blue-green dress that reminded Erwyn of the dragon's erstwhile scales.

"I thought you removed that spell." Chesric whispered in the sorcerer's ear, so he wouldn't upset the dragon any more than necessary.

"I thought so, too," Erwyn whispered back. "I wonder what spell I *did* re—"

Another thunderclap rocked the castle, followed by a whirlwind in the courtyard—centering on the dragon *cum* damselfly.

"Everyone duck!"

Erwyn's warning was unnecessary. Chesric had already dashed off to the relative safety of the nearest wall, and Viona had taken to higher ground when Virgil exploded.

> *Some spells take longer to work than others. And some spells take longer to convince* not *to work.*
>
> Sorcerers Almanac
> Section Six: On the Successful Use of Magic

"Sheesh! I can't think of a worse fate for a dragon." Virgil had his voice set on "boom" again.

Erwyn closed his eyes, covered his ears, and waited for the dragon to calm down.

"Listen, Erwyn." Virgil's voice came from a point in front of the sorcerer's face.

Erwyn opened his eyes.

"That isn't going to happen again, is it?" Virgil looked

concerned.

Erwyn didn't blame him. "I don't think so."

"What happened?" Chesric took several wobbly steps toward the boy.

"Delayed reaction." Erwyn scanned the dragon, then tried scanning the entire castle for residual spells. As far as he could tell, the coast was clear.

"Once more, with feeling." The dragon flexed his wings, glanced apprehensively at the top turret, then launched himself. In seconds, he had sailed over the top of the castle and out of view.

Erwyn stood watching the skies. "Gullible dragon," the boy murmured.

"What do you mean? The spell was gone, wasn't it?"

"Yes. But if I had been in his place, I'd have at least done some research before taking off like that. I mean, Fenoria might have set more than one booby trap for him. And I *am* just a journeyman. I could have been wrong."

"Why didn't you mention it to him?"

"I didn't think of it until just now." He tore his eyes away from the sky. "Okay. Let's go see the princess and get this over with."

Erwyn followed Chesric through a long, twisting, turning passage. Doors opened on all sides, leading to unknown rooms and places. Chesric stopped at none of them.

"How'd you manage to find the princess in such a short time? There must be hundreds of rooms in this place."

"Easy," Chesric replied without stopping. "All the other doors are locked."

"Not a very good way to prevent her from being found, if you ask me."

"True. But maybe nobody expected us to get this far. Or maybe something terrible will happen when you wake her. Ah, here we are."

"Here" turned out to be the end of the passage. The hall was blocked by a large, heavy-looking, beautifully carved door.

Erwyn would have liked to spend some time admiring the workmanship that went into making that door. Days maybe. Months even. At least until someone else came along to wake up the person behind it.

Unfortunately, Chesric didn't let him stall that long. The old knight swung the door open to reveal a chamber worthy of the entrance.

Thick, royal-blue carpets covered the floor from one wall to the other. The walls, too, were completely covered. Hand-woven tapestries hung from ceiling to floor, each bearing a different scene.

One depicted a typical hunt, such as Erwyn had known as a little boy. The horses, dogs, and hunters were lifelike to the smallest detail.

Another hanging showed a fantastic battle between a tiger and a white unicorn. The animals seemed ready to leap from the walls.

Between the tapestries were tall columns, carved into the likenesses of mythical beasts—or maybe not so mythical, Erwyn decided, thinking about the dragon he'd just been talking to. In fact, one of the columns looked a lot like Virgil.

In the ceiling was set a round opening through which sunlight streamed. Erwyn wondered what kept the rain out as he let his gaze travel the length of the sunbeams to the figure in the middle of the room.

He had saved looking at the room's occupant until last. Mostly because once he saw her, he might be too nervous or worried to check out the rest of the room.

His instincts were correct.

Princesses are not always imprisoned by evil *wizards.*
                                        Sorcerers Almanac
                            Section Five: On Things to Watch Out For

Princess Fenoria rested on a dais in the exact center of the chamber, or close enough to the center to defy distinction. Unlike the rest of the room, the dais was unadorned, unless one counted the princess herself.

She lay on the platform like a life-sized china doll. Her blue and silver satin dress sparkled in the sunlight, cascading over the edges of the dais. Volumes of shiny black hair had been spread out from her head, fanlike, to tumble over the sides of the platform. Her hands were clasped across a tiny waist, and she seemed to be holding something.

Finally, Erwyn allowed himself to focus on her face. He hadn't really expected anything spectacular. As a result, he was shocked.

Princess Fenoria was not only beautiful, she was phenomenal. She had flawless olive-hued skin and a perfect oval face. Her lips were red, her cheeks like roses. Her nose was the perfect size for her face and was perfectly straight, except for . . . the heck with it! Erwyn didn't need to catalogue every feature. What mattered was, she was gorgeous. Kissing her might not be so bad, after all. He wondered briefly when his opinion of kissing girls had changed.

"Come on, quit stallin' and get it over with."

"I'm working up to it."

"Work faster."

Erwyn looked at the girl again, but the mood was gone. She was still pretty, but he was no longer in danger of getting all sappy about it.

Slowly, the young sorcerer approached the dais. He took a moment to wipe the sweat from his palms before he closed his eyes and bent to give her a long-lasting kiss.

"Geez, that was great. But next time could you try for the lips? I think you bruised my nose."

The princess was awake. She sat up, smoothing her hair and patting her dress into perfect folds.

"Boy, I've been waiting for a small slice of *forever* for someone to come and get me out of this place, ya know what I mean? I thought I'd never get out of here, let me tell you. Say, what did you say your name was, sweetheart?"

"Uh, Erwyn."

"Well, I don't mind telling you, I'm glad to get up off

that dais. My back is simply killing me. And these shoes . . ."

Fenoria One slipped her arm through Erwyn's and dragged him toward the door.

"They're just not the right size. You just can't get a good cobbler these days. Not to mention this dress. Blue really isn't my color, you know. . . ."

"Chesric!" Erwyn looked to his friend for help.

"Gesundheit. Anyway, as I was saying, I really ought to wear something in less natural colors, say light pink, or maybe peach and teal. Something to offset the drab color of my eyes, and my skin, and my hair . . ."

An eternity later, they reached the courtyard, with Chesric and Kerissa trailing behind. Virgil was nowhere to be found. Erwyn hoped he'd been able to get away without springing any more traps. On second thought, he almost wished the dragon would come back and finish him off.

Better a quick death by dragon fire, than being chattered to death . . .

" . . . and then there's this castle. It's *so* drafty. Why do they always have to lock princesses up in drafty old stone castles, anyway? I've half a mind to report this to my daddy, as soon as I can get back to him. I wonder how long I've been asleep. . . ."

So it went, across the courtyard, through the passage, and out the gates. Once outside, Erwyn paused to retrieve his wand from its pocket. Apparently, the thornbushes hadn't given up just because the princess had awakened.

"Geez! Would you look at this place? You'd think it was haunted or something. Why do they always have to use a gloomy place like this to lock people up in? I mean, why not put them someplace more cheerful like a beautiful ivy-covered cottage in the wood, with a white picket fence, and lots of trees and rose bushes and . . ."

Erwyn was beginning to doubt the girl had actually been kidnapped at all. Maybe her father had *given* the princess to Fenoria Two. Maybe he paid the witch to take the girl away. Erwyn certainly wanted to. He looked around, but there were no witches in evidence.

He stuck the wand into the hedge and enlarged the subsequent hole until it was large enough to accommodate even Fenoria's mouth. It was also large enough for him to see the spectacle that awaited them outside the castle grounds.

34

Castle Sandwich

(Or, Help! Help! The Gang's All Here)

Provoking an attack from a more powerful mage is dangerous. Provoking one intentionally is suicidal.

Sorcerers Almanac
Section Six: On the Successful Use of Magic

While they'd been exploring the castle, the rear guard had been busy.

Devydd and Lariyn were bound and gagged and lying on the ground. Devydd seemed to be taking things philosophically. That is, he was busy trying to undo his bonds and ignoring the large, pointy objects that were aimed his way.

Lariyn's face was bruised and puffy, her tunic torn. She must have put up quite a fight; there were more men guarding her than Devydd.

Several of the damselflies were hanging from the point of a pike. In a net. Erywn could hear them whining and complaining, something about wrinkles and crushed wings.

Then there was Sharilan. As his gaze locked with hers, Erwyn had a fervent desire to be back in the relative safety of the castle. Even the losing hand of a game of three-handed poker was preferable to facing the sorceress.

She seemed to like to travel with large groups, for in addition to the seven men guarding Lariyn, Devydd, and the damselflies, there were ten more pointing their toys at Erwyn, Chesric, and Kerissa. And then there was the army.

It was hard to be certain how many soldiers there were, and Erwyn was fairly certain Sharilan wouldn't let him take time to count. At a guess, there were—dozens.

"I see you've made good use of the wand," Sharilan commented. Her voice was huskier than Erwyn remembered. He also didn't remember the hard edge in her tone or the icy chill running up his back when she spoke.

"I did my best."

"Now, if you would be so kind as to return it, please. Along with the silver sphere *dear* Fenoria is carrying."

Erwyn glanced at the girl clinging to his arm and the shiny ball she held. He'd forgotten she was there. It was the first time she'd been quiet since he'd awakened her.

"No way." Erwyn pushed the princess behind him as Chesric and Kerissa closed the space between themselves and him.

"I didn't go to all the trouble to put this castle here and lure the princess into it, just to be defeated by a mere journeyman. It's bad enough my sister tried to keep me from succeeding, with her damn snowstorms and dragons. You haven't got a chance."

"I can try."

"You think you can best me where my sister failed?" Sharilan's eyes narrowed. "Very well!" Blue light crackled between her fingers as she signaled her henchmen.

It occurred to him that he'd just made a bad decision. After all, here he was, an inept journeyman sorcerer, about to take on a master sorceress and her entire army (at least, he *hoped* what he saw was all she had) with only two warriors, plus a damselfly or two. Not the best odds.

Of course, he had an ace up his sleeve, or, rather, in his pocket. He hoped it would work. All he needed was a few minutes and someone to distract Sharilan.

"Viona," he whispered to the damselfly, without taking his eyes off of Sharilan.

"Yes, Erwyn?" He noticed she did *not* come out of folds of his cloak where she had hidden earlier.

"Could you do me a favor?"

"As long as it doesn't mean coming out in the open."

"I'm afraid it does."

"Uh-uh."

"You mean you're just going to leave your friends hanging there? You're not willing to help them? I'm surprised at you!"

The damselfly peeked out from under the material. She looked a little limp.

"What do you want me to do?"

"Nothing much. Just distract Sharilan for a couple of minutes."

"Nothing much," Viona mimicked. "Your idea of 'nothing much' and mine are a little different."

"Come on, it's not that difficult. All you have to do is just fly past her nose or something. And stay out of reach of those blue sparks flying from her hands."

"Right. Sort of like dodging raindrops."

"Exactly. But not until I give you the signal."

Viona grumbled a little more, then sailed into the air and headed toward Sharilan. While Erwyn and the damselfly had been conferring, the guards had moved Devydd, Lariyn, and the net closer to Erwyn's group, presumably to give the sorceress a larger target. That way she could kill them all at once, instead of a few at a time.

Erwyn kept his eyes glued on Sharilan while the sorceress slowly, very slowly, built up the power in her lightning spell. She smiled as she did it, and Erwyn felt certain she was building her power slowly so the suspense could build along with it. It was working. Erwyn's palms itched and his neck muscles were tight.

Blue light crackled and flashed up to Sharilan's wrists. Erwyn continued to stare, sweat trickling down the back of his neck. The pin was almost in position. He nodded slightly, hoping that Viona would recognize his signal and Sharilan wouldn't. He also hoped that Sharilan wouldn't be ready before he was.

Suddenly, Sharilan ducked in her saddle, waving her hands as though to shoo away an insect. Not the most healthy of reactions, considering the spell she was in the process of casting. Unfortunately for Erwyn, she remembered to damp down the lightning before she solved his problem for him. The pin was in place, though, and Erwyn nodded again.

Sharilan turned back to her captives. In spite of Viona's efforts, she was still smiling. So was Erwyn, as he waited for her to start casting her spell again. She disappointed him, though.

"On second thought, I think I'll let my men take care of you. It'll last longer that way." She turned her horse.

"Too bad," Erwyn muttered.

The sorceress didn't notice. Addressing the man with the pike, she said, "Kill them all, then bring me the wand and the sphere." With that, she rode away.

"Rats! She was supposed to fry us, not spit us."

"You must be joking!" Chesric whispered back. "At least against these guys we've got a fighting chance."

"You don't understand." Erwyn sighed, exasperated. "If she *had* tried to zap us, the battle would be over already."

"You're right. I don't understand."

" 'ere, now." One of the guards was addressing them. "Stop whisperin' and untie those two." He indicated Lariyn and Devydd. "And take their gags off. We can't go executin' 'em with 'em lyin' in the dirt like that."

The guards had a strange sense of fair play. It seemed that they couldn't kill anyone with his or her arms tied up. They preferred to line their victims up face to the wall for a nice little round of back-stabbing.

"I don't mean to tell you how to do your job, kid," Devydd said when Chesric had removed his gag, "but it seems to me that now would be a good time to practice your sand castles. Get my drift?"

Erwyn did. "Be nice if I could manage to . . ."

"To what?"

"Oh, nothing."

Erwyn's mind flicked to the expanse of sand he'd seen just south of the enchanted castle. It was convenient how Sharilan's army just happened to be assembling there. If only he could . . . oh, well. He could try that later, if he survived.

He took a quick peek at their executioners, thought about the sand some more, then concentrated on building the castle he wanted. He heard the men take a few steps in their direction. Then . . .

"Hey! What th—" That was one of them now.

"T'ain't hardly fair. You stop that this instant!" There went another one.

"I hate fighting against mages!"

The air behind them filled with more muffled cries of outrage.

The group turned around. Behind them stood the sand castle, right where Sharilan's men had been. Actually, the men were still there, but the castle had been built around them. Erwyn was rather pleased with that. He figured it took a bit of finesse to build a castle *around* someone.

Of course, it wasn't a very big castle. But then, there had only been sixteen or seventeen men about to kill them.

It was adequate. It also had walls about three feet thick.

"Should take them a while to get out of that one."

"I don't see any doors or windows," Kerissa observed.

"There aren't any," Erwyn replied. "That's why it will take them some time to get out. Longer, if none of them has anything to dig with."

"So what do we do now?" Devydd was being practical.

"We've got to get rid of that army somehow."

"That's terrific." Devydd fingered the hilt of his sword. "Just the six of us against an army. You folks won't mind if I just go find myself something else to do, will you? Something a little less—terminal?"

"Now's yer chance, young fella." Chesric placed a hand on Erwyn's shoulder.

"Huh?"

"Yer chance to practice some more of that magic of yers. We'll race around the castle here and catch up with the army. The rest of us'll keep the riffraff from slicin' you to ribbons, while you take out the bad guys."

"Are you kidding?"

"Beats waitin' around here to get slaughtered."

"Moot point." That was Devydd again.

"Uh-oh."

The army had caught up with them.

35

Hole In One

(Or, Sisters, Sisters, There Were Never Such Devoted Sisters)

Overconfidence can be your greatest asset, as long as it is your opponent's and not yours.

Sorcerers Almanac
Section Three: On People and Their Influence

The soldiers were really only part of the army, but they were running in the companions' direction, and screaming loud enough to wake the dead. Fortunately, they could only run four abreast once they got between the storybook castle and the sand castle.

"Do something!" For someone who had a low opinion of magic-users, Kerissa was sure asking a lot.

"I'm not sure I can," Erwyn shot back. "Magic isn't like breathing, you know. You have to stop sometime."

"You have to stop breathing sometime, too. And if you don't do something, we'll all get to experience it, you know." Chesric had to add his two gold pieces' worth.

"Whatever happened to you holding off the riffraff?"

"That was before the riffraff started trying to off us first!"

"All right. Just don't expect miracles!"

Erwyn gathered his remaining energy into one last burst.

For lack of a better idea, he just started adding another room to the sand castle. He thought the guys in the first room were digging through that wall, anyway.

While the group watched, a wall formed halfway between them and the men who were running toward them. It grew sideways until it almost reached the thorn hedge, then took an abrupt right-angle turn away.

"Uh-oh."

Erwyn groaned at Devydd's now-familiar warning. His aim had been a little bit off. Seven or eight of Sharilan's soldiers had slipped through the wall before it was completed, and they were still headed in the companions' direction.

"You guys are going to have to handle this," Erwyn said wearily. "I'm beat." He sank to the ground to watch.

To Erwyn, it was the most spectacular example of sword-fighting he had ever seen, but then, he'd never seen any real swordfights.

Chesric accounted for three of the enemy, his sword flashing brightly in the sunlight. Devydd took out two more. Kerissa and Lariyn handled the rest, however many that was. It was pretty intense for a while, then all was still, except for a lot of heavy breathing.

After a few more minutes, Erwyn relaxed. While he rested, the rest of the group waited tensely for someone else to come looking for them. No one did.

They couldn't sit there forever, though. Finally, they decided to follow Chesric's advice and go looking for the rest of the army. How many more could there be? Twenty? Thirty? No sweat. Well, maybe a little sweat.

They walked slowly around the sand castle toward where they supposed the rest of the army was. Princess Fenoria, whom Erwyn had blissfully forgotten in the heat of . . . er . . . sand castling, snuggled up as close as she could get to him. If she got any closer, Erwyn decided, he'd have to find a larger set of clothes.

Everyone who still had a weapon had it out again. As a group, they rounded the last corner of the sand castle . . .

and froze in their proverbial tracks.

"Wow! I never realized how much sand it takes to build one of those." Devydd let out a low whistle.

"Me, either. That's amazing." Kerissa's voice held a touch of awe.

Erwyn was a little impressed himself. He didn't know whether his subconscious had taken control or just thinking about the location of the sand had influenced the spell. Well, whatever caused it, the results were spectacular. Sharilan's entire army had conveniently fallen into the hole left by Erwyn's sand prison.

"I hate to bring this up, but Sharilan's still on the loose here somewhere." Leave it to Chesric to put a damper on things.

Maybe he should have saved the damper for later. With a crack of lightning and a cloud of smoke, the sorceress herself appeared in front of them.

"Speaking of whom," Erwyn murmured. Aloud, he said, "Back so soon?"

"I should have known better than to leave important business to incompetent clods."

"Well, thanks for the compliment, but . . ."

"Silence!" The sorceress glared down at Erwyn. "I thought I had chosen the right tool to free the princess. It seems, however, that you are no ordinary fool. Nonetheless, you will soon be a dead one."

"Suits me," Erwyn replied, silently hoping his plan would work. He'd only get one chance.

That stopped her for a moment. The last thing Sharilan expected was for Erwyn to agree to her killing him. The rest of the group was having doubts about his sanity, as well.

It didn't take her long to recover. She stared thoughtfully at him. "You have courage. Perhaps it will be of service to me someday." Something with little prickly feet ran up Erwyn's spine. Was it what she said, or the way she said it?

"I think I will bottle you up for a while, until I think of what to do with you." She began her usual windup for her spellcasting. What a ham!

"Oh, put a cork in it, Sharilan!" he scoffed.

"You insignificant little . . . I ought to—"

"Yes?"

Lightning crackled, leaping from one hand to the other as Sharilan glared at Erwyn. He tried to look as smug as he could. If the sorceress didn't actually *cast* her spell, it would do him no good at all. He had to force her hand.

"Hold it, Sharilan, sweetie! If you think I'm going to let you blast these people to kingdom come without sticking my nose in, you got another think coming."

"Fenoria!"

Was it Erwyn's imagination, or was Sharilan a teensy bit upset?

The latest arrival at their little rendezvous was slightly shorter than Sharilan, with light brown, curly hair and dimples. She wore a pink tutu and ballet slippers and, at the point she entered the fracas, she hovered about four feet off the turf. This put Sharilan at a disadvantage, since she was standing on the ground.

"In the flesh, Sister, dear. Why don't you just take a hike, huh?"

As Sharilan's spell fizzled out again, Erwyn groaned in mental agony. Some days, you can't get zapped no matter how hard you try.

"Not a chance, you stupid bimbo. I worked hard to get that ball. It's mine!"

"Well, excu-u-use me! You're out of luck, Miss High-and-Mighty. The current owner isn't through with it yet. And who are you calling 'bimbo'?"

"Oh, pardon me. *Bimbette*. I forgot you haven't attained full bimbo status yet."

"You ought to know. You've been Queen Bimbo for years."

"I've half a mind to . . ."

"Gee, that's the first time in years we've agreed on anything. That you've got *half* a mind."

"I oughta send you clear into the next dimension!"

"You and what army?"

Erwyn was beginning to get the impression that Sharilan and Fenoria didn't get along too well. He wasn't about to get in between them, though.

"I'm going to tell Mother on you!"

"Listen to you. You sound like a little *baby*. Here, baby, take this."

During the argument, Sharilan had been working on another spell. Now she literally threw it toward her sister, casting it as she would a net. Fenoria Two recovered from her surprise in time to put up some kind of shield, using a strange wand with a star atop it.

She needn't have bothered. The white glow the sorceress tried to fling onto her sister never got any farther than Sharilan's hands.

Like smoke being blown into the smoker's face, the white cloud swelled to envelop its creator. It billowed higher and higher, hiding the sorceress completely.

From inside the cloud came a single exclamation.

"Oh, shit!"

Then a gust of wind blew the cloud away, leaving no trace of the sorceress. Sharilan was gone.

"Where did she go?" the princess asked in a bewildered voice.

Erwyn wondered about that himself. "I don't know," he said. There must have been something odd about the way he said it, though, because Chesric looked at him strangely.

"You sure know something." The old man eyed him suspiciously for a moment. "Come on, out with it. What gives?"

"Well . . ." Erwyn stalled for a moment more, then shrugged. "You remember that silver pin Sharilan stuck me with when we first met? The one she was using to tune in on me?"

"Yes, but what does that have to do with this?"

"Everything. I levitated the pin onto Sharilan's dress.

When she tried to cast a spell at her sister, it recoiled on her."

"But I thought you said you fixed it so she couldn't use the pin anymore."

"No, I fixed it so she couldn't use it on *me*. I did a little creative spellcasting so that, when she tried to zap me, it would backfire."

"But she wasn't aiming at you."

"*That* part I don't understand. Unless . . ."

"Unless what?"

"Unless she thought the connection was still active. If she had tried to drag me into performing the same spell on her sister . . ."

"It would backfire on her," Chesric concluded.

"Maybe." Erwyn still wasn't certain. He was just glad his experiment worked.

"The question is," the Fairy Fenoria added, looking at Erwyn the same way Chesric had, "what, exactly, was the spell she was using?"

Epilogue

"Well, at least Sharilan's gone for the time being." Erwyn sighed. What he needed now was some good, old-fashioned boredom.

"And I'm free at last," Princess Fenoria added, snuggling up to Erwyn and batting her eyelashes.

"Uh, right." Erwyn found himself blushing. "Has anybody seen the damselflies lately?"

"Over here, Erwyn, honey," Viona called.

"I mean, the *rest* of the damselflies."

No one had. Some of them had been missing since before Princess Fenoria had been located. The remainder had disappeared after they had been released from the net.

"Oh, well. They'll turn up sooner or later. Probably sooner than we'd like. So what happens now?"

"What do you mean?" Chesric was being dense.

"You were all tagging along to help me free the princess. Now that she's freed, I expect you'd all like to go on your separate ways."

In spite of his words, Erwyn was half hoping they would decide to stay with him. If it hadn't been for their help and coaching, he'd have ended up dead, or worse. But he didn't want to ask. Truth was, he didn't like admitting that he no longer wanted to go it alone.

"I think I'll go find myself a place where a sword or a set

of nimble fingers are needed more than a spellbook. I've got some ideas about how Viona could help me, you know what I mean, kid?" Devydd spoke softly as he stared off into space. "I'll catch up with you some other time."

"I understand." Erwyn smiled sadly. He hated to admit it, but he'd miss them. "Maybe I'll see you around."

"Hold on there a minute, boy." Chesric grabbed Erwyn's elbow. "I didn't say I was leaving. Heck, things are just now getting interesting. And I think the ladies, here"—he indicated the Marlians—"might have a thing or two to say about yer leaving without them, too."

"Sharilan's still got the Tetraliad, remember?" Kerissa hesitated, remembering what had happened to the sorceress, Then she added, "Or someone does. Anyway, you promised to help find it. We aren't going to let you out of that deal. Besides, you're kind of handy to have around. Sometimes."

"I want to go home!"

They all looked at the princess. Fenoria stood there, her lower lip stuck out. It had been five whole minutes, and no one had paid any attention to her.

"We'll get you home somehow, okay? Just don't cry. I can't stand crying."

"Oh, thank you. You're so wonderful!" Fenoria snuggled up to Erwyn again.

"And no kissing!"

"Aw, you never let a girl have any fun."

"I wish I could stay to help." Fenoria Two approached the young sorcerer. "But I have work to do elsewhere. I suspect that you'll have all the help you'll need."

The witch/fairy smiled at Erwyn. There was something about her eyes . . . something that reminded him of a moonlit night at the edge of an enchanted forest.

Then she was gone. Just like that. She took Sharilan's army with her, too, leaving nothing but a huge, empty hole.

When Erwyn turned to survey what was left of their "battlefield," he was thinking aloud. "What I want to know is: Why did Sharilan pick on me? There are fifty other journeyman sorcerers out traipsing around somewhere. I want to know what I did to deserve all this."

"What I want to know," said a crotchety old voice from a crotchety old man who had somehow managed to sneak up on them, "is who's going to clean up this mess in my front yard?"

"Your front yard?"

"Yes. I live here. This is my castle. What's the matter, you dense?" The old man glared at them with his watery blue eyes.

He just *happened* to have several shovels with him, too. Erwyn signed. This could take a while.

As all of them, with the exception of the princess (she was far too delicate for such menial labor), began shoveling the sand back into the hole, Chesric turned to Erwyn with one last comment.

"You know, I'll be glad when you've sufficiently recovered to do something about this."

Erwyn sighed heavily, trying to shovel faster. "So will I, Chesric, so will I."

The old man at least had the courtesy to provide them with lunch. Halfway through filling the hole, he shuffled out of the castle with a platter of cheese, fruit, fresh bread, and wine that was so cold, it was almost painful to swallow.

After the meal, Erwyn announced that he was ready to try filling the hole by less mundane means. Nothing too dramatic. He simply levitated as much of the sand as he could comfortably move, and dropped it into the opening.

When the job was finally over, Erwyn was again exhausted. Kerissa, Lariyn, and Chesric cleaned up the mess while the sorcerer slumped to the ground.

Their task complete, they gathered in a tent conveniently left behind by Sharilan's army. They finished the wine, and then the old caretaker, whose name turned out to be Faylen, brought out another platter of food. While the rest of the group stuffed themselves, Erwyn sat down with his journal.

The dragon was vanquished, the princess saved, and the sorceress had vanished before our eyes. I, personally, dispatched most of the enemy with my most powerful spell. They will not bother us again soon.

The princess must be returned safely to her father's castle. I must, in all good conscience, see that this task is accomplished. The old knight and the Marlian warriors have opted to remain with me. Ever will there be adventure at a sorceror's side . . .

"E-r."

"Huh?"

"Sorcerer is spelled *s-o-r-c-e-r-e-r*."

Erwyn snapped his book shut and glared at Princess Fenoria.

"What the hell are you reading over my shoulder for? This is supposed to be private!"

"Well, you needn't get so huffy, and so *loud*. I mean, really, you didn't hang out a 'Do not disturb' sign or anything." She flounced off in a huff.

Erwyn smiled, shaking his head. In some ways, truth was stranger than fiction. But fiction was easier to write.

The sun was setting, and a chill breeze had blown in. Summer was almost over, and autumn would soon be here. He'd made it through most of his first year as a journeyman sorcerer. Only three more to go.

Maybe he'd even get used to all the adventure and excitement. . . .

"Ouch!"

Erwyn started at the sound of Viona's high-pitched squeal.

"Unhand me, you little slut! And get out of my hair!" Fenoria's shout followed a split second later. "I'll teach you to pull the hair of a princess."

"Princess, schmincess!"

There was a muffled *whack!* and Viona squealed again.

Erwyn sighed and headed toward the scene of the battle. Some forms of excitement he could do without.